THE TOWMAN'S DAUGHTERS

*The Wild Onion Ltd mystery series
from David J. Walker*

A TICKET TO DIE FOR
A BEER AT BAWDY HOUSE
THE END OF EMERALD WOODS
ALL THE DEAD FATHERS
TOO MANY CLIENTS *
THE TOWMAN'S DAUGHTERS *

* available from Severn House

THE TOWMAN'S DAUGHTERS

A Wild Onion Ltd Mystery

David J. Walker

This first world edition published 2011
in Great Britain and in the USA by
SEVERN HOUSE PUBLISHERS LTD of
9–15 High Street, Sutton, Surrey, England, SM1 1DF.

British Library Cataloguing in Publication Data

Walker, David J., 1939–
    The towman's daughters.
    1. Kirsten (Fictitious character : Walker) – Fiction.
    2. Dugan (Fictitious character) – Fiction. 3. Wild Onion,
    Ltd. (Imaginary organization) – Fiction. 4. Private
    Investigators – Illinois– Chicago – Fiction. 5. Detective
    and mystery stories.
    I. Title
    813.5'4-dc22

ISBN-13: 978-0-7278-8066-6   (cased)

All Severn House titles are printed on acid-free paper.

Severn House Publishers support The Forest Stewardship Council [FSC],
the leading international forest certification organisation. All our titles that
are printed on Greenpeace-approved FSC-certified paper carry the FSC logo.

MIX
Paper from
responsible sources
FSC
www.fsc.org   FSC® C018575

Typeset by Palimpsest Book Production Ltd.,
Falkirk, Stirlingshire, Scotland.
Printed and bound in Great Britain by
MPG Books Ltd., Bodmin, Cornwall.

To John Donahue
Juancho
hero, friend . . . gone too soon

ACKNOWLEDGMENTS

This is a work of fiction. The organizations and characters are imaginary or are used fictitiously. Even so, I am grateful that they showed up and seemed pretty real to me.

I am also grateful to very many actual persons, including: Danielle Egan-Miller, my agent, and her entire staff, for their unflagging support; the people at Severn House, especially James Nightingale, for believing in Kirsten and Dugan and what they had to say; Pat Reardon and Jerry Silbert, lawyers who helped me sort out a few legal issues; and all the Red Herrings, especially Libby Fischer Hellmann and Michael Allen Dymmoch, for their generosity and insight.

ONE

He'd knocked down a few, sure, but Dugan couldn't blame what happened only on the alcohol. After all, he hadn't been totally wasted when he stepped up to rescue Isobel Cho from that gunman at Wancho's Towing.

It was Friday night, or actually around one o'clock Saturday morning, and being a hero had definitely not been on Dugan's to-do list. No way. He just wanted to retrieve his car – Kirsten's Camry, actually, she being out of town until probably Tuesday – and go home and sleep until noon. It seemed a perfectly reasonable idea at the time. Of course he *was* a little juiced up, and mad as hell, and not about to hand over two hundred bucks for a half-hour's parking.

It had been years since Dugan was out socially on a Friday night – or any night, for that matter – without Kirsten. But he'd spent most of the day at the Attorney Disciplinary Commission, trying to hang on to his law license, and when he got back to his office it was almost six o'clock. Larry Candle, one of the three lawyers who worked for Dugan, said he was meeting a few guys at Twin Anchors, on Sedgwick, for ribs. Dugan, against his better judgment, agreed to go along. A couple of hours later they ran into another guy Larry knew, and had a couple of beers with him. One thing led to another, and Dugan somehow got the idea that he and Larry should get Kirsten's car and drive up to a place on Manheim Road, near O'Hare, to check out a poker game they'd heard about. So they did that, and it didn't take long to discover the game was way out of their league. They left – the first intelligent decision Dugan made that whole night – and drove back downtown, where he dropped Larry off at his condo and then headed for home.

Without Kirsten, though, home exerted less of a pull, so he stopped off at a place called Cawley's Tap, on Diversey. He'd worked halfway through a Dewar's on the rocks, when this glassy-eyed, long-legged girl in a short leather skirt put a move

on him and – making his second, and last, intelligent decision
of the night – he downed part two of the scotch, grabbed his
jacket, and was out the exit . . . just in time to see the Camry
being towed down the street. The hot dog stand across from
Cawley's was closed, so why should anyone care if he parked
there? And he sure hadn't seen any *No Parking* sign.

He ran over and looked again, though, and, yes, the sign was
there. Way up on the wall, with the light above it burned out.
The sign said: 'Unauthorized vehicles will be towed to Wancho's
Towing.' It gave an address and a phone number . . . and told
him it would cost him two hundred dollars to get the car back.

'Two bills my ass!' Dugan yelled, as the tow truck and the
Camry disappeared around the corner. He dug into his pocket
for his cellphone . . . and remembered he'd shut it off and left
it in the car.

It was quite a warm middle-of-the-night for Chicago in June,
and there were plenty of loud-talking, weekend-loving people on
the street. He got a cab easily. The driver was a Sikh or something, wearing a turban, and tried to talk Dugan out of going.
'Better you go in the morning, when your thoughts are more
clear-cut,' he said. 'Then you pay your money and forget about
it. With such people, one cannot win.'

'Thanks for the advice,' Dugan said. 'But just take me to
goddamn Wancho's.'

If the Sikh hadn't driven like a maniac maybe Dugan would
have had time to cool down, and to give some consideration to
the things he'd learned about Wancho's and its thugs a year earlier
when he'd sued them on behalf of a client. But when the cab
pulled up to the place he was still mad as hell . . . and convinced
his thoughts were as 'clear-cut' as they needed to be.

So maybe the alcohol did have a part in getting him to Wancho's
that night. But the rest of what happened? Chalk it up to fate,
or bad karma, or whatever.

In a neighborhood marked mostly by vacant lots and abandoned
factories, Wancho's was essentially a huge fenced-in parking lot
– not much smaller than a football field – with an office. The
office was a one-story concrete block building on the north side
of the street, with eight-foot-high chain-link fencing extending
out from each side. The fence ran along the sidewalk in each

direction, ending at a railroad embankment on the west and a boarded-up, two-story brick warehouse on the east. One section of the fence, near the office, was an electronically-operated gate that opened and closed by sliding sideways on a track-and-pulley system.

The fence was obviously old, but in decent shape, with angled barbed-wire along the top and aluminum slats woven through the links to make it difficult to see through. Even where a few of the slats were broken or bent, it was too dark in the lot for Dugan to pick out the Camry. It was bright inside the office, though. The entrance door and most of the front wall were glass, and he could see into a waiting area with half a dozen cheap plastic chairs. Against the back wall stood an ATM machine, and beside that was a cashier's window. Very convenient, Dugan thought, to be able to get cash so you could ransom your own car back from a bunch of thieving crooks.

The Sikh had offered to wait, 'in case there occurs difficulty in getting your vehicle back,' but Dugan waved him away. Other than the cashier, there were four people inside the office: two slick-haired young toughs – Mexicans, he was certain – standing near the cashier's window, facing a man and a woman who had their backs to the entrance. The woman wore a bright-red spaghetti-strapped sundress, and had long dark hair and a deep tan. Her escort was a broad-shouldered, dark-skinned black man, with a shiny shaved head and an electric-blue short-sleeved sport shirt hanging loose outside his jeans. He had one muscular arm – his left arm – wrapped around his lady's shoulders, squeezing her close to his side, and he was nodding his head up and down like he was talking to her . . . or maybe to the Mexicans.

The couple started walking backwards toward the entrance, which – Dugan realized later – should have raised a red flag. But just then he was busy being pissed off about the car and the barely visible *No Parking* sign. As he got closer, he did sort of half-wonder why the two didn't finally break off their embrace and turn around and walk out frontwards. But they never did, and just as they backed up to the door he got there, too.

'I got it,' he called, as he yanked it open.

The black guy must have been planning to hit the door with his upper back, and when the door wasn't there he lost his balance and started to fall backwards. '*Damn!*' he yelled, and flung his left arm out to get his balance, letting go of the woman.

She screamed and the guy grabbed at her, but he was still stumbling backwards, and would have gone down, except he fell right into Dugan's arms. Which is when Dugan saw the nickel-plated pistol in the guy's hand and suddenly realized he'd been dragging the girl out the door.

'Oops, sorry,' Dugan said, wrapping his arms loosely around the guy's body from behind and stepping back, as though tangled up and trying to keep them both from falling. The guy struggled to get his balance, but Dugan kept pulling him and then, yanking hard on his right arm, he stepped out of the way and let the guy fall, arms flung wide, to the sidewalk.

At about six feet, the man was a little shorter than Dugan, but bulky, and landed on his back and hit his head on the concrete. The gun flew out of his hand and Dugan heard it skitter along the sidewalk, off where it was dark.

Right away the guy was up on his knees, looking around for his weapon. It wasn't in sight, and he got to his feet and turned toward Dugan, who assumed that by then the Wancho's people must already have called the cops.

'Jesus, sorry,' Dugan said, listening for sirens. 'Didn't mean to get in your way.' He raised his hands. Conciliatory. 'But I'm *with* ya. Sons o' bitches took my car, too, and—'

'Fuck you,' the guy said, mad as hell. He took a step toward Dugan, then obviously changed his mind and turned to find his gun.

Dugan didn't like that idea. He ran up behind the guy and yelled, 'Hey, over here!'

When the man spun around, Dugan swept his right arm across and, fist clenched, slammed the heel of his palm into the guy's left ear, then came back with the heel of his other hand, up and hard into his chest.

It was a basic technique, practiced a thousand times in the last year or so, and the man should have stumbled backwards and dropped like a sack of rocks. But this was one tough thug. He charged, and Dugan pivoted aside and slipped out of the way as the man went right on past. His momentum, with a little help from a shove in the small of the back, propelled him forward too fast for his feet and he tripped off the curb with his arms spread wide and sailed head first on to the street, and slid his face along the concrete.

Even so, as Dugan finally heard the sound of approaching sirens, the man got to his feet again. At that moment, though, a black Cadillac sedan slid up. The driver said something Dugan couldn't hear and the man jumped in, and the Caddy was gone. Then the cop cars, wherever they were headed, wailed past on some street a block or two away, and they were gone, too.

By the time Dugan got inside the office, neither the two young Mexicans nor the girl he'd saved from the gunman were in sight. He tried the door beside the cashier's window, where they must have gone, but it was locked. He stepped over to the window. It was bulletproof glass with a metal slide beneath it to put your money in . . . money they stole from you in return for your stolen car.

A heavy-set young Latina scowled at him and spoke through a round metal grate set in the glass. 'Can I help you?'

'Yeah,' he said. 'Where'd those people go?'

'Peeble?' Chewing her gum and acting like she didn't understand him. '*No entiendo.*'

'*Los hombres,*' he said, '*and la . . . la chica. Donde van?*' Miss Davis, his old Spanish teacher, would have been proud. 'Where did—'

'You here to pick up a vehicle, sir?'

'You're damn right I am, but . . .' He gave up. 'A Camry. They just brought it in. And if you think I'm gonna pay—'

'Wait, please.' She swiveled away from the window and typed on a keyboard off to her left. Finally she turned back. 'Your vehicle will be out in front.' She pointed. 'No charge.'

He turned toward the front door, and saw the Camry already coming out the gate and being parked at the curb. They obviously didn't need an ignition key around here. He started for the door, then turned and went back to the window. 'Listen,' he said, leaning toward the glass, 'who was—'

A door burst open in the wall behind the cashier, maybe ten feet back, and one of the two Mexican toughs came out, and behind him the woman in the red dress. Finally came a different man, an older, beefy-looking guy.

'Hey!' Dugan called.

The three of them stopped and stared at him, wide-eyed.

'I'm the *one*,' he shouted, pointing at his own chest. 'I saved her!'

The woman took a step his way, but the younger punk yanked on her arm and dragged her toward a different door, which the older guy opened. One of the straps of her dress had slipped off her shoulder.

Dugan was too surprised at being ignored to think what to say, but as she was pulled through the door the woman hiked the strap back up over her shoulder and pointed a finger right at him. 'Dammit!' she yelled. 'Why couldn't you mind your own—'

The door closed behind her.

Hoping the tow thugs hadn't stolen his phone, he ran outside to the Camry. A man stood beside the open driver's door. Tall and wide, with a nose that over the years had been battered nearly flat against his face, this one was a thug-and-a-half. And he didn't step aside from the car door as Dugan approached.

Instead, he nodded politely. '*Señor* Cho is grateful for your help,' he said. 'This is a good deed he will not forget.'

'Bullshit.' Dugan, wondering what part of Mexico *this* huge guy could be from, looked up at him. 'Whoever that woman in red is, *she* doesn't think I did something good. I'm calling the—'

'No.' The guy rested his fist on Dugan's shoulder. 'Listen carefully, *señor*.' He pressed down and the fist felt like one of those iron shot-put balls Dugan's cousin used to heave in high school. 'The "woman in red" you speak of, she is the daughter of *Señor* Juan Cho. Your actions here have saved you so far two hundred *dolares*. And now, what happened you will keep to yourself. Because this way you will save yourself also very much trouble, *amigo*.' He grinned. '*Entiende?*'

'Yeah,' Dugan said. 'I get it.'

TWO

'**J**uan Cho?' Kirsten couldn't believe it. 'That's the guy's *name*?'

'Yeah, he— Hold on.' Dugan was pulling her wheeled carry-on bag through level four of the parking garage at O'Hare airport. 'There it is,' he said, pointing, 'two rows over.'

When they got to the Camry he put her bag in the trunk, then handed her the keys, taking for granted she'd drive. Which was fine with her, although she was wiped out, having spent the last ten hours or so getting home. So she set her Starbucks cup on the roof of the car and gave him another hug, their fourth since they'd met in the baggage claim area, each one longer and more . . . how to put it? . . . 'interesting' than the last, and finally untangled herself and got behind the wheel.

It was late Sunday afternoon. She'd been in Seattle because of a divorce and child custody fight out there that led to the mother running off with a three-year-old. The father was convinced they'd gone to Chicago and, not wanting to involve law enforcement, hired Kirsten through one of his lawyers here. She'd found mother and daughter camping out in a thousand-square-foot hotel suite in Trump Tower. That was a year ago, and Kirsten was paid and forgot about it. Meanwhile, the whole sorry mess had swollen and festered and was finally set for trial. She'd gone out there last week and, after numerous delays, was scheduled to testify on Monday. Then the lawyers notified her late Saturday afternoon that 'all disputes have been resolved.' They didn't say how, and she couldn't have cared less. She'd learned during her stay in Seattle that her client was easily as despicable as the little girl's mother. They both deserved to be tried, found guilty, and sentenced to a lifetime of living together. The kid, though, deserved better. Kids deserved parents who—

'Hello? Anyone in there?' Dugan was trying to get her attention. 'They're piling up behind us.'

She looked around and discovered she'd apparently just paid the cashier on the way out of the garage and they were still sitting motionless beside the booth. 'Sorry,' she said, and drove on.

'Want me to drive?' Dugan asked.

'No, I'm fine. Just jet-lagged.' She paused. 'So, where were we?'

'We were on level four, before you negotiated that spiral ramp at about sixty miles an hour. I mean, I know you're anxious to get me home and we can . . . you know . . . get reacquainted, but Jesus!'

'You're exaggerating. But anyway, you were telling me about this guy who owns Wancho's Towing.'

'Oh, right. Name's Juan Cho. His father came from

somewhere in China and anglicized the last name. But his mother's from one of those towns across from Texas on the Rio Grande. I guess that's why he hires all Mexicans . . . and not the honest guys who'll work two-and-a-half jobs to feed a family.'

'What, no Chinese?'

'He was raised Mexican. Besides, there's not that big a pool of Chinese to choose from,' Dugan said. 'And the ones that get in are all . . . like . . . chemical engineers.'

'Or violinists,' she added. 'But anyway, how'd you find out the guy's name?'

'I learned it a year ago, when I sued Wancho's Towing for a client who needed body work for both his Jeep and himself after a run-in with a Wancho's crew.'

'Really? You never told me about that case.'

'Yeah, well, it was barely filed before it got dismissed on a pre-trial motion. Juan Cho was in court the day the order was entered. My client, no bargain himself, didn't want to pay for an appeal. So I let it die. But I'd already done some checking and heard lots of bad stories about Mr Cho and his business practices.'

'He probably starts the stories himself,' she said, 'to make a No Parking sign with "Wancho's Towing" on it something people take seriously.'

'Anyway, back to Friday night's adventure. Like I said, Larry Candle and I went out for ribs.'

'I'd call any evening spent with Larry a "disaster," not an adventure . . . but where does Wancho's Towing come in? I mean, you don't even own a car.'

'If you keep interrupting,' he said, 'I won't finish before we get home.'

'So? Why the deadline?'

''Cause we can't talk after we get home. I have champagne chilling, and supper to heat up, and after that . . . you know . . . there's the fun stuff.'

Traffic was heavy from the airport into downtown, and Kirsten drove and drank her coffee, wondering if she could stay awake for 'the fun stuff.' She let him tell her the whole story, even the parts he wasn't especially proud of. Which, she was certain, was most of it. His fellow Aikido students, though – at least the less-disciplined ones – would have been thrilled.

By the time he finished they were almost at their condo. 'I should have known,' she said, 'that I couldn't go off and leave you alone.'

'Hey, I got your car back in good shape . . . and it didn't cost anything.'

'Didn't cost anything *yet*,' she said.

'Meaning what?'

'I'm just saying . . . you never know.'

'Anyway, Cho's got a daughter named Isobel – with an "o" – who's college age. That had to be her. And the older guy was Cho himself, holding the door while she's screaming at me and one of the punks is pulling her through it.'

'What about your friend with the gun . . . did you get a look at the license plate of the car that picked him up?'

'No, it happened too fast and I—'

'Right. So . . . no idea who he is?'

'Not a clue, and I'm hoping he knows as much about me.'

'I hope so, too. But Mr Cho, he had your car . . . *my* car . . . and he'd have found out right away who owns it, and it's an easy leap from me to you. So my suggestion? Follow the advice of the big guy with the twelve-pound fist.'

'I suppose, but . . . Hold it. Where'd the "twelve pound" figure come from?'

'You said his fist felt like one of those iron balls your cousin threw in high school. That's what the shots weigh in high school, twelve pounds.'

'OK . . . and how do you know that?'

'Damn, Dugan, I'm a private detective. I know stuff.'

'Uh-huh. Good. So then, genius, here's a tougher question: What do we do with the gun?'

'Gun?'

'Specifically, a Double Eagle Mark Two, Series Ninety, forty-five caliber Colt semi-automatic. The one the black guy dropped. Right now, I got it wrapped up and under your suitcase back there in the trunk.' He paused. 'Seemed like a good idea at the time.'

THREE

D ugan sat in a conference room at his office nursing a growing headache as two accountants tried to help him understand a complicated settlement agreement. His client, Myles McGonigle, suffered a spinal injury and would need specialized medical care and equipment for the rest of his life, so the proposed settlement was a 'structured' settlement, designed to provide a series of payments to Myles over an extended period of time. The complications arose because no one could predict exactly what care he'd need, or what rehab equipment and technology might become available in the future.

Dugan was about to call a timeout when Mollie buzzed him. 'Kirsten's on the line,' she said. 'Says she has the information you're looking for.'

'I'll take it in my office.' He stood and nodded to the accountants. 'Sorry,' he said, although the opposite was true, and he was sure they knew it. He waved his hand over the papers spread out on the table. 'Keep working on breaking this down to where I can understand it, OK? Think: "sixth grader."'

Heading down the hall, he marveled that it was only ten thirty, Monday morning, and Kirsten apparently already had what they wanted. Marveling, yes, but not all that surprised. She still had some good cop contacts. She'd been a homicide detective – and well-respected by brass and rank-and-file both – when she quit to go private.

In his office, he picked up the phone. 'What the hell?' he said. 'What took you so long?'

'Very funny. Is it locked in your office safe?'

'It is.'

'Good. Then you're in possession of a weapon reported stolen on Saturday morning by its owner of record, a guy named Tyrone Beale.'

'So, if he's a registered gun owner, at least he's not a

convicted criminal. That fits with what Isobel Cho seemed to be saying . . . that he was trying to help her, not kidnap her.'

'And you're assuming the man you sent flying into the concrete, twice, was Beale.'

'I can't help it if the guy lost his balance. And I know it might have been someone who stole the gun from Beale, or someone who *bought* it from someone who stole it from Beale. But chances are it was Beale. How soon do you think you can find out anything about him?'

'Here's what I got: Tyrone Anthony Beale. Thirty-nine years old. African American. Six years in the Marine Corps. Twelve years with the Cook County Sheriff's Office. As of a year ago he's a licensed private detective in the state of Illinois, in business for himself.'

'Really. So . . . do you know him?'

'Never heard of him before today. But I'm told he hires himself out as a "Professional Security Driver."'

'Uh-huh, and what does he drive?'

'It's not what. It's who. Low grade VIPs . . . mostly entertainers, actors, authors pushing books, people like that. They come into town, they need someone to drive 'em around. But Beale specializes in the ones wanting security services as well as transportation.'

'Like a bodyguard?'

'Yeah. I bet it's usually an ego thing on the client's part.'

'So let's assume it was Beale who I . . . who had the balance issues Friday night. I'm not sure he ever got a very good look at me. And if he did, no way he'd have recognized me, right?'

'Far as I know,' she said, 'you're no more famous than he is.'

'You think? Anyway, I'll turn that forty-five in to the cops this afternoon.'

Dugan went back to the accountants and at eleven thirty, just as he was getting a handle on the structured settlement agreement, Mollie buzzed him again. 'I know you said hold your calls,' she said, 'but I couldn't get rid of this one. The guy claims you'll want to take his call. Name's Tyrone Beale.'

'Damn,' Dugan said. 'Does he sound happy?'

'What?'

'Put him through.' He waited, then hit the flashing button. 'Mr Beale?'

'Yeah, I—'
'It's nice to hear from you. I suppose you're calling about
your . . . about the property you misplaced.'
'Right. We should—'
'Lunch is on me,' Dugan said. 'You pick the spot.'

FOUR

D ugan took a cab – a three-mile ride up Lake Shore Drive
– and got there first and checked the place out. The lunch
crowd was heavy, but the service looked fast. Before
long Beale arrived, looking like he'd stepped out of *GQ* in blue
slacks and a tan leather sport coat over a yellow turtleneck. It
was the same guy, all right, down to the ugly abrasion on the
left side of his face, as though he'd scraped it across some
concrete. He wasn't smiling.

They nodded to each other and walked over to order their
lunches, Dugan figuring that since it was on him the guy would
pick one of the more expensive entrées. And he did. He ordered
the Chicken Supreme, a grilled chicken breast sandwich on a
caraway bun. How much can you spend at the Safari Café,
basically a hot dog stand at the Lincoln Park Zoo? 'Lettuce and
hot sauce,' Beale said. 'No mayo, no fries.' He carried his own
bottle of Evian to wash it down. This guy thought ahead. And
watched his weight.

Dugan chose the Double-Dog-Special, with fries and a Pepsi,
and Beale led the way to a park bench set in the grass a few yards
back from the wide walkway known as the zoo's 'Main Mall.' They
sat on opposite ends of the bench, laid out their lunches between
them, and dug in. The sky was blue and the grass was green, and
if there hadn't been business to attend to, Dugan would have been
happy just to sit there in the sun, munching on his fries, watching
all the kids run around, and listening to the monkeys chatter and
the exotic birds scream in the distance. Maybe the upside of losing
his law license – which looked like a pretty sure thing just then
– would be having the time to enjoy places like this.

But there was business to attend to, and Dugan spoke first.

'Friday night? That was a mistake. I'd had a few pops and I wasn't thinking very straight to begin with. Then I saw the gun and . . . well . . . you know . . . Sorry.'

'Uh-huh.' Beale took a swig of his water. 'How'd you know this morning what I called about?'

'Would I have thought it was some *other* Tyrone Beale? Maybe selling legal malpractice insurance?'

'No, I mean, how'd you know the guy you sucker-punched was named Tyrone Beale?'

'I got the number off your gun and got a little help from . . . from a friend . . . one who knows people.' Dugan pointed his hot dog at Beale. 'But you, how'd you know *my* name – to call *me*?'

'I took the plate number off your ride . . . your wife's ride . . . and I know a few people myself.'

'So we're even then,' Dugan said, although he was certain Beale had already left in the Cadillac before the Camry was brought around to the front of Wancho's.

Beale touched his fingertips to the left side of his face. 'Not exactly even,' he said. 'Anyway, is that it? That bulge there in your jacket pocket?'

'Got some ID?'

Beale showed him his driver's license and Dugan took the gun from his pocket – wrapped inside a brown bag – and gave it to him.

'Feels kinda light,' Beale said, and set the bag on the bench. 'Got another pocket?'

'Oh . . . yeah.' Dugan passed him a second brown bag, smaller, which Beale put beside the first one. 'The clip,' Dugan said. 'I removed it. So if for some reason a cop stopped me, at least the damn thing wouldn't be loaded.'

'It's not a "clip,"' Beale said, 'it's a "magazine."' He finished the last of his sandwich, then opened both paper bags. He inserted the magazine and slid the weapon into a holster under his arm. He didn't seem to care who might have been watching, but at the same time moved so smoothly and quickly that probably no one but Dugan saw the gun.

'You reported it stolen,' Dugan said. 'Now I guess you'll have to say you found it.'

'Uh-huh. I take it you didn't fire it.'

'Nope.'

'So who knows what happened at Wancho's?'

'You, me, and Juan Cho and his people,' Dugan said. 'And Isobel.' He watched Beale watching him. 'And I suppose you told whoever hired you to get, or keep, Isobel away from her father.'

Beale looked more curious than ever, but didn't ask how Dugan knew what he knew. 'I didn't see anyone there old enough to be her father.'

'He was there,' Dugan said. 'I saw him. I've seen him before.'

'And are you saying you didn't tell anyone what happened?'

'One of Cho's people advised me not to.'

'I'm guessing it was more than "advice." But I'm also guessing you told the "friend" who helped you get my name. Would that be your wife? The wife who runs a private detective agency called Wild Onion, Ltd.?'

'I have only one wife.'

'And you told her.'

Dugan shrugged.

Beale twisted the cap tight on his water bottle and slid it into his jacket pocket. He squeezed one of the brown bags Dugan gave him into a tight ball and put it, along with the wrappings from his sandwich, into the other bag. He stood up and looked around, doing a three-sixty turn. 'All this anti-terrorism stuff,' he said, shaking his head. 'Hard to find a barrel to toss your trash in.'

'So . . . no grudges?' Dugan asked. 'I mean, I wouldn't exactly call it a sucker-punch, not when the punchee's going after his gun.'

'Grudges waste energy,' Beale said, and with his free hand he pulled a card from his lapel pocket and gave it to Dugan. 'Anyone you know ever needs a security driver, call me. Meanwhile, if you ever get the idea you should discuss what happened with anyone?' He was sounding very serious. 'I'd say you should think again.'

'That's pretty much what Cho's guy told me, and he had a very heavy fist.'

'I'm sure he did,' Beale said. 'And I'm thinking neither one of us wants to find out just how heavy Mr Cho and his people can come down.' He gave a solemn goodbye nod, turned away from Dugan, and headed for the gate out of the zoo, looking from side to side as he went. Once a marine, always a marine. Always on the alert for trouble.

Or maybe looking for a trash container.

FIVE

K irsten stood off to the side, pretending to study the colorful visitors' map she'd picked up on her way into the zoo, but in fact peering out from under the bill of her cap. It was a khaki-colored baseball cap, with *Lincoln Park Zoo* on the front in red lettering. She'd just purchased it in the gift shop, so it wasn't likely to draw Dugan's attention.

They'd agreed that after he gave the gun back to Tyrone Beale they would forget about the whole incident, put it behind them. Easy to say, but not so easy to do. Not for her. So here she was, watching his back and not telling him about it. Of course she'd probably tell him later. And of course he'd probably be pissed off when she did.

From about hundred yards away she saw him turn over the gun to the husky black man who had to be Tyrone Beale. She'd had a busy morning, both on line and on the phone, but hadn't learned much but basic facts about this guy who'd apparently been hired to whisk Isobel Cho away from her father. His features looked familiar, as though he were related to someone she should know, but she couldn't imagine who it was.

She didn't know a whole lot yet about Isobel, either; but a few interesting, even intriguing, bits had popped up. Interesting that the daughter of this guy who builds up a rather notorious tow truck empire attends a Catholic high school for girls just north of the city, then trots off to Massachusetts, to Tufts, one of the 'Little Ivies,' where she graduates with honors in four years. But even more intriguing – and this gleaned from a few gossip column snippets – that she comes home romantically linked with a young lawyer named Jamison Traynor. Quite a leap for the Cho family, because Jamison, a recent hire in the Chicago office of the DC-based firm of Gillem & Cox, was the son of Eleanor Traynor. And Eleanor Traynor? She was the junior US senator from Illinois.

So Kirsten watched until, with their brief picnic over, Tyrone Beale and Dugan nodded their goodbyes. Beale headed for the entrance and, after a slight detour to a trash barrel, was gone. He moved with an athlete's grace and a fast stride, and Kirsten knew she'd have to hustle to stay with him. At the entrance gate she glanced back at Dugan. He was sitting – sprawling, actually – with his outstretched arms draped over the back of the bench, his face turned up toward the sky . . . probably wishing he could spend all afternoon at the zoo.

She turned her attention back to Tyrone Beale. He led her west, out of Lincoln Park and on to Lincoln Avenue, talking on his cellphone as he walked. She wasn't sure what she hoped to accomplish by this spur-of-the-moment surveillance, particularly because Beale seemed to be keeping an eye out for a taxi. There weren't many on the street, and if an empty one came along and he snared it, she would have had little chance of flagging down another one and following him.

As it turned out, her concern was half-correct. Beale climbed into a car that pulled up and stopped beside him, and the car sped off, leaving her behind. It wasn't a cab, though. It was a long black Cadillac sedan, with a livery license plate, the kind of plate issued to a limousine service. She memorized the number and was sure the vehicle would be registered to Tyrone Beale, the self-styled 'Professional Security Driver.'

But more important than that, when the limo drove past her, before stopping for Beale, it was going pretty slowly and she'd glanced over and gotten a clear look at the driver, and couldn't believe her eyes. She *knew* the guy. Or at least knew who he was.

His name was Andrew, or it was the last time she'd seen him, anyway. That was . . . how many years ago? Five? Six? But the day itself wasn't one she'd ever forget. The two of them had stood face-to-face in a bright little kitchen, with three bodies lying on the floor around them, each body leaking blood on to the tiles. She'd held a semi-automatic pistol in her hand. It was Andrew's pistol, and she'd held it pointed at Andrew's chest.

Her hand had been steady, but her mind wavering back and forth. She'd thought almost too long, in fact, before she let Andrew walk away. Or run, actually. And not just away from her, but away from the cops who were on their way . . . to arrest him and charge him with murder.

SIX

Once Beale was out of sight Dugan sat on the bench again, feeling the breeze on his cheeks and noticing how the sunlight was filtered through the rustling leaves above him. It came to him that he spent way too much time at a cluttered desk in a climate-controlled cave, and way too little time in the fresh air and sunshine. Still, a guy's gotta make a living. So, as a compromise, he decided to walk the three miles back to his office. He sighed and got to his feet.

As he walked he thought about Juan Cho, and Isobel Cho, and Tyrone Beale. Kirsten was right. The whole business was no concern of his. On the other hand, he *had* been a participant, albeit an unwitting one. And not a hero . . . at least not in Isobel's eyes. Beale hadn't denied being hired to get Isobel away, or keep her away, from her father. What was the problem between them? Whatever it was, it would take a hell of an intra-familial spat to move one party to hire an armed bodyguard.

Maybe Beale and the Cho family drama were none of his business, but they were certainly more interesting to think about than, say, the apparently inevitable suspension of his law license, just for giving a few bucks to a cop or two once in a while for recommending his legal services to accident victims. More interesting, too, than pondering that complicated structured settlement agreement waiting for him back at the office. Still, the McGonigle case was a big one, and the fee would go a long way toward bridging the no-income gap until he got his license back. Which brought up that nagging question he'd rather not think about: Did he still *want* the damn law license?

Not really.

Or *did* he?

That's what was ping-ponging through his mind when he came to his senses and found himself standing on the marble-floored lobby of his downtown high-rise, pushing the call button for the elevator up to his cave and his cluttered desk. He checked his watch. He'd taken a forty-five minute walk . . . and he hadn't paid one damn bit of attention to the fresh air and the sunshine.

When he got up to his suite the receptionist was signing for a FedEx delivery, and he gave her a nod and went on through. He waved at three secretaries at their work stations as he passed three empty lawyers' offices. He knew where the lawyers were. Fred Schustein and Peter Rienzo both had workers' compensation hearings expected to last all day. Larry Candle was in a conference room at the other end of the suite, taking the deposition of a supermarket produce manager in a slip and fall case involving a wayward leaf of spinach and a fractured skull.

Dugan's secretary and office manager, Mollie Wavers, had a desk right outside his office, but she wasn't there, which was a surprise. And another surprise: the door to his office was closed. It was rarely closed even when he was in it, and never when he wasn't.

He had a hunch. He picked up Mollie's phone and tapped out Kirsten's cell number.

Kirsten answered with, 'Hey, Mollie. You back already?'

'Hey, yourself,' Dugan said. 'What are you doing in my office?'

'Shhh,' she hissed. 'I don't want Larry to know I'm here.' Larry Candle drove Kirsten nuts, and she went to great lengths to avoid him, which wasn't easy because Larry worshipped her. 'And as to what I'm *doing* . . .' He heard the rustle of papers. 'I'm straightening up the mess on your desk.'

He slammed the phone down, and ran over and threw open his office door. 'Stop! I know just where everything—'

But all she was doing was sitting on the one little section of his sofa that didn't hold stacks of files, eating an apple she'd cut into quarters. '*Gotcha!*' she said.

He went behind his desk and sat down. 'Did I ever tell you that you were a pain in the ass?'

'Not that I can recall. Want part of my apple?'

He shook his head. 'Where the hell is Mollie?'

'Restroom, for God's sake. Enjoy your lunch?'

'Got a lot to catch up on right now,' he said, and made a production of picking up his phone. 'See you at dinner. Tell you how it went down.'

'I already *know* how it went down. I asked if you enjoyed it.'

'Oh?' He put the phone down.

'You're a lawyer. Did you warn Beale that carrying a gun

around in the city of Chicago, even unloaded, can get you jail time?'

'Nope. I'm not *his* lawyer. But I handed it over in a plain brown wrapper.'

'Two brown bags, actually,' she said. 'And Beale took the Colt from one and loaded it with the magazine from the other, and slipped it into a holster under his left arm.'

He sighed, recalling his certainty that no one could have noticed what Beale did with the gun. He rested his forearms on his desktop and leaned forward. 'We agreed that I'd return the gun and we'd forget about the whole thing. So why were you lurking around? Afraid I couldn't handle Beale by myself?'

'You already proved you could "handle" him, by bouncing him around on the pavement. I got a good look at the side of his face. I was there because I just can't shake the feeling that trying to "forget about the whole thing," isn't going to make it go away.'

'Yeah, well, it *is* interesting to think about, but whatever's going on, it doesn't involve us.'

'Of course not. Still, I'm wondering, did Beale say how he ID'ed you?'

'From the Camry's license number. When they drove off in that Caddy they must have hid somewhere nearby, and he got a look at the plate.'

'Was it Jamison Traynor who hired him to get Isobel away from her father?'

'He didn't deny that *someone* did, but I didn't ask if it was someone named Jamison Traynor. Mostly because I never heard of anyone named Jamison Traynor.'

'He's Isobel's boyfriend. And he's the son of Eleanor Traynor.'

'Jesus.' He shook his head. 'Senator Eleanor Traynor, another poster child for attractive airheads who manage to make it big through money and the miracle of media politics.'

'And to think,' Kirsten said, 'not so long ago men had a lock on that category.'

'Right, the good ol' days. Anyway, her son's name didn't come up.'

'And what about Beale?' Kirsten asked. 'Does *he* plan to forget about the incident? At least once the side of his face heals.'

'It sounds that way. He said that getting Juan Cho pissed off wasn't a good idea, for either him or me.'

'Good. But back to that Cadillac . . . I guess you don't know if it had a livery license plate.'

'No idea. All I know is it was black and long – but not a stretch limo.'

'And the driver?'

'A man. I think he was black, but it was dark and I didn't get a good look at him. Why?'

'A long black Cadillac stopped and picked up Beale today, and the driver was a black man.'

'And?'

'And you've got a lot to catch up on right now,' she said, and stood up and headed for the open door. 'See you at dinner. Tell you all about it.'

'Hold on.' He stood up. 'Tell me—'

'I'll pick up a couple of chicken salads. See you at home.' And she was out the door.

In fact, Dugan *did* have a backlog to catch up on, and he told Mollie to hold his calls while he waded through a mound of correspondence, court pleadings, and phone messages. It was way easier to lose himself in the never-ending flow of cases than it was to ponder what he really wanted to do with his life, and when Mollie buzzed him he was surprised to see that it was after five o'clock.

'I'm on my way out the door,' she said, 'and that guy Tyrone Beale's on the line again. Says it's important.'

'OK, put him through.'

Beale came on the line. 'I don't suppose you're watching the Channel Five news,' he said.

'I don't— I mean . . . why?'

'They're on to something else now, anyway. But they had a story on about Isobel Cho. You know, the girl you left with her father . . . against her will. Seems her friends, and some co-workers at a day camp where she volunteers . . . and her boyfriend, too . . . they're all getting pretty worried. Nobody seems to know where she is.'

SEVEN

The next morning, Tuesday, Dugan was making breakfast and watching the story about Isobel Cho on the local news. It was in second place, behind a 'road rage' shooting on the Dan Ryan Expressway. They showed what looked to be a graduation photo of Isobel, then a shot of Wancho's Towing. The news guy said there'd been no official police comment about the 'possible disappearance,' but that 'sources close to the matter' said the police were 'looking into the situation,' and that there was 'no evidence of foul play.'

When the screen switched to some guy convincing himself to tell his doctor about his erectile dysfunction, Dugan hit the mute button on the remote and went to the refrigerator and got out a carton of eggs. He opened it and took out one egg, then set the carton on the counter and looked over at the stove . . . and saw greasy black smoke swirling up from the pan he was frying bacon in.

'Hey Kirsten!' he yelled, bending over to search along the wall under the cabinets. 'Where's the switch for the exhaust fan?'

'Where it's always been,' she called back, and then appeared in the doorway, holding her robe closed with one hand, toweling her hair with the other. 'It's behind— Hell, *Dugan*!'

She dashed past him and he turned . . . to see flames shooting up from the frying pan, licking awfully close to the curtain on the window over the counter. Kirsten did a frantic 360-degree spin, as though looking for something. 'Damn,' she said, and spread out her towel and draped it across the flaming pan. She turned off the gas and then snatched the damp towel off the pan. The fire was already out. She hip-checked him out of her way and reached behind the coffee maker to turn on the exhaust fan.

'Nice work,' Dugan said, as the smoke cleared. 'But . . . do that last part again.'

'What?' She was shaking her head and inspecting the towel, which had what he considered some pretty insignificant scorch spots. 'Do *what* part again?'

'That sort of nudge thing.' He stepped in and bumped his hip against hers. 'Like a little dance step.'

'You are a lost cause,' she said, and walked out of the kitchen and down the hall.

'I never did care much for that pink towel set,' he said, and followed her, but by the time he got there she'd locked herself in the bathroom.

Heading back up the hall he looked down and was surprised to discover that he still had the egg clutched in his hand. Or part of it . . . the gooey part . . . along with a few pieces of broken shell.

Dugan was sentenced to a solo breakfast, but they shared a cab ride downtown. The driver was one of those guys who are convinced that no pedestrian or vehicle would ever dare cross in front of them, and roared through every intersection at breakneck speed. He *did* make every light that way . . . sort of. Meanwhile, Dugan tried not to look out the window and Kirsten concentrated on her iPhone, sliding the tip of her finger back and forth across the screen. Dugan had never gotten into the apps stuff, and really didn't even know what she was doing.

'Hate to interrupt,' he finally said, 'but we have to decide what we're gonna do.'

'Not a problem.' She didn't look up from the phone. 'I'll get a new towel set at Macy's and you scrub the soot off the walls. Oh, and there's raw egg on the—'

'Very cute,' he said, 'but you know that's not what I'm talking about.'

'Oh, then you must mean Isobel Cho. I've just been reading about her.' She looked up and winked at him, and then got suddenly very serious. 'My suggestion? Same as I said last night. Do nothing, at least for now. Until I get a handle on what's going on.'

Dugan glanced up at the driver, but no way was the guy listening. He was too busy playing Grand Prix driver and arguing with someone on his hands-free cellphone. 'And later,' Dugan said, 'how do I explain not going to the cops with what I saw?'

'What's to explain? The girl apparently went out with friends Friday night. When you saw her it was obviously after she'd left her friends, and she was with her own father, in his place of business. Still Friday night.'

'Early Saturday morning.'

'Right.' She slipped the phone back into her purse. 'The important thing is, she was with her father.'

'But she was trying to get away from him.'

'When it was all over, it may have appeared that way to you,' Kirsten said, 'but did she actually *say* that?'

'Of course not. Not exactly. She yelled at me and asked why I didn't mind my own business. Then her father and another guy pulled her through a door and shut it behind them.'

'So she did *not* tell you that she didn't want to be with her father.'

'But I'm sure she—'

'Hey, we're working on what you tell the cops about why you haven't said anything. OK?'

He shrugged.

'Anyway, sometime on Monday a friend . . . and we assume the friend was Jamison Traynor . . . reported her missing. You had seen her only briefly, on the previous Friday night.'

'Saturday morning.'

'Dammit, Dugan, one a.m. Saturday is Friday night, especially for purposes of your story.'

'OK. But if there wasn't "foul play," there was a very strange incident, something the police would want to know about.'

'We don't even know,' she said, 'how seriously the cops are taking her so-called disappearance at this point. She's an adult, and can come and go as she pleases.'

'Taking it seriously or not, if someone claims she's missing, you have to know the cops have at least spoken to her father.'

'Agreed,' Kirsten said. 'But we don't know what he told them. If he saw the "strange incident" you saw, and if he thought it was important, maybe he already told the cops about it.'

'I don't know if he saw everything I saw, but his thugs sure did. And how could he *not* think it's important? A guy with a gun pulling Isobel out the door . . . then me getting in the way and the guy running off.'

'Let's be more precise.' Kirsten frowned. 'What you saw was Isobel leaving Wancho's Towing with a guy, but then the guy ran into you and tripped and fell. Then he got up and left. As he was falling you noticed for the first time that he had a gun, but you never saw him pointing it at anyone.' She paused. 'Am I right?'

'Well, technically, yes. But—' He gasped as the cab suddenly veered to the curb and stopped, sending both of them straining against their seat belts. Dugan looked out and realized they'd already gotten to his building. 'But I'm—'

'And Isobel ended up staying there with her father.'

'True. And I didn't actually *see* Tyrone Beale holding off Cho's thugs with a gun. And Isobel didn't actually *say* she didn't want to be with her father, or that she wanted to leave with Beale.'

'So you could interpret what you saw one way or another. But as far as explaining why you haven't gone to the cops . . . if you ever *need* to explain . . . the facts themselves aren't all that clear. Also, why would you ever imagine that an incident that happened on Friday night had anything to do with Isobel's disappearance, or *possible* disappearance, two or three days later?'

'I'd sure love to be the lawyer cross-examining me if I made *that* claim,' he said. 'But OK, for now I just sit tight. Except what about—'

'Hey, people!' the cab driver broke in. 'You are sitting all day here, or what?'

'Hey, yourself,' Dugan said. 'Relax. The meter's running.' The driver's cell rang and Dugan turned back to Kirsten. 'What about Beale? When he called to tell me it was on TV about Isobel being missing I should have asked him if he'd talked to the cops. But he hung up before we got that far. I better call him today.'

'Hold off on that, too,' Kirsten said. 'But let's you and I stay in close touch. If Beale *did* talk to the cops, and depending on what he told them and what Juan Cho told them, they might be contacting you. And I want to be there when you talk to them.'

'They won't let you sit in.'

'We'll cross that bridge,' she said, and smiled . . . sweetly. 'Meanwhile, we don't know what Beale told Jamison Traynor, either. Or whether he was even working for Traynor. We're assuming he was, but he didn't *say* so, and—'

'Hey, people!' It was the cabbie again.

'OK, OK,' Dugan said. 'I'm getting out. She's staying in.' He opened the door and added, 'Drive safely, will ya? And stay off the goddamn phone.'

One can always hope.

EIGHT

D ugan stood on the curb and watched the cab lurch away with Kirsten. He knew she'd just come off a case where she'd made a huge fee, mostly for sitting around waiting to testify . . . at a trial that got settled. She didn't seem to have any other clients right then, but he couldn't be certain of that. He *did* know, however, although she hadn't said so, that she was into this Isobel Cho thing already, big time.

He'd known all along that she couldn't *not* be, once she'd heard about his walk-on part in that drama at Wancho's Towing, and how one of the players had warned him to keep it to himself, to save himself 'very much trouble, *amigo*.' But despite the threat, and all the half-assed excuses for keeping quiet Kirsten could dream up, they both knew that if Isobel didn't show up, and soon, he'd have to go to the cops with what he saw.

He went inside the building with all this churning through his mind, and then was pleasantly surprised at the calm that came over him on the elevator ride up to his office. That had to be because he was headed back to his daily routine: reviewing court documents, arguing with insurance adjusters, reassuring clients who struggled with disabling injuries and fear of the future. He was damn good at what he did.

Yeah, but do I like *what I do?*

At five after nine he was at his desk going through yesterday's mail, when Mollie put through a call from Larry Candle. 'Hey, Doogs, I'm on my cell, on the way to court,' Larry said. 'Nine o'clock call.'

'You're late,' Dugan said.

'*Nulo problemo.*' Larry had his own brand of Spanish. 'I'm thirteenth on the call. Anyway, I just ran into this guy in our building lobby. He looked familiar, but I couldn't place him. He seemed to know who I was, though, and he wanted me to call and tell you to meet him right away . . . out front on the sidewalk. I told him he should just call and—'

'He didn't tell you his name?'

'Nope, but the side of his face is all scratched up and— Oops! *Excuso mio.*' Dugan heard a jumble of angry voices speaking at once, and then just Larry again. 'Jesus, Doogs, it's a jungle out here. Gotta watch where you're goin' all the time. Anyway, the guy's probably a wacko. But I'm headed into the courthouse, so . . . gotta go.'

'Wait. Larry?' But the call was over, so Dugan slipped on his jacket and went out to Mollie's desk. 'I'll be out for awhile.'

'How long?' Sometimes it was hard to tell if Mollie worked for him, or he worked for her. 'Jeff Jones will be calling,' she said, 'about the Castro case. And you—'

'I have my cell if anything important comes up.' He was walking away by then, and called back. 'But only if it's *really* important.'

He could trust Mollie to sort out the *really* important from the *usual* important. Meanwhile, forget the comforting law office routine. And for now he'd forget Kirsten's advice to do nothing until she got a handle on what was going on. His own handle had just appeared – in the form of Tyrone Beale – and he should grab it, and see what door it opened up.

'We can talk while we walk,' Beale said. He started off at a fast pace, and Dugan joined him.

What the hell? Why not?

It was a beautiful warm day, but the *GQ* look Beale had sported at the zoo was gone. Today it was sneakers, khakis, a baggy golf shirt – and to get to 'baggy' with Beale's build you had to start with size XL and then some – and a White Sox cap on his shaved skull. Heading north on Clark Street, Dugan thought they must look like a typical lawyer-client pair, hustling along the crowded sidewalk toward the Daley Center, the courthouse where Larry Candle was doing his thing on the nine o'clock call.

Beale seemed preoccupied, and they walked for a few minutes, but didn't talk, until Dugan decided it was up to him. 'You lose track of my number?'

'Huh?' Beale seemed startled, as though he'd forgotten Dugan was there. 'Oh, your phone number? No.'

'Then why not just call?'

'I wanna leave a light footprint.'

'Oh,' Dugan said, 'I see.' Which he did, sort of. By that time they were passing the Daley Center and might have been headed for the State of Illinois Building, but they quickly went past that, too. 'You . . . uh . . . you seem a little strung out,' he said.

'Tell me 'bout it.'

'Actually,' Dugan said, 'the "tell-me-'bout-it" ball is in your court.'

'OK, yeah, I guess it is. But I'm . . . thinking.'

'Uh-huh.' Dugan paused to let Beale elaborate, and when nothing came he said, 'You know, you're not giving me a lot of incentive here to continue this dance.'

'I understand,' Beale said. By then they were waiting for the *Walk* light under the El tracks at Lake Street. 'I guess you trust me, right?'

'What?'

'I said, I guess—'

'I heard you. What are you talking about?'

'You must've done some checking on me, and you had no problem giving me back my gun. So you must kind of trust me. I hope so, anyway, 'cause now I want you to come with me.'

'Come with you? Where?' *Jesus, was it really such a great idea to be out here with this guy?*

'My place. Not far. Near the old Hubbard Street courthouse. You haven't talked to the cops yet, right? I mean, about Friday night?'

'It was past midnight,' Dugan said. 'So Saturday morning.'

'OK, but you *haven't*, right?'

'Talked to the cops? No. Have you?'

'No.' The light changed and Beale started across Lake Street. 'Thing is, someone showed up this morning at my place, and wants to talk to you.'

'Someone like who?'

'Like Isobel Cho . . . if she's still there.'

It would have been only fifteen minutes on foot, but Dugan waved down a cab and they took it north across the river and into an area where, before the economy tanked, new high-rise condo buildings had been springing up seemingly every week. Now construction had mostly stalled, with some half-built towers sitting there, silent and forlorn.

They climbed out of the cab on a block that had a construction site – basically a huge abandoned hole in the ground behind tall chain-link fencing – running all along one side of the street, and a row of 1920s' vintage two- and three-story buildings on the other. Some of the buildings had been rehabbed during the last economic boom; most still languished forlornly. Bars anchored the two corners, with modest shops and retail businesses in between. The upper floors were intended for commercial offices, it seemed, and not apartments, although it appeared that most were vacant.

In the middle of the block was a beautifully restored red brick building with two street-level businesses: a White Hen Pantry and a place called Lo-Kee Cleaners & Alterations. Beale led the way into the cleaners, a bright, modern-looking establishment. To their right an elderly Asian woman – probably Korean, Dugan guessed – sat at a sewing machine. She glanced up at them, but returned at once to her work. Straight ahead a younger woman – also probably Korean – stood behind a counter, sorting through a huge pile of clothing. She said nothing, but looked up and nodded at Beale.

Beale didn't break stride as he turned and slid sideways through a narrow break in the counter. Dugan followed and they passed among rows of plastic-sheathed clothing hanging on racks. Beyond the racks, near the rear wall, Beale turned left and they went through an unlocked door into a sort of vestibule, with three more doors. One was wide open and led into a storeroom which was obviously part of the White Hen. A second was closed and had a small frosted-glass window, and must have led out to the alley. The third was also closed. That one Beale unlocked and pulled open.

They went through and let the door swing shut behind them. It was a solid metal fire door which Dugan saw could be pushed open from the inside with a panic bar, no key needed. A few feet ahead was a set of stairs leading up. 'I'm at the top, on three,' Beale said, and led the way. 'Place is zoned commercial, but I did some work for the building owner – Mrs Kee, the one at the sewing machine, whose son runs the White Hen – and I have an apartment up here, behind an office. I haven't been here long, but it's a nice set-up.'

At the second floor landing there was another closed fire door and a second flight of stairs. 'Hope you have a classier entrance for clients,' Dugan said, following Beale up.

'Yeah, there's a front entrance for clients, through a street door between the cleaners and the White Hen, with a more formal stairway and an elevator. I usually enter and leave the way we came, through the cleaners, or else through the alley entrance. I like to avoid the public eye. I like this building, too. It's solid and secure.'

'And Isobel Cho,' Dugan said, as they climbed the stairway, 'you don't even know if she's still here?'

'She was here when I left, but she wasn't locked in, and she's pretty unpredictable. I think she'll be here, though. My going to get you was her idea.'

'Me? How does she even know who I am?'

'She doesn't. Not really. But she wanted to talk to the guy who stuck his nose into what was happening at Wancho's.'

'Great. So she can yell at me again?'

'No. I think she's looking for help.'

They reached the landing and by then it was a little late to turn back. 'I smell coffee,' Dugan said, 'and . . . burnt toast, I guess. Was she alone?'

'Yes.'

Beale unlocked the door – again, a heavy fire door – and they stepped directly into a high-ceilinged room; once probably an office or a storeroom, now equipped as a kitchen.

Isobel Cho was there, sitting at a square wooden table, spreading cream cheese on a toasted bagel. And she was *not* alone.

NINE

'Well, well,' Kirsten said, lifting her coffee in salute, 'look who's here.'

'What the hell?' Tyrone Beale seemed stunned. 'Dammit, Isobel, who *is* this person?'

'Oh my God!' Isobel's eyes widened. 'Don't you *know*? I thought you and she were working on a case together.'

'What case? I don't even *know* this . . . this . . .'

'Careful,' Dugan said, laying a hand on Beale's shoulder. 'This *person* is my wife.'

'And the case we're working on together, Mr Beale,' Kirsten said, 'is the disappearance of Isobel Cho.'

Within minutes things had settled down and they all had their own mugs of coffee, with more brewing in Beale's Mr Coffee. The bagels and cream cheese were courtesy of Kirsten.

'Only four bagels, though,' she said. 'I didn't expect to run into Dugan here . . . or Isobel either.' She handed the bag to Beale. 'Isobel and I each took one, and Dugan's already had way too big a breakfast. So that leaves two for you.'

'Uh, thanks.' Beale looked at Dugan and lifted the bag, offering to share, but Dugan waved him off.

'They're blueberry,' Kirsten said. 'And better when they're toasted.'

While Beale headed for the toaster oven on the counter, Isobel sat in silence, looking as though she felt out of place among her elders. Not intimidated, though. More like . . . self-assured, confident. Maybe even condescending. *Or*, Kirsten thought, *trying to appear that way, anyway.* She had on wide-leg faded jeans and flat shoes, and a see-through long-sleeved blouse, worn unbuttoned over a dark-blue tee. Her black hair was up in a sort of casual twist. No make-up, and no need for it. Very young. Very attractive.

Beale slid the two bagels into the toaster oven and Dugan sipped his coffee, both men acting as though nothing in particular were drawing their interest. Especially not Isobel.

'Your business card, Mr Beale,' Kirsten said, as he sat back down, 'lists nothing but an email address and an unlisted phone number.'

'I know,' he said. 'So how'd you find me?'

'Trade secret.' She smiled. 'It wasn't easy, though, and I pride myself on—'

'Right,' Dugan said, 'you're the best. But for now, would somebody like to explain what the hell is going on?'

'Great idea,' Kirsten said. 'Let's start with Isobel.' *And maybe see how self-assured she really is.* 'She and I were just chatting when you guys came in. Right, Isobel?'

'I wouldn't say "chatting,"' Isobel said, her voice strong, but also a little strident. 'I'd say you were lying to me.'

'Who, me?' Kirsten widened her eyes in mock surprise.

'Yes. I only let you in because you made it seem like you and Mr Beale were working on a case together. You implied you were an employee of his, or his partner or something. And—' The bell on the toaster oven interrupted her and Beale went for his bagels. When he was seated again, Isobel continued, 'You said you were here with breakfast, implying that you always did that.'

'So, if I "implied" things, I didn't exactly say them.'

'You deliberately led me to believe things which weren't true. That's a *lie*.'

'Really.' Kirsten shrugged. 'Well, nobody's perfect.'

'*Perfect* has nothing to do with it.' Isobel leaned forward, obviously thinking she was ahead in the match, about to charge the net. 'I don't approve of lying, and furthermore—'

'You want "furthermore"?' Kirsten broke in. 'Then "furthermore," knock off the crap about how lying – which I did *not* do – offends the hell out of you and your damn principles. Let's get to the point.'

'I . . . you . . .' Isobel was clearly speechless. The condescension – or superiority or whatever it was – was gone, replaced by simple shock, like she'd taken a slap in the face.

From interrogating God-knows-how-many suspects in her cop days Kirsten knew how to segue, seamlessly, from kindly big sister to cold-hearted bitch. And she loved that game. But she'd accomplished the breakthrough she wanted, and this wasn't a suspect. This was a person she actually liked already, for some reason. 'Look Isobel,' she said, easing the edge out of her voice, 'you came here to Mr Beale's office because you had a problem. And I guess Mr Beale here thought getting Dugan involved might help somehow. Right?'

'No.' Isobel shook her head. 'That was *my* idea.' Her voice softer now. 'I asked who that man was who . . . who interfered. I mean, he was obviously trying to help, to do the right thing, and he didn't waste time thinking about it. He just went right ahead and, you know, he accomplished what he tried to do. So I asked, and Mr Beale said he had talked to the man and he thought the man was, like, trustworthy.'

'Uh-huh,' Kirsten said, 'a trustworthy guy who doesn't waste

time thinking. Makes sense to me. Thing is, though, with Dugan
you also get *me*. Clear?'

Staring back at her, Isobel nodded. 'I . . . I guess so.'

'Good. And you know what? I'm going to help you.' Kirsten
hardly believed she'd gone ahead and said that. But damn, she
had just finished working for a guy she'd disliked at first sight,
and the sentiment only got worse, despite a very handsome fee.
Isobel Cho she liked at first sight. And she had a feeling that
sentiment wasn't going to go away either. 'If you want me to,'
she added.

'Yes, I do. But I mean . . . the thing is . . . I don't really have
any money of my own.'

'Oh, well . . . we'll talk about that later.' Not wasting time
thinking seemed to be the operative procedure here. 'For now,
tell us: What's the problem?'

'The problem? I . . . it's hard to . . .' She stared down at the
mug on the table in front of her, squeezing it with both hands
as though it might run away and leave her there.

'Look at me,' Kirsten said, 'and—' She stopped short, because
when Isobel raised her head there were tears shining in the corners
of her eyes.

'I'm sorry,' Isobel said. 'Everything's just so . . . give me a
minute, OK?'

'Take your time.' She could tell Isobel was determined not
to cry. 'It's OK.' She felt like hugging the girl, but held back.
'Let's do it this way: you listen, and I'll describe what I think
brought us to this point. And if you . . . or Mr Beale . . .
have—'

'*Beale*'s enough. You can skip the "Mr" part,' Beale said.

'Right. So if you, or Beale here . . . or Dugan, for that matter
. . . have anything to add, or to correct, just break in.' She looked
around. 'How's that sound to everyone?'

They all nodded, including Isobel, who seemed to be regaining
her composure.

'So,' Kirsten began, 'someone hired Beale to keep an eye on
you. The "someone" wasn't you, and it wasn't your father. It
was Jamison Traynor.' She paused.

No one said anything, but Isobel's eyes widened and Beale
gave a slight nod.

'Whatever it was that triggered the hiring of . . . well . . . of a bodyguard, I don't believe the idea was to protect you from your father. So—'

'No, not my father,' Isobel said. 'I mean, I was ignoring him, but I wasn't *afraid* of him. The thing is, I'd had this . . . this feeling. I guess I was nervous, anyway, because someone had broken into our apartment and took some cash and an iPod one of my roommates had left on the table. We were all nervous, but we had new locks put on and it seemed OK. And then I started getting this feeling, like someone was watching me. Like . . . like a stalker. I'd think I saw someone, and look around, but then I wouldn't see anyone. I mean, I was getting scared, and I mentioned it to Jamison.'

'And it was his idea to hire Beale,' Kirsten said.

'Yes. Then I tried to downplay it. I told him not to, but he has . . . his family's quite wealthy, you know, and he said it was worth it to see if there really *was* someone.'

'The idea was to watch,' Beale said, 'and if some guy's really stalking her, to get his identity and then scare the . . . the crap outta him. But also, of course, to step in if she was actually in danger. She wasn't happy about the whole idea, and she never let me hang around very close to her. So Friday night I'm across the street and I see her come outta the restaurant by herself. She had went in with her girlfriends and—'

'It was late,' Isobel said, 'and I wanted to be at the gym early Saturday, so I left before they did.'

'Wasn't like the street was totally deserted.' Beale was spreading cream cheese on his second bagel. 'There was a few people coming and going. Some looking for cabs. And I could tell that's what she was doing, too. Then these two Hispanic-looking guys step up outta nowhere and get her into a car before I can do anything. It happened fast and they were smooth, and I really couldn't tell if she knew them, or agreed to go.'

'And you had a car handy?' Kirsten asked.

'Of course. So me and my . . . my driver . . . took off after 'em, hanging back, to see where they're going. Finally they pull up to Wancho's Towing, and I'm thinking, "Jesus, her old man's place. Good thing I didn't stick my nose in." Then all the sudden I see her fighting like a crazy woman . . . scratching, punching, clawing . . . while the two mopes pull her outta the car. They're dragging her inside the office there, and she's holding back, until one of 'em hauls off and slaps her on the head. *Wham!* So that's it. I go in after her.' He paused. 'And I woulda got her out, too, except . . .' He waved his bagel toward Dugan.

'Yeah . . . well . . .' Dugan looked apologetic. 'Like the lady said, "Nobody's perfect."'

'So, Isobel,' Kirsten said, 'do you think it could have been your father who was behind whoever you felt was stalking you?'

'No. I asked him and he said no. And I believe him. Plus, I'm not even positive someone *was* stalking me.'

'OK. But anyway, that night he sent someone to pick you up and take you to him. And that's because you wouldn't do what he wanted you to do, right?'

'Right,' Isobel said, looking surprised. 'But how did you—'

'Damn,' Dugan cut in. 'What kind of father would—'

'Um . . . Mr Trustworthy?' Kirsten handed her empty mug to him. 'Would you . . . ?' He took the mug without even a roll of his eyes, and she continued. 'And what your father wanted, Isobel, was that you stop seeing Jamison Traynor.'

'Yes.' Isobel stared as though Kirsten were a Tarot reader, getting it right.

'But you don't like to be told what to do,' Kirsten went on. 'And of course you didn't stop seeing Jamison. Your father insisted, but what could he do? You're of age. You're not living at home, and he apparently didn't know *where* you were living.'

Dugan set Kirsten's coffee on the table. 'Anyone else for a refill?'

Isobel shook her head, not taking her eyes off Kirsten, and Beale said, 'I'm good.'

Dugan took just his own mug and went back to the coffee maker.

'Anyway, Isobel,' Kirsten went on, 'when you wouldn't come in and talk to him, he sent his men to find you and bring you in . . . to *drag* you in if they had to.'

'Which brings us,' Dugan said, standing beside the table, 'to Fri— I mean Saturday morning.'

'What we're up to is,' Kirsten said, looking straight at Isobel, 'what's the deal with your father and you? Why fight so hard, when you knew they were just taking you to him?'

'I just . . . You were right when you said I don't like to be told what to do.' Isobel picked up her mug and stood.

'I'll get it,' Dugan said, and snatched the mug from her hand.

She was stalling and he obviously saw that as clearly as Kirsten did. 'You just go ahead with your story.'

'Right,' Kirsten said. 'Go on. Once you see they're taking you to your father's, why not relax and just go in and talk to him?'

'For one thing,' Isobel said, sitting again and taking a deep breath, 'those two . . . idiots . . . they never said who they were. I was terrified.' She took her refilled mug from Dugan. 'Thank you.'

'No problem.' Dugan still didn't sit. He seemed restless. The room had an alcove to the right of the door into the rest of the apartment. There was a window in the alcove and he wandered over there with his coffee.

'Go on, Isobel,' Kirsten said.

'You're right, when I saw where they were taking me, I stopped being scared of them. I got mad. I have a really bad temper. I just kinda lost control. And they're grabbing at me and pushing me around, and—'

'But a few minutes later,' Kirsten said, 'that part's over and Beale's gone, and then you're yelling at Dugan for interfering. Why? After all, it was only your father. Why not just sit and let him scream about how he doesn't approve of your choices? And then walk away and do your own thing. Happens all the time.'

'I yelled at him,' Isobel said, pointing at Dugan, 'because I was upset. And anyway, my father never screams. Sometimes I wish he would.'

'OK, we'll come back to that, too. So then what happened?'

'My father took me home, and *kept* me there. At home. *His* house, I mean. In my old room . . . but locked in.'

'Ah, a captive, then. All day Saturday, and then Sunday. But sometime early Monday morning you left. Tell us how that happened.'

'Glad to hear there's something you don't know,' Beale said.

'Actually, I think I *do* know.' Kirsten smiled. 'I think her father *let* her go.'

'Bullshit,' Beale said. 'That's not what he told the cops.'

'And you know exactly what he told the cops?' Kirsten asked.

'Well, from the news reports you can—'

'No,' Isobel interrupted, 'she's right. The fact is, he let me go.'

'What the hell,' Beale said. 'So why'd you show up here telling me you're on the run from your old man, and you can't possibly go to the cops.'

Isobel slapped her palms on the table and leaned forward. 'I did *not* say I was running from my father. I said I was scared. And I *am*. The thing is, I have this . . . this feeling someone's been following me, or . . . like . . . watching me. And it's *not* my father.' She leaned back, and now seemed suddenly on the verge of tears. 'I'm *not* making this up. And I *can't* go to the police. If you don't want to believe—'

'Excuse me, eveyone.' Dugan was looking out the window as he spoke. 'But from here I can see just a bit of the street. And . . . did somebody mention police?'

TEN

D ugan leaned to the side, to get a better angle. The window was in a part of the building that jutted out over a gangway, and the view was too narrow for him to see just where the two men were headed after they left their double-parked dark green Chevy Tahoe.

'You sure they're cops?' Kirsten asked. 'And sure they're coming into this building?'

'No, and no,' he said. 'They—'

A long buzz, then three shorts, sounded from somewhere toward the front of Beale's apartment.

'Make that: No, and yes,' Dugan said.

'Goddammit.' Beale was on his feet. 'They're down in the vestibule.'

Another long and three shorts, and by then Isobel was standing, too. Beale looked pissed off; Isobel, scared. Kirsten, though, sat calmly where she was, which impressed the hell out of Dugan. Although, come to think of it, why *not* calm? The cops certainly weren't after her, or him either.

'They must've followed you here,' Beale said, pointing a finger at Kirsten.

'Not a chance,' she said. 'If they followed anyone, it was you and Dugan. Or Isobel. But who's to say they followed anyone? If they wanted to talk to you, they could find you. I did.'

Again a long ring, and three more shorts.

'Shouldn't someone answer it?' Isobel said.

'That's up to Beale,' Kirsten said. 'None of the rest of us lives here.'

'I'm not answering.' Beale shook his head. 'But damn, I hope they don't have a warrant or something.'

'If they do,' Dugan said, 'you don't have to worry about letting them in. They'll be bustin' down the door any minute.'

'Maybe.' Kirsten shrugged. 'Thing is, you're not even sure they're cops.'

'So,' Dugan said, 'let's find out.' He set his coffee on the table, turned, and went out the door he and Beale had come in by, and down the back stairs.

He hurried through the cleaners and out the front door. The Tahoe was there, still double-parked where he'd seen it from Beale's window. It was empty, so the cops – or non-cops – were still inside the building. He noted the plate number as he ran to the entrance door between Lo-Kee Cleaners and the White Hen.

He got to the plate glass door just in time to see the two men go through a second glass door, the one between the outer vestibule and a larger lobby beyond that. He pulled open the outer door, but too late, and the second door closed before he could get to it, with a noticeable click of its lock. The men, who had obviously not seen Dugan, headed up a wide set of stairs and disappeared from view.

From its façade he'd seen that the building was renovated, and the inside smelled of paint and varnish. Both the vestibule itself and the lobby beyond were well-lit and spotless, with freshly painted walls, golden oak woodwork, and gleaming tile floors. On the wall to his right a new, but antique-style, call panel held buttons beside name slots for eight offices on the second floor and eight on the third floor. Not many renters had yet moved in, because only two slots were filled for the second floor, a child psychologist and a graphic designer; and one for the third: SECURITY DRIVING.

Someone from the second floor must have buzzed the two men inside – so much for Beale's "solid and secure" building – so Dugan hit both of those buttons. A long and three shorts, copying the men's rhythm. He got one response from the intercom. 'Police again?' a man asked, sounding irritated. 'I just buzzed you guys in.'

'Yeah, well, I was outside and missed the door. Hit the button again, please. Nothing you need to worry about, but it's important.'

There was a buzz and the door clicked, and Dugan went into the lobby. He bypassed a very small, probably very slow, elevator and headed for the stairs. It was an open staircase with smooth wood banisters, with a turnaround landing halfway up each flight. The two men would already have been at the top by the time he started up, so he moved quickly. When he reached the landing between the second and third floors he could hear the men knocking loudly on what must have been Beale's door.

He called out, 'Excuse me. Can I help you?' and climbed the rest of the way up.

Wide hallways at the top, both brightly lit by skylights, led off to the left and the right. To his left the hall led past four office doors, two on each side, and ended with a door with an *EXIT* sign above it. To his right, where the men were, there were four more office doors and the hall dead-ended at a blank wall.

One of the two men was tall, slim, and hard-looking, with a narrow, pointed face. The other was shorter, maybe five-eight, and squat. Both in sport coats. Both with the look of men sensible people didn't mess with. They sure *might* have been cops.

Dugan started toward them. 'Can I help you?' he asked again.

'We don't need any help,' the squat man said. He had a deep, raspy voice, like a toad. Matching his body shape and his wide, deeply-lined face. 'You just go about your business,' Toad said.

Dugan kept walking their way. 'Right,' he said. 'Except . . . this building *is* my business.' He already had his cellphone in his hand, holding it in a way that not even a nervous cop could mistake it for a weapon. He thought of reaching into his pocket for a business card, but these guys might think he was going for a gun. 'I represent the building owner, Mrs Kee, and if there's a problem I can get her son up here right away.' He lifted his cell and waved it toward them. 'He's just down in the White Hen and—'

'You got a hearing problem, Jocko? I said everything's fine.' Toad's eyes bulged and he leaned forward, clearly to intimidate Dugan, make him back off.

Dugan stopped walking, but didn't step back. 'Actually, that's not what you said. You said you didn't need any *help*, which is a completely diff—'

'Unless you wanna be arrested, sir,' the taller man said, his voice strangely thin and strained for such a tough-looking man, 'you'll leave this area. Right now.' But no show of badge.

'Oh,' Dugan said, 'in that case . . .'

He turned and strolled back toward the stairs, not hiding the fact that he was making a call on his cell. He speed-dialed Kirsten, and when she answered he spoke loud enough for the men to hear. 'Police? Yeah, look, I'm here at Lo-Kee Cleaners.' He paused, then gave the address, paying no attention to whatever it was that Kirsten was saying. 'These two sort of *violent*-looking men just forced their way into the building here and went upstairs, where our tenants have offices.' He turned at the stairway and started down, raising his voice as though he were scared. 'Yes . . . and hurry. I think they have guns.'

Then he ran like hell down the stairs.

From inside the cleaners Dugan watched the two guys who *could* have been cops – or *some* sort of law enforcement, even if they didn't want to show IDs – come out of the building and drive away. He turned to the woman behind the counter. 'I need to get through the door to the back stairs, to get up to Mr Beale's place again.'

'Mr Beale, he leave you message.'

'A message?'

'He say two women gone somewhere. They catch you later. Say he catch you later, too.'

Just then Dugan's phone vibrated. He hoped it was Kirsten, but it was Mollie.

'What's up?' he asked.

'Jeff Jones needs you,' Mollie said. 'They just finished jury instructions and he's "*this* close," he says, to settling Castro with the jury out. But he needs you at the courthouse . . . to talk to Mrs Castro. They're in twenty—'

'I know. Judge Prendergast. I'm on it.' They'd been working on the Castro case for three years. It was a big one, and Perlita Castro was . . . well . . . more than a little high-strung.

Out on the sidewalk, looking for a cab, he went into his text messages. There was one from Kirsten. It said: 'All cool. Got idea. Later.'

Damn. Some people have all the fun.

ELEVEN

B y the time she got Dugan's bogus 911 call, Kirsten had already herded Isobel down the back stairs and into a little storage room where there was a door out to the alley. Beale had insisted on staying put upstairs and getting rid of the signs of their breakfast. He said if the men were persistent enough he'd eventually answer his door. If they were cops he'd be cooperative, but not let them inside unless they had a warrant – which neither he nor Kirsten thought likely, since they hadn't already broken in.

'And if they're not cops?' she'd asked.

'Then,' he said, with a perceptible squaring of his shoulders, 'they certainly won't be a problem.'

She thought he was overdoing the macho thing a little, but – not without some reluctance on her part – she and Isobel left without him.

Dugan's call gave her no chance to talk and she couldn't tell whether he thought the men trying to get in were cops or not, but he certainly wasn't enthusiastic about them. And Isobel was more than anxious to get away from them, whoever they were. She was clearly very afraid of something, or someone, and for some reason she didn't want to talk to the police.

Kirsten thumbed out a quick text message to Dugan, then opened the alley door and looked out. No one there, so they hurried down the alley and out on to the street where she'd parked her car. She'd gotten an idea.

They got in the car, and as Kirsten started the engine, Isobel asked, 'Shouldn't we . . . like . . . check on your husband?'

The question surprised Kirsten, and it made her like Isobel even more. 'Dugan?' she said. 'He'll be fine.'

'Uh, OK. That's good, I guess.' Isobel slumped back in her seat. 'I haven't slept for two whole nights. Where are we going, anyway?'

'Where do you *want* to go?'

'I . . . nowhere. There's nowhere I can think of to go.' She paused, then said, 'You must think I'm crazy.'

'You could be, I guess,' Kirsten said, 'but the evidence on that isn't in yet. Meanwhile, let's just drive around awhile, while you think about the best way to tell me what's going on.'

'There's nothing more to tell, so there's nothing to think about.'

'Yeah, right. So you think about nothing. I'll drive.'

'Good.' Isobel stretched her arms out in front of her, as though reaching out for the windshield. 'Because I'm *really* tired.'

Right, Kirsten thought, *not to mention* really *trying not to look afraid.*

Isobel had her head leaned back and her eyes closed, and Kirsten drove north on La Salle Street. It was strange how things so seldom turned out the way she'd expected, or planned. Her interest had been in protecting Dugan from any trouble that might head his way if Isobel stayed missing and he had to go to the cops with what he'd seen at Wancho's Towing. But then Isobel showed up and, before she knew it, Kirsten found herself signing on to help the girl. Her offer had been pretty much instinctive, and—

'You don't have to help me,' Isobel blurted out.

'I thought you were asleep,' Kirsten said.

'Just kinda dozing. But I looked over and saw you were thinking and, like, shaking your head to yourself. I bet you wish you didn't say you'd help someone who can't pay.'

'That's a bet you'd lose.'

'Yeah? Well, then you're thinking, "Her father has money, " or "Her boyfriend has money," and you're hoping—'

'Isobel, please. You're *not* a mind-reader, and that's *not* what I'm thinking. I promised I'd help you, and I will. Believe me, getting paid is one of my favorite things. But it's not the only thing, or the main thing. I just made a bundle doing something I didn't enjoy doing, for someone I didn't like very well. Which means I'm free for a while, to pick and choose. And what I'm choosing to do is to help you. If you want me to. Fact is, I can't always figure out my motivations myself. Let's just say . . . things even out.'

'What about Mr Beale?' Isobel asked. 'You think *he'll* help . . . without getting paid?'

'He might. He likes you.'

'I don't know about that. Jamison was the one who hired him, you know, and with me he was always kinda . . . standoffish. All business.'

'Oh? And you wanted him to come *on* to you, did you?'

'*No!* I'm just saying . . . Most guys . . .'

'Anyway, he might help, because he likes you,' Kirsten said. 'Plus, he likes *me*.'

'He never even *saw* you before today.'

'So? Neither did you. And *you* like me. Right?'

'I don't know,' Isobel said. 'I guess the evidence isn't in on *that* yet, either.'

Kirsten glanced over, caught Isobel smiling at her own cleverness, and said, 'To help you, though, I could use a little more information.'

'Yes, well, I guess there *is* a little more I could tell you.' Isobel yawned and stretched her arms again. 'But can it wait a little? 'Cause I'm not kidding. I'm *really* tired.'

It seemed like the truth, and not just a delaying tactic. 'I've got plenty to think about just now, anyway,' Kirsten said. 'You stop trying to read my mind, and take a little nap. Then we'll talk.'

A few minutes later Kirsten pulled on to Lake Shore Drive. Isobel had tilted the back of the bucket seat back as far as it would go and was unconscious almost at once, really out of it this time. It wasn't very safe to ride in a moving car that way, almost lying down, but Kirsten let the girl sleep, and concentrated for a few minutes on making sure no one was following them.

Going back to Beale's place made no sense. Beale had her number and he could call if anything interesting happened. Dugan might call, too, but her guess was that by now he was back at his office and in the middle of something. He worked very hard . . . which, of course, might be changing soon. She wondered if his law license was really going to be suspended. If so, it surely wouldn't be a long suspension, she thought, not just for paying a few cops to give his business cards to accident victims. He'd never gotten many clients that way in the first place, and he didn't do it at all any more.

More importantly, when the suspension was over, would he go back to practicing law? They weren't super-rich, but they already had a bigger stash stored up than she'd ever thought she'd see. But if he didn't practice law, what would he do? She knew he'd love to get more involved in her cases, and he'd already been a help to her on more than one occasion. In fact, she'd never find a more perfect partner. Except . . . dammit . . . she didn't *want* a partner.

She got out her cellphone, and stuck the ear bud in and tapped out a number. The call went through, and she asked a few questions and got the answers she wanted, thank God, and she signed off. Through it all Isobel seemed dead to the world, but it wouldn't have mattered if she'd heard Kirsten's end of the call, anyway. A few minutes later she swung the Camry on to the Irving Park exit off the Drive. At that point Isobel did stir, and shifted her weight around. But she sank back again at once.

Kirsten didn't really feel bad at all about her offer to help Isobel, regardless of whether she'd be paid. What she'd said about just raking in a large fee was true. But there were other reasons, too. For one thing, *something* was going on with Isobel, and whatever it was, whoever was following her . . . or *watching* her . . . Dugan had gotten himself involved. That meant Kirsten had to stay close, stay where she could see how things developed, for *his* sake.

Besides, she was feeling at loose ends these days. No clients, but also – and this had a lot to do with it – no sign of the baby they'd been trying so hard for, and she needed something else to wrap her mind around. It had seemed so natural . . . so *right* . . . to reach out to Isobel, who, beneath the apparent bravado, seemed truly to be lost . . . alone on a raft, struggling with winds she couldn't control.

Kirsten, who always wanted to be in control, knew what that was like. She'd found herself in such situations too, more than once. Those were scary times, times that cried out for outside help. And so far someone had always been there for her. So why shouldn't she do the same for someone else once in awhile?

It was intriguing, too, that two of those 'someones' – people who'd been there for her – were showing up again. One of them Kirsten knew as Andrew, the man Tyrone Beale had described, after a noticeable beat of hesitation, as his 'driver.' And the other? The other was someone she'd just invited into the game. And when Isobel met him, Kirsten would get the chance to watch one more bewildered person try to wrap her mind around a very curious force of nature.

TWELVE

'Hey!' Kirsten reached over and gave Isobel a shove. 'Wake-up time!'

'Yeah, OK. In a minute.' Isobel shifted around, turned her back on Kirsten and then was still again.

'C'mon, wake up. We're almost there,' Kirsten said. She stopped at a red light and shoved Isobel again, harder. 'Shouldn't have let you lower the seat like that, anyway. It's not safe.'

This time Isobel managed to sit up, and to raise the seatback to an upright position. She shook her head as though to stir up her brain cells. 'What did you say?' Her speech was sluggish and she looked awful . . . or at least, Kirsten thought, as awful as Isobel *could* look, damn her. 'I don't understand.'

'If you've got the seat reclined and we have an accident, you—'

'No,' Isobel said, 'I mean, we're almost *where*?'

'We're almost where we're going. But first we have to talk. Remember how I guessed that your father had deliberately let you go?'

'Oh, so now it's a "guess"? A little while ago you said you *knew*.'

'Call it an "educated guess." I knew that Tyrone Beale would have told his client, Jamison Traynor, what happened Friday night, and that Jamison would have tried to get through to your father, wanting to talk to you.' The light turned green and Kirsten accelerated. It was stop-and-go all along on this part of Irving Park, which was fine with her, because she was in no hurry. 'My guess is your father stonewalled Jamison, so Jamison went to the police and said you were missing, and were last seen at Wancho's Towing. Your father's the kind of guy that cops don't mind hassling, and he doesn't need that kind of attention. So he decided to let you go before it got that far.'

Isobel was silent through all that, but hadn't gone back to sleep. Kirsten glanced over and saw once again that expression of someone watching a psychic get it right.

'It's not really that hard to put together,' Kirsten said. 'But now we come to the tricky part.'

'Tricky part?'

'Yeah. I'd have thought . . . and I bet your father did, too . . . that as soon as you knew you were free to go you would notify the police, or at least call Jamison, or one of your girlfriends, and tell them you weren't missing, that you were OK. But either you didn't tell anyone, or—'

'I didn't tell anyone.'

'And you stayed hidden.' A cab was trying to move over into her lane, and Kirsten let it in. 'So,' she said, 'who are you hiding from?'

'I don't know.'

'OK, we'll come back to that later. And you can't go to the police. Why is that?'

'My father . . . well . . . it's complicated. But I guess I have to tell *someone*. My sister and I, we—'

'A *sister*? I didn't even know you had a sister. Your mother . . . she died . . . a long time ago, right?'

'Yes. Breast cancer.'

'That must have been hard for you.'

'Yes, well, it was eleven years ago, and . . . Anyway, my sister . . . she's actually my *half*-sister . . . she's nine. Her name's Luisa.' She stopped, then reached over and put her hand on Kirsten's arm. 'Look, this is all confidential, OK?'

'You have my word. Go ahead.'

Isobel returned her hand to her lap. 'OK,' she said. 'Luisa's mother was Chinese, and she and my father weren't married. I never even knew—'

'Hold on a minute,' Kirsten said. She took her phone from her purse again and speed-dialed a number.

'Yeah?' The man sounded angry, but what else was new?

'That appointment? I need another fifteen, twenty minutes.'

'Yeah,' he said, and hung up.

'Right,' Kirsten said to the dead phone, 'I'm looking forward to it, too.' She turned to Isobel. 'There's a park up ahead, not too far. We'll stop there and talk.'

A few minutes later they came to Horner Park, one of the city's largest neighborhood parks, acres and acres of baseball diamonds and soccer fields that stretched for half a mile beside the north branch of the Chicago River. Kirsten turned on to the street that ran along the west edge of the park, and then on to a drive that curved around and led to a parking area near the field house. The few cars in the lot at that time of day were all up close to the building. She found a spot near the other end, in the shade, facing across a baseball diamond where twenty or thirty small kids and a couple of adults were engaged in some sort of organized races in the outfield. Well . . . *semi*-organized, anyway. A soft breeze brought the screams of the kids and the smell of fresh-cut grass through the open car windows.

'Back to Luisa,' Kirsten said. When she twisted in her seat to look straight at Isobel she could see beyond the girl and keep an eye on the entrance to the lot. 'Why did you say her mother *was* Chinese?'

'Because she died. In China. My father told me. I never met her. I never even *knew* about her, or about Luisa, until my father brought Luisa home one day. She wasn't even a year old then. My father's part-owner of a very small business in China . . . just a few people making, like, party favors and things . . . and he's always gone there a lot. Sometimes he would spend a week at a time there. Not so much any more. Now it's usually a few days at a time. Anyway, I never knew anything about my sister's birth. She was born in China and he brought her here from there, but he would never say anything more about it, and I don't ask any more. He's raised Luisa since the day he brought her home. Of course he's always had help with her . . . and with me, too, I guess. We don't have any relatives around here, but we always had a nanny.'

'OK, but you were explaining why you're in hiding, and why you can't go to the police.'

'Yes, well, I said it was complicated. I'll start with Friday night. When my father sent those men to take me to him, I was furious. As soon as we were alone he started telling me again that I had to stop seeing Jamison, and I told him I was an adult and he couldn't tell me what to do. I told him we'd already had that argument, too many times, and it was over, and that's why I'd been ignoring his demands that I come see him. He was angry and I was angry, and we ended up with him actually having me locked in my room. I couldn't *believe* it.'

'Yeah, well, it's not even *legal*, Isobel. You could have him—'

'I know, but he's my father, and . . . Anyway, I wasn't

mistreated, and they brought me all my meals, but I was kept in my room for two whole days, with no phone, no computer, no way to contact anyone. He knocked on my door a couple of times, but we're both . . . well . . . pretty stubborn, and I totally refused to speak to him. But then, Sunday night, he came again, and we'd both cooled down by then. We talked, and I saw something I'd never seen before. My father was . . . he was *different*.'

'Different how?'

'He was . . . Well, first, my father is a *very* strong man. I mean, people think he's terribly mean and harsh. And he *is*, I guess, in his business. The tow trucks and the men who work for him and all. But with Luisa and me he's not. He travels a lot, and even when he's home, he can be . . . *distant* . . . I guess. But he wants only the best for us, and wants us to be *our* best. Especially with our education. He can be very demanding, you know, like he insists we speak only Spanish at home, to him and to each other, so we stay bilingual.' Isobel paused, maybe realizing she'd gotten off-track. 'Anyway, the main thing is, he's always strong, figures out what has to be done, and does it. No hesitation, ever. In my whole life, I never saw one tiny bit of fear in him. Not of anyone, not of anything.'

'Until Sunday night.'

'Yes,' Isobel said, 'until Sunday night. Like I said, we'd both cooled down. And this time there was no argument. He said he'd thought it over, and that I was an adult now, and that even if he could send men to bring me to see him, he realized he couldn't really *make* me do *anything*. He said that I was free to go, because he knew he'd been wrong to lock me up.'

'Uh-huh,' Kirsten said, 'not to mention that the cops were about to get involved.'

'Yes, he told me . . . like you said . . . that Jamison had reported me missing, and that he didn't want to have to deal with the police. The thing is, for all of his bad reputation, my father's never been arrested or anything like that. But he said he had to be careful with the police. Still, I'm sure that wasn't the only reason he let me go. I'm sure he honestly realized he'd done a stupid, wrong thing. He apologized . . . I can't imagine how hard that was for him . . . and I'm sure he was sincere about it.'

'Fair enough. Anyway, did he say what he was afraid of?'

'My father would never *say* he was afraid at all, of anything.
What he said was he was sorry and I should go back to my
apartment and my friends, and live my life. He said he'd never
order me again to do anything, but then he said he was *asking*
me to stop seeing Jamison. I said I respected his wishes, but that
if Jamison and I broke up it would be because one of us wanted
to, not because of one of our parents. I told him—'

'Hold on. I just thought of something,' Kirsten said. 'This
relationship has been going on for . . . what? . . . a couple of
years?

'About that.'

'And has your father been against it all along?'

'Not that I know of. And that's why . . . I mean, I couldn't
understand it.' Isobel spread out her hands, palms up. 'He's
known about it almost from the beginning, and he never said he
didn't approve. Not till, like, a month ago or something.'

'And what are his objections?'

'Well, up until Sunday he'd always say things like, "Your
backgrounds are so different," or "You live in two different
worlds." Totally bogus arguments.'

'Totally,' Kirsten said, although to her mind they weren't,
which was irrelevant just then. 'So . . . what did he say on
Sunday?'

'When he said he was *asking* me to stop seeing Jamison, I
said "We're not as different as you think," and he just sat there
and didn't say anything for a long time. Finally, though, he said
I must never tell anyone what he was about to say. Then he said
the *real* reason was because there were people who didn't want
Jamison and me to be together. I said, "I don't care what *people*
want or don't want." He said he didn't either, usually, but . . .
but that these people were very serious, and very powerful. And
that's when I saw what I'd never seen before. He was
frightened.'

'And it's not himself he's frightened for, is it,' Kirsten said.

'No.'

'It's your sister.'

'I . . . yes, but . . . how did you know that?'

'Why else would you have spent all that time telling me about
Luisa? So . . . what did he say?'

'He said that as long as I stayed away from Jamison everything would be fine. But that if I didn't, we . . .' There were tears welling up in Isobel's eyes. 'If I didn't, we could say goodbye to Luisa. They would send her back to China.'

THIRTEEN

K irsten reached into the back seat of the Camry for a box of tissues and gave it to Isobel. 'Your sister,' she said, after Isobel had dried her eyes, 'is she . . . undocumented?'

'I never . . . I suppose I don't really *know*.' Isobel gave a helpless shrug. 'I never thought about it. She's just . . . you know . . . just my father's daughter, and my little sister. I mean, she goes to school and everything. She's not, like, a secret. She's cute, and bright. And I love her . . . almost like she's my daughter, y'know? . . . and she loves me.'

'Does she have a passport?'

'I have no idea. I'm sure she's never been out of the country. I don't know what the law is, but my father's pretty smart, and he has lawyers he could ask, and he obviously thinks these people can carry through on their threat. He warned me not to tell anyone at all about this, but . . . but now I've told you. You won't . . . I mean . . . even the police, if they hear about it . . . they might . . .'

'I promised confidentiality,' Kirsten said, 'and I keep my promises.' Just then she saw a car – an old, old Ford, 1960s' vintage she thought, and rose-colored – pull into the parking lot and come their way, but it passed behind them and kept on going, all the way to the field house. 'These "powerful people,"' she said, 'does your father know who they are?'

'I guess he must know. But he didn't tell me, and I didn't ask. I was too shocked to think of asking anything.'

'So you left your father's house,' Kirsten said. 'When? That very night?'

'No. Early Monday morning, like about five o'clock.' The old Ford had U-turned by the field house and seemed headed back out of the lot, but went past them and parked three spaces down.

'. . . and then I couldn't possibly sleep,' Isobel was saying, 'so I got up and—'

'Hold on,' Kirsten said. She was looking past Isobel, and was startled to see the hard-top roof of the Ford begin to separate itself from the windshield, then lift and retract backwards. 'Damn,' she said, 'a convertible.'

'What are you—'

'Look behind you,' Kirsten said.

Isobel twisted around in her seat and the two of them watched as what appeared to be the trunk lid of the Ford – except that it was hinged at the rear, near the bumper – rose up like an opening clam shell, and the car top folded and settled itself down into what would have been the trunk. Then the clam shell slowly swung down into place again. The driver opened his door and, with what Kirsten thought was remarkable dexterity for someone his size, extracted himself from the front seat.

He was a huge man, built tall and wide, like a Pepsi machine. He was dressed all in black, including a short-sleeved shirt that showed enormous biceps and forearms. This guy made Tyrone Beale look like the 'BEFORE' picture in a Bowflex ad. His deeply lined face had prominent cheekbones and large, deep-set eyes, and a thick mustache drooped along both sides of his mouth. His hair, black turning gray, was long and shaggy and by no means stylish. He closed the car door, then bent and reached behind the front seat, and came up with a hat and put it on. It was a black, narrow-brimmed fedora and would still have been too small even if he'd shaved his head.

The man seemed completely unaware that there were two women in a nearby car gawking at him. He checked the Ford's rear deck, apparently making sure it had snapped into place over the folded top, and then walked over to a long bench that sat on the third base side of a baseball diamond's empty infield. The bench was actually two benches, placed end-to-end, for use by one of the teams during a game. He sat on one of them and looked out toward the kids running around in left field.

'That . . . that *person*,' Isobel said, 'I don't like the looks of him, or the way he's staring out at those little kids. What is he *thinking* about?'

'I don't know,' Kirsten said. 'Let's go ask him.'

'No way. Are you kidding?'

'Nope.' Kirsten opened her door and got out, and went around to Isobel's door and opened it, too. 'C'mon,' she said. 'He's waiting for us.'

'What? Are you a friend of his or something?'

'Let's say he's a friend of *mine*. I don't know if Cuffs thinks of anyone as an actual friend of *his*. But if he does, I'm probably it.'

Isobel got out of the car and, in almost a whisper, said, 'That's his name? *Cuffs?*'

'It's a nickname. A long story . . . from his days as a cop. But let's go. I'll introduce you. Because, if I have my way, the two of you are going to be spending some quality time together.'

As they walked together over to where Cuffs sat, Kirsten said, 'If you want my help, and you're determined to stay hidden, Cuffs is the man.'

'But I told you, I can't pay any—'

'Did I say anything about paying? He'll be compensated, one way or another. Besides, he owes me a favor.'

He sat with his back to them, and as they drew nearer to him, Kirsten called, 'Hey Cuffs, nice ride.' He didn't answer. He was an acquired taste, but she really *did* like Cuffs. That can happen when a guy saves your life . . . and you save his. 'How ya doin'?'

'I'm above ground.' He stood and turned to face them, and looked even bigger close up. His scowl was maybe a bit less intimidating than usual, which was about the best one could hope for from him. 'This the one?' he asked.

'Yep.' Kirsten turned to Isobel. 'Isobel Cho,' she said, 'meet Milo Radovich.' Then to Cuffs she said, 'I told her she can call you "Cuffs."'

Isobel took a tiny step forward and reached out as though to shake hands, but Cuffs stayed where he was and smoothed his mustache with a forefinger. 'Am I s'posed to care what she calls me?' He didn't wait for an answer, but said, 'Your Juan Cho's daughter.' A fact, not a question.

'Yes,' Isobel said. 'One of them. He has two.'

'Uh-huh. Juan Cho. I never met the sonovabitch. But I don't like him. That a problem to you?'

'A problem? I don't even—'

'Not a problem, Isobel,' Kirsten said. 'Cuffs doesn't like *anybody*.'

'Oh? And he's the person who's supposed to be . . . like . . . my bodyguard?'

'I'm not *supposed* to be anything,' Cuffs said. 'And I'm not *like* a bodyguard. I keep you safe. Or I drive away alone. It's up to you.'

'Good. Then it's a done deal,' Kirsten said.

'Maybe.' Cuffs stared down at Isobel. 'The last guy you had watching out for you obviously wasn't up to the job. With me, it'll be different.'

'It wasn't his fault. I insisted he stay across the street, and—'

'Bullshit. He agrees to stay across the street, and you get grabbed, it's his fucking fault. Period. You want my protection, you do what I say. Got it?'

'You know what?' Isobel said, her voice suddenly filled with anger and frustration. 'You're a nasty, mean person. And a bully, too. I don't like you, and—'

'Good. Then we understand each other.' Cuffs turned and rearranged the two benches so he could sit on one and the two women on the other, and they could face each other. They were long, heavy, wooden benches, and he moved them like they were cheap plastic lawn chairs. 'Sit down,' he said. 'We'll talk. But keep it short.'

FOURTEEN

Kirsten did the talking. Cuffs asked a question here and there, and either she or Isobel answered. Isobel didn't seem to be warming up to him, which was no surprise. Finally, Kirsten said, 'That's everything I know so far.'

'Uh-huh,' Cuffs said. He turned to Isobel, 'So, two things. Why didn't you just stay at your old man's place? And when you left, where'd you go?'

'He said I could stay there, but I thought about it, and I decided I wanted to stay hidden. I knew, though, that if I did that, pretty soon the police would come looking for me at my father's house. I didn't want him to get into trouble, so I planned to leave Monday afternoon, yesterday, without telling any—'

'Hold on,' Kirsten said. 'You told me you left at five a.m.'

'I know I did. I'm saying what I *planned* to do was rest all morning and then leave after lunch, but I left when the sun was just coming up.'

'Why so early?' Cuffs asked.

'Because Luisa's nanny . . . she always gets up real early . . . she said there was a car parked a little down the street from our house with two guys in it, just sitting there. And I looked out and I thought, "My God, the police, they're already here." So I decided I had to leave right away. I grabbed some stuff and I left, out the back.'

'Are you sure,' Cuffs asked, 'that they were cops?'

'Well . . . I guess I don't know for sure. I looked out and saw the car with two guys, and they just looked that way to me. And, you know, I was already afraid the police might come.'

'Why didn't you get your father?'

'My father . . . I mean he might have been asleep . . . but lots of times he stays out all night and doesn't get home until almost breakfast. I never wanted him to know I knew about that . . . and I don't ever bring it up. He's entitled to his life. Besides, I was in a hurry, and if the police were there, what could he do about it?'

'The car the men were in,' Kirsten said, 'what kind of car was it?'

'It was . . . I don't know cars very well. It was some kind of SUV or van or something. Dark-colored, I guess.'

'Uh-huh,' Kirsten said. She looked at Cuffs and he looked back at her and shrugged, and she did, too.

'OK,' Cuffs said, turning back to Isobel, 'then what? I mean, after you left.'

'Then I . . . I got cash from two different ATMs and I just wandered around all day yesterday in a couple of different shopping malls, trying to think what to do. When it got to be evening I thought of going to a motel, but you always hear how they can trace you by your credit card, and . . .'

'"They" can trace you?' Cuffs asked. 'Who's "they"?'

'You know. People in movies, when they're after people.'

'This isn't a movie.'

'I know. Anyway, I'm just saying what I did. So then . . . I have this woman friend who runs . . . She's older. She's . . . a nun. Her name's Andrea and she taught me in high school, and we got to be kind of close. Now she runs a women's shelter. It was getting late last night and I didn't know what to do, and I called her. The shelter was full, but she said I could spend one night there, on a cot. So I did. I couldn't sleep, though. Then this morning I knew I had to go to *someone*, and all I could think of was Mr Beale.'

'Tyrone Beale. The guy who lets a young girl push him around. Jesus.'

'He didn't . . . Anyway, he seemed honest, and Jamison, my boyfriend, heard good things about him. Also, he seemed like . . . like he wasn't afraid of stuff.'

'Musta been afraid of *you*,' Cuffs said.

'Are we keeping this short, or what?' Kirsten said. 'Go ahead, Isobel.'

'OK . . . well . . . I was thinking maybe Mr Beale knew people who, like, had ideas or something.'

'Ideas?' Cuffs asked. 'About what?'

'About . . . I don't know . . . about what to do.' She paused. 'And then I thought about that man who showed up at my father's business, and kept Mr Beale from getting me away from my father, and I asked Mr Beale about him, and—'

'And Beale went to get him . . . him being Dugan,' Kirsten said. 'And what did you think Dugan would do?'

'Yeah,' Cuffs said, 'you're not doing so good at telling us what the hell you want *anybody* to do.'

'I know.' Isobel sighed. 'OK, but there's more than one thing. First of all, I already said that I had this feeling that someone was following me, and not my father. And I'm afraid they'll start that again if I walk back into my life. And whether they do or not, I'll have to break up with Jamison. And I'm just . . . Well, the thing is, I *would* do it, to keep my sister here. I'd do *anything*. The problem is, if someone can really get Luisa sent back to China, who says that would be the end of it? Who says the same person won't order my father . . . or me . . . to do something else? So I'd rather have people think I'm . . . well . . . missing or something, until . . . until I'm not sure what. And meanwhile, I can't let the police, or anyone else, find me.'

'Uh-huh.' Cuffs nodded and Kirsten thought his expression showed approval at the way Isobel was thinking. *Words* of approval, though, were not a big part of his vocabulary. So what he said was, 'You're saying you want me to keep you safe and outta sight while Kirsten finds out who was following you, and stops them. And then finds out if someone can really send your sister to China, and if they can, makes sure they can't.'

'I . . . I guess so,' Isobel said. She looked at Kirsten. 'Does that make sense?'

'I'm still trying to figure it out, but *your* thinking makes perfect sense. So you go with Cuffs, and I'll see what I can do.'

'I don't know,' Isobel said. 'He's not very . . . well . . .' She sighed. 'I guess I have no choice.'

'No choice? Poor baby.' Cuffs stood up. 'I'll call a you cab.' He held up a cellphone. 'Then you can make a choice about where you wanna go.'

'Go with Cuffs, Isobel.' Kirsten said, and she stood, too. 'The great thing is, you don't have to *like* him. He doesn't *care*. What I can tell you is that once, when I needed protection, he did the job and I'm still alive. And so is everyone else I ever brought to him.'

'Not quite everyone,' Cuffs said.

'Yes, well, that was a special case.' Kirsten turned to Isobel. 'You *do* have a choice, and your best choice is to get in his car and go with him.'

'I don't know,' Isobel said, 'what if I do, and then later I—'

'Christ,' Cuffs said, 'if you change your mind later, I don't give a shit. You don't wanna stay, you go. Oh . . . and if you don't do what I say, I go.'

'I . . . OK.' Isobel went around the Ford and got in the passenger side and closed the door. The seat was a bench seat and she sat as far from the driver's side as possible.

Cuffs opened the driver's door and slid in behind the wheel. He reached for the key, then stopped and looked up at Kirsten. 'Wanna buy a 1957 Ford Fairlane Skyliner?'

'No.'

'Good decision. It's a piece of shit. I only got it 'cause I took it from a guy. He wasn't happy, but he shoulda paid me what he owed.' He dropped his hat on the floor behind his seat and looked up at the sky. It was bright and blue. 'Funny thing. This is the first damn time I ever put the top down and it didn't fucking rain five minutes later.'

'See? Stick with me and your luck changes.'

'I hope so.' He nodded his head back toward Isobel. 'But I got my doubts.'

FIFTEEN

Kirsten stood there, feeling quite confident as she watched Cuffs and Isobel drive away. Confident that Isobel was in good hands, that is. Not so confident that she herself had any clear understanding of what the hell was going on . . . or what she could do about it.

Not that there weren't ways to start digging into it. There were people to talk to, like Juan Cho and Jamison Traynor, for starters. An immigration lawyer would also be helpful. Then there was Tyrone Beale. She could talk to him about what was beginning to look like a separate problem altogether. She couldn't get over the feeling that those two guys knocking on Beale's door were there for Isobel. And that didn't seem to fit with the threat to send Luisa back to China.

Still, first things first. She reached into the Camry and got her cellphone and speed-dialed her favorite number.

'Hey,' Dugan answered. 'Everything go all right? What's up?'

'Long story. But you sound sort of . . . I don't know . . . upbeat or something.'

'Don't I always?'

'No.'

'I'll have to work on that. Meanwhile, I just settled another case for another upbeat sum. I'm thinking a little suspension might be just what I need, to give me time to spend the fees.' He paused. 'What about you? Where are you? Have you solved the Isobel Cho matter yet?'

'I'm in Horner Park, watching some kids running around as part of what I think must be a day camp. And Isobel Cho? Not quite. What about those men at Beale's door? Cops or not?'

'Hard to say. They had the look. But no show of ID, and they beat it fast when they thought I was calling 911. I got their plate number, too, and it doesn't look like Chicago PD to me. Plus, they're in a Tahoe.' He recited the number, then asked, 'At this point, do we even know what this Isobel Cho thing is about, or what we're up to?'

She wasn't sure she liked the *we* and the *we're*, but she let it go. 'It's basically this: a beautiful princess leaves the castle she grew up in, visits the village, and falls in love with a commoner. This angers the king, who captures her and locks her in the tower. Later he releases her and tells her she's free to go back to life in the village. Except she discovers that if she *does* go back, she must choose to give up one or the other of the two people she loves most in the whole kingdom. So she decides to go into exile for awhile, under the watchful eye of a cold-hearted, but dependable, ogre, until a beautiful hero can come along and fix things, so the princess can go back to her life. Got it?'

'Not entirely. First of all, I wouldn't call the son of a US senator a "commoner."'

'It's an allegory. It limps a little.'

'And the beautiful hero,' he said. 'Is she a fairy godmother? Do I know her?'

'She's a good witch, not a fairy godmother,' Kirsten said. 'But otherwise, yes.'

'And you said you were in Horner Park. Doesn't a hard-hearted, despicable ogre I know live in a cave out that way somewhere?'

'I said "dependable," not "despicable."' Kirsten checked her watch. 'Gotta go. I might be late tonight. Don't spend all that settlement money without me.'

After a few more phone calls, one of which made her seriously doubt the veracity of Juan Cho, it took Kirsten about an hour to drive home from Horner Park, ditch the Camry, and get to Seneca Park in a cab. When she got there she spotted Tyrone Beale sitting alone on a bench, waiting for her, but she ignored him and took a reconnaissance walk around the park. Which didn't take long because, if Horner Park was one of Chicago's largest neighborhood parks, Seneca Park, a block east of Michigan Avenue's Magnificent Mile, was one of its smallest. She'd become a member of the Museum of Contemporary Art the previous year and figured she better visit the place a few times to get her money's worth, which is how she got acquainted with Seneca

Park. It was right across the street from the MCA and was basically a patch of grass with a well-equipped play lot and some shade trees. It was restful there, and grass and trees were easier to look at than anything in the MCA, which made perfect sense, since clearly 'easy-to-look-at' and 'restful' weren't what the MCA was about.

She finally entered the park and strolled right past Beale and on toward the play lot, where six or seven noisy pre-schoolers were chasing each other around the swings and climbing equipment. Three young moms – too few moms for the number of kids, she thought – stood together off to the side, chatting, but keeping watchful eyes on the children. There were a couple of nearby park benches, both vacant.

Kirsten could have been taken for one of the moms, she thought – even if she was maybe a *little* older – and she sat on a bench and stared at the kids, trying not to think about whether she'd ever have one, and finally Beale joined her. He left plenty of space between the two of them, as she'd suggested.

'I apologize for the cloak and dagger stuff,' she said, making a point of not looking at him, keeping her eyes on the play lot, and then laughing and turning casually toward him. 'But those two guys *did* show up at your door this morning, so we can't ignore the possibility that there's been a tail on either you or Isobel.'

'Yeah, right. Or on *you*,' he said. 'Are you working for Isobel?'

'I'm trying to help her. I told her I would, and I am. Maybe you can help, too.'

'Maybe.' He paused. 'Where is she, anyway?'

'Actually, I don't know.' Which was true, technically.

'Bullshit. She left my place with you.'

'She did. But, as you may have noticed, she makes up her own mind about things. She went her way and I went mine. I can't hold her against her will.'

'Jesus.'

'Anyway, you're better off not knowing where she is. We don't know who might be looking for her.'

'What, you think I can't take care of myself?'

'I think what you don't know you can't tell,' she said. 'Jamison Traynor, is he still your client?'

They were both still looking everywhere but at each other,

acting as though they were strangers, exchanging a few casual words. 'Who is . . . or who was . . . my client,' he said, 'is my business.'

'Yes, it is. And my helping Isobel is *my* business, but in case you've forgotten, I just shared that fact with you. Why? Because we're both on the same side here, assuming Jamison hasn't fooled you completely, and is secretly out to harm Isobel. You don't think that's true, do you?'

'No.'

'Then tell me if he's still your client, for God's sake.'

Beale looked up at the sky, as though searching his mind for any downside to telling her, but apparently couldn't find one. 'He hired me to take care of Isobel, and I didn't succeed. So . . . still my client?' He shrugged. 'I don't know.'

'Have you talked to him since Friday night?'

'Of course. I called him right away. About one thirty, maybe two, a.m., Saturday. Woke him up and told him what had just gone down.'

'You give him all the details?'

'Mostly,' he said. 'Everything except about my gun. I told him how Isobel went with two men, apparently willingly, and how I followed them all the way to Wancho's Towing and went inside. I said she told me the men worked for her father, but that she didn't wanna talk to her father. I said I tried to talk them into letting her go with me, but there wasn't much I could do. That there was another guy there, and there was no sense getting anyone hurt. I mean, it was her *father's* place.' He paused, then added, 'I'm pretty sure Jamison told all that to the police.'

'When did he do that?'

'How do I know? Sometime between then and the next time I talked to him.'

'Right. And when was that?' She found herself moving reflexively into a blunt, aggressive tone of voice . . . even though she knew that wasn't smart. 'When's the next time you talked to him?'

'What *is* this, a goddamn interrogation, for Chrissake?'

'OK, sorry. Take it easy.' Speaking to herself as well as to Beale. 'Like you said, we don't know what's going on. I'm just trying to get the picture.'

'Yeah, alright.' He breathed out and seemed to relax. 'We had a couple more phone conversations on Saturday. He couldn't get through to Isobel's father, and the police weren't taking him seriously since she was last seen at her father's place. And then he called last night, said the cops told him her father said she'd spent the whole weekend with him and she was fine.'

'But Jamison was still worried?'

'He was, like, frantic.' Beale reached down and untied and retied his shoe, apparently to show how much he was into this *casual* act. 'She hadn't called. He didn't know where she was. He didn't ask me to do anything, but he called me, so I guess he hasn't fired me.'

'Have you talked to the police?'

'They talked to *me*. I told them everything I told Jamison.' Beale paused. 'They talk to your husband?'

'No, but if they do I'm sure he'll tell them much the same as you did. No need to bring up the gun.'

'I'm wondering if those two guys who took her to Wancho's told the cops about the gun.'

'Probably not,' she said. 'No one got hurt, and I doubt they're the kind to share *anything* with law enforcement.'

'I hope so,' he said. 'So tell me, if you're helping Isobel, and you want my help, who's she afraid of? And what's she afraid they'll do?'

'The "who" she doesn't know, and maybe you can help me find out. The "what" I'm not going to tell you. For two reasons: one, I don't know enough about it to make it helpful to tell you; two, I promised her I wouldn't.'

'Uh-huh.' He shook his head in obvious disgust. 'And you expect me to help you on that basis?'

'I expect you to help me help Isobel, which will help your client, Jamison.'

'That's bullshit. What am I, your errand boy?'

'I'm not even gonna *touch* that one,' she said.

'You getting paid?'

'By Isobel? You heard her. She says she has no money of her own.'

'By her father?'

'I've never spoken to Juan Cho, and I'm not counting on anything from him, or from Jamison either.'

'But I bet you wouldn't turn down money from either one of them.'

'If the time comes when someone wants to demonstrate some gratitude, I'll consider the offer . . . as long as the demonstrator isn't part of the problem.'

'You saying you think one of those two *might* be?'

'I only mean to say . . . for I guess the third time in the last ten minutes . . . that, like you, I don't know yet what's going on.'

'But you've talked to Isobel,' he said, 'and you know more than I do, and you're keeping me in the dark.'

'Yes, that's how it has to be, for now.'

Beale stood up and stretched his arms, acting like a man totally at ease. 'Well, honey,' he said, his tone anything but relaxed, 'I don't do business like that. If you need me bad enough, fill me in.'

'Mr Beale, you could be a help to me, in getting Jamison's cooperation, for one thing.' She didn't stand, didn't look at him. 'But I don't *need* you, or anyone, badly enough to break my word.'

'Really.' He blew out a deep sigh. 'Well then, you have yourself a nice day.' He turned and walked away.

SIXTEEN

At about six thirty that Tuesday evening, Dugan was in his office reviewing a set of interrogatory answers drafted by one of his law clerks. He was down off the high of the huge settlement in the Castro case, and well on his way to a renewed appreciation of the mind-numbingly tedious aspects of his law practice, when Larry Candle called.

'Hey Doogs,' Larry said. 'Just called so you wouldn't be worried about me.' Which Dugan wasn't. 'I finally finished taking Meyer Manowsky's dep. See ya when I get back in.'

'It's late,' Dugan said. 'Why don't you just go home?' *And let me finish up here in peace.*

'Are you kidding? After playin' Squeeze-the-Sleazeball with Manowsky since noon? Guy tried to wriggle out of every question I asked. And his lawyer, Sybil Maguire? Woman's got no sense of humor. I'm too tired to go home.'

Dugan, who couldn't recall ever seeing Larry look fatigued, could imagine what Manowsky and Maguire must be feeling after an afternoon spent with the ever-ebullient, ever-irritating, Larry Candle. 'What you mean,' Dugan said, 'is that you want a couple of free beers from the office fridge.'

'Jeez, Doogs, it's not about the beer. It's about the chance to unwind, decompress, shoot the shit with my mentor.'

'I'm your *mentor*?'

'Yeah, well, *kind* of. Anyway, I don't wanna talk about the Manowsky dep. I wanna ask you something.'

'I'll be here,' Dugan said. 'Take your time.'

Dugan always got a lot of work done during the evenings. His staff, including Mollie, was gone by five fifteen. That was an office rule he tried to strictly enforce. Fred Schustein and Peter Rienzo, the lawyers who handled his workers' compensation cases, loved the rule, and were usually gone by then anyway. Dugan, of course, wasn't subject to his own rule, and always stayed late. As did Larry Candle, who wouldn't recognize a rule if it crawled up his leg.

Larry, contrary to the expectations of those who thought he was a total screw-up – which was just about everyone in the universe, including Kirsten – was surprisingly diligent. Better yet, he knew the personal injury game as well as anyone. He'd even had his own firm for awhile, with ads in the *Yellow Pages* that screamed: LARRY CANDLE, THE LAWYER FOR THE LITTLE GUY!

Dugan had heard of Larry years ago, but first met him when Larry hired Kirsten to find a witness he'd lost. His ads had a photo of him, chin high, arms crossed, wearing a determined scowl and a pinstripe suit. Sort of a Schwarzenegger look. But in real life he was more of a slightly shorter, slightly rounder Danny DeVito. Kirsten succeeded in finding his lost witness, but Larry's law firm bit the dust; and when that happened Dugan, to Kirsten's great dismay, took Larry on as an associate . . . and wasn't at all disappointed.

Which wasn't to say Larry couldn't be a pain in the ass.

Dugan had set aside the interrogatory answers and gotten lost in thoughts about the possible suspension of his law license. Was it a good thing or a bad thing? How would he keep the office in operation while he was gone, so there'd be something to come back to . . . if he *wanted* to come—

'Hey, Doogie pal!' Larry bounced into Dugan's office with four bottles of beer. He opened two of them, handed one to Dugan, and took a long swig from the other. 'Aaahh,' he sighed, and lowered himself into one of the client's chairs. His feet barely reached the floor. 'Nothin' like good ol' ice-cold Moose Drool.'

'Ice-cold what?' Dugan stared at the label on the bottle he'd just taken a drink from.

'Moose Drool. From Montana. Big Sky country. Whaddaya think?'

Dugan took another pull. 'Not bad.' Larry was in charge of ordering the office beer. That used to be Mollie's job, but Larry didn't like her selections, which leaned toward Miller's and Bud, anything on sale. 'So,' Dugan said, 'what is it?'

Larry lowered his bottle, which was already close to empty, and said, 'They call it a brown ale, and—'

'No, Larry. I mean . . . what's your question?'

'Oh, *that*. Well, it's not so much a question. It's just . . .' He leaned forward in his chair. 'It's just I wanna tell ya, I know it's gonna be a tough situation, and I'm ready to do whatever I can to help.'

Caught by surprise, Dugan said, 'Yeah, well, if it really happens I'll have to figure out how to keep the office up and run—' He stopped, suddenly realizing that so far his possible suspension was only a confidential discussion between his lawyer and the Disciplinary Commission lawyer. Larry wouldn't know anything about it. 'Uh . . . help with what?'

'You know, with that missing girl case. Isobel Cho. Kirsten's working on it, right?'

'Isobel Cho?' Dugan knew Larry's antennae were always extended, but he still never failed to be amazed by how little the guy missed. 'Watch the news, Larry. The cops say she wasn't missing at all. And anyway, why would you think she has any connection with *me*? Or Kirsten?'

Larry grinned and knocked down the last of his beer. 'I figured it out. I finally put a name to the face of that guy who asked me to have you call him this morning. Tyrone Beale. I used to see him in court sometimes, when he was with the sheriff's office. And the news? Eleanor Traynor's son and Isobel are an item, y'know, and the senator must be keeping a lid on the media. Not much about the case the last day or so. But when the story first broke they said Beale was the last person known to have seen the girl.'

'And that means I'm involved with her? Because Tyrone Beale wanted me to call him?'

'Well . . . that . . . plus the fact that you been out of the office more in the last two days than any time since last year, when the cops tried to stick a murder on you.' Larry grinned and gave Dugan a conspiratorial wink. 'Not to mention the look on your face when I brought the girl's name up a minute ago.'

'That was a look of surprise, Larry.'

'Yeah, right.' Larry grinned again. 'Anyway, if you *did* have something to do with it, Kirsten would be involved, right?'

'If I did, maybe she would . . . or maybe not.'

'Whatever,' Larry said.

'Tell you what, *if* I ever have anything to do with Isobel Cho, and *if* I need some help, *maybe* I'll ask you.'

'Great,' Larry said. "Cause *if* you ever asked, I'd mention something I saw on the Internet. A week or so ago. I don't remember where. But I think it was in a comment on some blog or other. Someone was asking whether anyone else heard a rumor about that airhead Senator Traynor being vetted for a vice-presidential run, but it being super hush-hush.' He grabbed the opener and popped the cap off a second Moose Drool. 'Anyway, I'm happy to help any way I can, partner.'

'Anything comes up, Larry, I'll let you know.' Dugan would have objected to Larry's use of the "P" word – they were most definitely *not* partners – except that Dugan's lawyer said one way to keep his office running while he was suspended might be to make the firm into a partnership before he left. 'Meanwhile,' he said, handing Larry a manila folder, 'you can be happy to work on these interrogatory answers. That new clerk doesn't quite get it yet.'

'Will do, chief.' Larry stood up. He took the folder, his half-finished beer, and the unopened fourth bottle, and headed for the door.

Larry was scarcely out of sight before Dugan reached a decision. 'Hey, Larry!' he called.

Larry reappeared in the doorway. 'Yeah?'

'Just for the hell of it, see if you can dig up that rumor again. Or anything else along those lines.'

'*Mucho bueno*,' Larry said. 'Glad to be of service. And oh, by the way . . . lemme know if you need any help with that suspension business.'

SEVENTEEN

It was early evening, and Kirsten knew it was time to take a run at Juan Cho. She didn't expect getting in to see him would be easy. She called ahead and was informed that 'Mr Cho is . . . um . . . out,' and, 'Uh-uh, I don't know when he'll be back.' From all accounts, though, Cho was a hands-on business owner, so she got in her car and headed for Wancho's Towing.

When she got there it was much as Dugan had described it. The compound lay on the north side of a wide, but not very busy, east-west street. A tall chain-link fence extended out from both sides of a small, one-story building, with slats weaved through the links so you couldn't see through. There was street parking in front, and she parked the Camry and got out.

It had been the middle of the night when Dugan was here, so he couldn't have seen everything she saw now. But she couldn't explain how he missed the large roof-mounted sign that said:

WANCHO'S TOWING
A MORE LIVABLE CITY, ONE NUISANCE CAR AT A TIME

He'd been right about the neighborhood, though. It must have been zoned commercial or industrial, because the buildings – at least half of which appeared vacant – were mostly warehouses and factories. What had once seemed to be an unstoppable march of condos and townhouses spreading out from downtown had come to a halt a mile or so to the east, stalled by a faltering economy.

The sliding gate beside the building was wide open and she walked in to take a look. The building had obviously been a gas station fifty or sixty years earlier, and the wing that once held the service bays – probably now the business office, with the overhead doors walled up – jutted out from the rear. From there the property stretched out to the north, an empty rectangle, easily as long as a football field, maybe longer, and about a third narrower, with the building, where she stood, in the south end zone. The entire property was surrounded by the same type of chain-link fencing, running along both sidelines and across the north end. A railroad embankment ran north and south, just beyond the fence along the west border.

It may once have been a parking lot for a factory, and it was certainly much larger than was needed for the thirty or forty cars, and several boats, that were stored there just then. The parking lanes had been paved years ago, and now were part broken asphalt, part gravel. Surprisingly, a few widely-spaced, scraggly trees had grown up along some of the rows, mostly way up toward the north end.

A tow truck turned off the street and came in through the gate, and she had to step aside. The driver gave her a decidedly unfriendly stare as he passed, and she went back to the sidewalk and inside the building. The air conditioning in there was keeping it way too cold, and there was a chemical odor as though the Orkin man had just visited. A young guy, in one of those thin jackets they wear on the floors of the commodities exchanges, sat on a hard plastic chair, apparently waiting to pick up his car.

She went to the bulletproof cashier's window and stared at a heavy-set young Latina woman in a long-sleeved sweater who was playing solitaire on the computer beside her. 'I want to talk to Mr Juan Cho,' Kirsten said.

The young woman barely glanced at her before turning back to her monitor. 'You wanna pick up a vehicle,' she said, 'I need ID, plus year, make, and plate number.' She spoke with more than a hint of an Hispanic accent.

'How's this for ID?' Kirsten asked. She held a driver's license up to the window.

'You gotta put it through here,' the woman answered. She waved her hand, without looking, at the metal slide beneath the window.

'You haven't looked at the photo,' Kirsten said.

'I'll look at it when—'

Kirsten rapped the edge of the hard plastic license against the window. It gave a satisfying *craack*, and she did it over and over – *craack, craack, craack* – until she finally got the attention of the woman . . . and of the commodities guy as well, who shook his head as though to warn Kirsten that getting mad did no good, not at Wancho's Towing.

'Look at the photo,' Kirsten said, and held the license flat against the window again.

The woman stared at the license. 'That's not your picture.'

'Good for you,' Kirsten said. 'Does it look like anyone you know?'

'It looks like . . . Oh my God! Is that . . .'

'Yes,' Kirsten said. 'Tell Mr Cho to call me.' She gave her cellphone number and the woman wrote it down. 'And I want that call *immediately*.' She turned, looked straight up at the security camera on the wall and nodded, and walked back out to her car and drove away.

She hadn't gone a block when the call came.

What better place to talk things over with Juan Cho, and not to let him just grab Isobel's driver's license and boot Kirsten out the door, than at a McDonald's around supper time? The one at Armitage and Western was quick and easy to get to from Wancho's, and was also near enough to the 14th District police station so that cops were probably in and out of there all the time. Perfect.

She ordered a Diet Coke and a chicken salad, and took it to a corner table where she could see the entrance into the parking area. As she sat down two uniformed officers got up from their table and left. There were maybe half a dozen other people scattered around the other tables, including two women Kirsten would have sworn were undercover cops. No one was sitting at the two tables nearest to her.

Five minutes later, after she'd finished her salad, she saw a white Ford Explorer pull in off the street and stop near the main entrance. A man in black pants and a green-and-white striped golf shirt got out of the front passenger seat and came inside, and the Ford drove ahead and out of Kirsten's view.

The man was around sixty, maybe five-eight, and muscular . . . if a little large in the paunch. His skin was a deep natural tan and his thick black hair was peppered with gray. He looked around, gave no indication he'd seen her, and went to the counter. He came away with a large coffee, took it to the drink dispenser and added ice to it, then came over and sat across the plastic table from her. He did not look like a happy puppy.

'How did you get my daughter's driver's license?' he asked, and though he kept his voice low, it was a deep, strong voice. 'Where is she?' He spoke excellent English, but with a strong Spanish accent, and she recalled Dugan saying he'd been 'raised Mexican.'

'I take it you're Mr Juan Cho,' she said, although she'd already seen a photo of him and didn't really need confirmation. He didn't answer, so she introduced herself and handed him a business card that said:

WILD ONION, LTD.
Confidential Inquiries
Security Services

He glanced at the card, and said again, 'How did you get Isobel's—'

'Isobel gave it to me.' In actual fact, she'd lifted it from Isobel's purse while the girl was asleep in her car. 'I'm working for her.'

'Where is she?' Cho was leaning forward, still speaking softly, but gripping the edge of the table with both hands, as though to keep himself from reaching across and choking her.

'I don't know. She doesn't want anyone to know.'

'She's safe?'

'I'm sure of it.'

'Why doesn't she notify the police of that, tell them that no one has harmed her?'

'Because if that were publicly known she would have to make a decision. Either she breaks up with the man she loves . . . or thinks she does . . . or she causes a terrible loss . . . to you as well as to herself.' She paused, and when he didn't respond, she added, 'Unless you lied to her about the threat to Luisa.'

Cho's eyes widened, and the hostile glare intensified. 'I told her to tell that to no one.'

'Yes, and you also told her you'd finally come to the realization that she's not a child, not some clueless, two-bit employee of yours, who'll do whatever you order her to do. You told her you

realized that she was an adult, responsible for her own decisions.'
She paused, then added, 'Or was telling her that a lie, too, like the
lie that Luisa could be sent back to China?'

Cho's lips drew back, revealing tightly clenched teeth, but then
he slumped down into his chair. 'A lie?' He shook his head. 'Did
you tell Isobel that I was *lying* to her about that? Because if you
did . . .'

He didn't complete the sentence, and Kirsten was suddenly
feeling unsure of herself. She'd been certain he'd been untruthful
with his daughter. But the guy was either one of the world's
greatest actors – which she didn't really believe – or he hadn't
deliberately misled Isobel. 'I suppose it's possible,' she said, 'that
you've fallen for someone else's lie.'

'What the *hell* are you talking about?' He sat upright again,
and put his palms flat on the table and leaned toward her. 'It's
time for me to leave. I don't know you, and I don't know that
you're really working for Isobel.'

'Ask her yourself. Does she know your cell number?'

'Yeah.'

Kirsten took out her cellphone and called Cuffs. 'I'm with
Isobel's father. Have her call him. Right now.'

Cho already had his cell in his hand. It rang almost at once
and he answered. 'Yeah, it's me. Hold on a minute.' Then he
stood up and walked outside. She watched through the window
as he paced back and forth and spoke into the phone.

It was pretty clear, both from his body language and his
expression, when she could see his face, that Isobel had quickly
verified that Kirsten was on her side, but the conversation
didn't end there. Cho was arguing with her. In a few minutes
he gave up, and came back inside and sat down across from
her again.

'Did she tell you where she was?'

'No.'

'Right. That way you don't have to lie when people ask you
where she is.'

'What did you mean,' he said, 'about me believing somebody's
lie?'

'I mean you told Isobel someone's threatening to have Luisa
sent to China. I'm saying the clear implication of that threat was
not that she'd be snatched illegally . . . kidnapped . . . and taken

to China, but that she herself is *subject* to being sent to China. Which would mean she's in the US illegally, and that whoever made the threat can cause to have her deported. Am I right?'

'Yeah, that was the clear meaning,' he said.

The restaurant was getting more crowded, and Kirsten was glad they'd gotten a corner table. 'Yeah, well, I know you were born in the US and you're a citizen. And in one short phone call I learned that the child of a citizen is by law herself automatically a citizen, whether she's illegitimate or not, or born here or not, or brought here via proper channels or not. So it's not possible that anyone . . . even someone with powerful government contacts . . . could have such a child deported.'

'And do you think . . .' He stared at her, as though amazed at what she was saying. 'Yes, you do. You think I don't *know* this law. You think I'm this . . . this ignorant peasant . . . who's way below your level of sophistication and education, who operates a business you find cheap and distasteful, using "clueless, two-bit employees," and so can be easily misled and intimidated.'

'Look,' she said, 'I'm not saying you're stupid. I'm only saying—'

'You're "only saying" that a simple-minded Chinese-Mexican guy like me can't *possibly* have known and understood for years what you learned today in your "one short phone call."' He lowered his head, and when he looked up he was smiling. A smile filled with contempt. 'My daughter has obviously not chosen wisely. You are not, Miss "Confidential Inquiries" Person, as smart as you think you are.'

Kirsten felt like a boxer rocked back on her heels. She hesitated, then took a deep breath and said, 'Maybe not, Mr Cho, but I'm smart enough to know that I've been wrong before . . . and that I will be again. So tell me what you think I'm missing. I'm told the law is straightforward.'

'Yes, and I am told the same thing.'

'So then . . . what's the problem? Why worry about an empty threat to send her to China?'

'The problem,' he said, 'is that Luisa does not fit under this straightforward law. The problem is that Luisa is not my daughter.'

EIGHTEEN

It had turned into a conversation that couldn't be conducted in a McDonald's that was getting more crowded by the minute, so Juan Cho and his driver led the way in the Ford Explorer and Kirsten followed.

At Wancho's she parked on the street and Cho ushered her into the waiting room, through the door into the room where the heavy-set young woman sat playing computer solitaire, and from there down a short hallway to his office.

'Have a seat,' Cho said. 'I need more coffee. What about you?'

'I'm good,' Kirsten said, holding up the Coke she'd brought from McDonald's.

Cho left, and Kirsten looked around. It was the sort of office one would expect in a converted gas station: about the size of one of the original service bays, with a dropped acoustic-tile ceiling, cheap wallboard, fake wood flooring, and a plain metal desk. On the desk were a phone, a Dell laptop, and a well-worn, paperbound booklet entitled 'Licensed Relocation Tow Companies of Illinois.' Behind it was a comfortable-looking executive's chair. There were two file cabinets, four metal chairs with cushioned seats, a tired-looking sofa, and a huge wall-mounted Sony LCD TV.

The room looked and smelled clean and fresh, with only a hint of oil and gas odor still hanging around. On the wall behind the desk were two large portrait photos: one of Isobel; the other of a charming little Asian girl. Between the two photos hung an engraved brass plaque, announcing that:

> *In recognition of his extraordinary professionalism*
> *and dedication to the towing trade and to the*
> *community he serves*
> JUAN CHO
> *is hereby enrolled in*
> THE ORDER OF TOWMAN
> *Sanctioned and presented by U.S. Towman Magazine*

On one side wall hung about a dozen eight-by-ten photos of Juan Cho posing with various presumably important people. She recognized only three of them: Muhammad Ali, George W. Bush, and Bruce Lee.

She was wondering whether the people in the photos had all had their cars 'relocated' by Wancho's Towing, when Cho returned with a huge white mug and sat behind his desk.

'That's Luisa, right?' Kirsten said, pointing to the portrait behind him. 'She's cute.'

'Yes, she is.' He waved his arm, as though pushing that topic aside. 'Let's not waste time,' he said. 'Isobel is young and, like you said, she *thinks* she's in love. But the odds against the long-term survival of this so-called love are . . . what? . . . fifty to one?'

'I don't know what the odds are. I do know that some people fall in love in their twenties, and stay in love until they die of old age. That's the plan I'm working on.'

'Yeah, well, lotsa luck,' he said. 'But it doesn't happen very often. A break-up is something just about everyone faces, sooner or later. And guess what, they survive it.'

'Uh-huh, and your point is . . .?'

'My point is you wanna help Isobel. Well, this isn't about Isobel. It's about Luisa. If Luisa is taken from her home, and sent to China, her life is over. *Period.* Understand?'

'Right, and no one—'

'I'm not just *saying* that.' Cho pounded the tip of a thick finger on the desk in front of him. 'I *know* China. There's too damn many people. In the cities they're crawling all over each other like . . . like ants in an anthill. Everyone's dirt-poor, in the cities *and* out in the country. And girls and women? They're like . . . I don't know . . . tossed out with the garbage. Poor people . . . and that's like ninety-nine percent . . . they got no say about anything. *Believe* me.' He held one hand out, palm up, toward Kirsten, as though begging her to understand. 'I've seen these things. I've described them to Isobel.'

'And I'm sure she understands, but—'

'But *nothing!*' Cho was clearly getting angry now, his dark complexion turning a deep red. 'I held back from saying this to Isobel, but I'll say it to you. Isobel is truly my daughter, but if she's willing to destroy the life of this nine-year-old child –' he lifted his hand and gestured behind him – 'this beautiful little sister of hers, for what is an adolescent, passing romance? Then Isobel is not someone I wish to consider my daughter.'

'Mr Cho, listen to me. *You're* the one missing something here. First, I'll grant you that it *might* be a passing romance, but you don't *know* that.'

'What difference does—'

'No, goddammit!' Kirsten pointed her finger at him. 'I listened to you. Now you listen to *me*. Do you think Isobel is willing to jeopardize Luisa's future for the sake of her own? She's *not*. Why the hell do you think she's chosen to stay in hiding? Because if she reappears, she'll have to break up with Jamison. And she believes . . . and whatever *you* think, it's her belief that counts . . . she believes no one has the right to force her into that. Still, she's willing to *do* that . . . she told me so . . . if that's the only way to save her sister. But she's chosen, instead, to stay out of sight for now.'

Cho stared at her. 'That makes no sense. Out of sight for how long?'

'Until I solve her problem.'

'That's not a sensible answer, either.'

'Or until someone else solves it. And so what if she breaks up with Jamison? She knows the problem won't end there. What will the next demand be?'

'I know that, too. But . . .' He shrugged. 'A person's gotta take one thing at a time.'

'Right, and it's time you and I got started. So . . . first question: What did—'

'What, you think *you* can do a damn thing about this? Bullshit.'

'I think someone has to do *something*. What're *you* doing about it? Anything? I mean, besides trying to get your other daughter to break-up with the guy she loves. It won't end there, you know.'

'I *told* you. I know that.' He drank some coffee, then set down his mug and stared at it. 'What I'm doing about it is nobody's business but mine.' He looked up at her again. 'Fuck it,' he said. 'Go ahead. Ask your questions.'

'What did they say when they made this threat? Did they say *why* they want Isobel away from Jamison? Did they put a time limit on it?'

'A time limit? Yeah, what the guy said was "for good." He didn't say anything about *why*.'

'OK, we'll get back to why. But let's start at the beginning. It was a man who spoke to you. Was that in person, or on the phone, or what?'

'It was in person. There were two men. One stayed behind my back the whole time, and I never did see him. It was in a bar and it was crowded, and I think he was sort of shielding us from other people, so no one else could hear.'

'But you're sure there were two of them, right? What bar? Where?'

'Two, yes. It was at this banquet place. The White Eagle, up on Milwaukee Avenue. I was at a wedding reception, and the drinks were free, but I didn't like the beer they had.' The story, obviously bottled up for too long, spilled out of him. 'The place is huge and there were some other parties going on, too, and one had a cash bar, and I went there to buy something I wanted.' He stopped for a breath.

'So . . . what happened?'

'Like I said, it was crowded and I had to wait awhile. And the bar itself was like a square around the center part where the bartenders were. So a stool opened up right by one of the corners, and I sat down. Right away this guy comes over and crowds in right next to me. "Excuse me," he says. Very polite, you know? But he's crowding me, you know? Obviously on purpose. And I could sort of feel another guy step up behind me. But that one never said anything.'

'So the guy beside you talked. What did he say?'

'I don't remember his *exact* words, but he said something like: "Mr Cho, nice to meet you." I said, "Yeah? Well, who are you?" He said that didn't matter, just that he had a message for me. I said, "A message from who?" but he just laughed. Then he said, close as I can recall, "The message is that we'd like you to talk to your daughter, Isobel. We'd like you to tell her to break off her relationship with her lawyer boyfriend." I couldn't believe it. Then the bartender came with my beer, and the guy actually paid for it. Like we were friends. I told him—'

'Wait. What did he look like?'

'I don't know. He was just an ordinary middle-aged white guy in a nice suit and tie. Like he coulda been at a wedding himself.

He was soft-spoken, not like a thug or some guy out to break your legs or something. Acting like he's just a guy making conversation. I told him I guessed he didn't know my daughter, that she was someone who made up her own mind. He said, "Oh, I know a lot about *both* your daughters, Mr Cho, and here's the thing." That's how he put it, the bastard, "Here's the thing," he says, "Isobel has to stop seeing that boyfriend of hers, and for good. Otherwise, Mr Cho, I'm afraid you'll have to say goodbye to Luisa."'

'Jesus, what did you say?'

'I asked what the hell he was talking about, and who the hell sent him, but he cut me off. Then he said two names, and they were the names of Luisa's mother and her . . . her real father. He didn't pronounce them right, but he had a little piece of paper and he was *reading* them. He said they were very sad, and missing their long-lost daughter. They wanted Luisa home with mommy and daddy. That was it. Then he told me I'd never see him again, and he left, and I turned around and the guy right behind me was gone already, and the guy who did the talking was out the door and gone, too.'

'So you know who Luisa's real father is, right? And he, and her mother . . . they're still living?'

'Yeah, I know 'em. I'm part owner of a little business over there . . . more hassle than it's worth, but there's people who work there who depend on it . . . and anyway, they're in the same village, up in the north. They're both still living. Her mother's . . . she's a decent person. But the father's a dirt bag someone should've put underground a long time ago.'

'So . . . what happened? How did Luisa—'

'I brought her here and I claimed her as my daughter. That's it. It's not important why I did it, or how I got it done, but it wasn't . . . y'know . . . through legal procedures. Her mother— No, I'm not gonna talk about that. The fact is, I did it, and Luisa's been my daughter ever since, in every possible way . . . except by blood. And that last part can be proved by DNA.'

'Maybe, if someone raises the issue. But who will? I know you don't want to discuss it, but I can't believe you took the child against their will, right?'

'Her mother begged me to do it, and it had to be right away. And her father? He'd as soon taken the girl out and left her under a bridge somewhere. Thing is, he's the sort of punk who'd say anything, if you paid him enough. He'd say he never knew what happened to his daughter, and now he's finally located her and he wants her back, wants to raise her. He'd say any shit they want him to say.'

'Uh-huh, and the guy who delivered the message didn't say who *they* were?'

'No.'

'And you'd never seen him before.'

'Right.'

'But somehow he knew he'd find you at this wedding. Was it a family member getting married? Or was it some well-known person or something?'

'No, just the son of a guy who works for me. Not a big event.'

'Uh-huh.' Kirsten nodded. 'And you have no idea who sent these guys?'

'I didn't say I didn't *know*. I said he didn't *say*. Think about it, for Chrissake. You got a couple of kids in a relationship that's looks like it's getting a little too serious. One's from big-time money, high society, political power. The other? She's from . . .' He swept his arms out, as though embracing his office . . . or his world. 'Who the hell do *you* think wants to break 'em up?'

NINETEEN

'**M**ore bubbly?' Dugan asked, as he refilled his own plastic wine glass.

'I believe I'm bubbled out.' Kirsten said. They were up on the roof of their condo building and she was lying on her back, on two layers of blanket she'd spread out as a cushion on the hard surface. 'Opening that second bottle was probably a mistake.'

'I don't think so,' Dugan said. 'Prosecco's like Jello. There's always room for more.' He set his glass carefully on the pebbly surface and lay back on his chaise lounge-style lawn chair and stared up at the sky. It was a warm, clear night, and the moon was bright, but ambient city light made it tough to see any stars.

Their condo was the third floor of a three-flat building and they had the only roof access. No fancy deck, just a roof. 'It's nice up here, isn't it?'

'Wonderful,' she said. She sat up, and he turned his head to look at her. She hugged her knees and rested her chin on them. It was a posture that didn't look very comfortable, but then, she'd always been more limber than he was.

He turned his head toward the sky again, easing the crick in his neck. 'I wonder why they call this an "anti-gravity" chair,' he said. 'I don't feel any lighter than usual.'

'Funny you should say that. I was wondering just this morning if you weren't putting on a few extra pounds'

'No way. I've never worked out so regularly, and so hard, in my life. That souped-up Aikido stuff Dr Sato teaches is wicked.'

'Is it mostly women?' she asked.

'You mean is that why I'm working out? Yeah, already they can't keep their hands off—'

'The *class*, dammit. Is it mostly women?'

'Oh. Only two women and five men. Six, if you count Dr Sato.'

'What are they like?'

'Three are just kids, early twenties or something. Then there's that guy I told you about, Foley. I think you know him. The guy that was in jail a while back? And then me and Dr Sato, who's about a hundred years old and tosses the rest of us around like popcorn. That's it.'

'I meant what are the *women* like?'

'Oh.' He paused. He loved these conversations. 'I don't know. Kinda . . . nondescript.'

'Yeah, right.'

'You know what?' He sat upright and knocked down the rest of his Prosecco, then looked at Kirsten again. *Damn. Who needs stars? Or a moon? Or even the damn sky, for that matter?* 'I'm a very lucky guy,' he said.

'Me too.' She was looking back at him. 'I mean . . . the "lucky" part.'

'Really? And . . . the baby thing? You're still OK with it?'

'Absolutely.' They'd reached their decision on that shortly before she left for Seattle, and hadn't really talked about it since.

''Cause I was really getting used to the idea of a kid, y'know?'

He still wasn't absolutely sure she didn't think fatherhood scared him. Which it did, but not *that* much.

'I know you were, and we still have time. And when it happens . . . if it happens . . . it'll be great. A new chapter.'

'I think we'd make pretty good parents,' Dugan said. 'Don't you?'

'Yes. *You* especially.'

'But you're still OK with—'

'I am, Dugan. Stop worrying. I mean, I *do* want to be a mother, but even apart from the expense, there's the waiting, and then the heartache when it doesn't happen. How many times can a person go through all that? The truth is, I already have a great life, great husband, love my work . . . mostly. And if a baby happens, I'll love that, too. As my mom would have said, "We just do what we do, and let God decide the big things."'

'Really? *My* mother would *never* have said "do what we do," not if the "doing" involved bodily fluids. My old man, though? He would have said that letting God decide is the coward's way out.'

'One,' she said, 'I'm not sure I believe in my mother's God. Two, your father's dead. Three, we made a decision, and we're not cowards. Which, not to change the subject, you proved again the other night . . . at Wancho's Towing, even if what you did wasn't very bright.'

'Yeah, well, I guess Isobel was right. She said I didn't stop to think.'

'There isn't always time to think.'

'You mean like when you blurted out that you'd help her? And then she said she had no money?'

Kirsten shrugged. 'I could have backed out at that point. But what the hell, I'd just collected a big fee, we were dropping the *in vitro* stuff, and I needed something to occupy my mind. And maybe the most important thing was that you were already involved, and I knew I'd want to . . . *you* know.'

'To keep an insider's eye on the situation? And make sure no harm came to your impulsive, vulnerable little hubby?'

'That about sums it up,' she said. 'And oh, those guys who showed up at Beale's? I had someone run the plate number you gave me. You didn't say differently, so I assumed it was an Illinois plate.'

'Right.'

'Well . . . if you got the number right . . . that was a stolen plate.'

'Oops. Well, believe me, that was the number.' He sipped some coffee. 'So . . . who *were* those guys? They must have been there because of Isobel. I mean, if they were looking for Beale they could have found him any time. *You* did. So they didn't just happen to show up when Isobel happened to be there.'

'I agree,' she said. 'But why? How do they fit in with that threat to Isobel's father? I mean, let's assume it came from Eleanor Traynor. Even though she's not up for re-election for another couple of years, she considers Isobel's involvement with her son so damaging to her politically that she makes this threat . . . and I guess it's perfectly legal to report something to the immigration people . . . about Isobel's little sister. But then why—'

'Hold on. Two things: one, I heard from a reliable source about a rumor going around that Traynor may be tapped as a vice-presidential candidate. Two, it's certainly not legal for an elected official to put the squeeze on a citizen by threatening to see that the laws are enforced. It's called . . . I don't know . . . extortion, for one thing.'

'OK, but suppose the VP rumor is true . . . as scary as it is to imagine Eleanor Traynor a heartbeat away from the presidency . . . and suppose she knows the threat's illegal and makes it anyway. None of that answers the question: Who were those men and why were they knocking on Beale's door?'

'How would they even know she was there?' Dugan asked.

'Everyone knew Beale had been caretaking her, so they might have been watching his place in case she went there.'

'That Tahoe wasn't there when Beale and I went in.'

'I didn't see it either. So maybe one guy was watching, and when he saw Isobel he called his partner and waited till he got there, in the Tahoe. Even if he noticed me going in after Isobel did, I doubt he'd know who I was, or that I was going up to Beale's.'

'He might have seen me, too,' Dugan said, 'with Beale, but maybe he wasn't paying attention to anyone going into the cleaners.'

'Anyway,' she said, 'they came in because Isobel was there. But *why*? They weren't police, or at least not police in an official capacity. The stolen plate establishes that, and besides, the department's official position all along has been that Isobel's not a missing person.'

'Maybe,' Dugan said, 'Senator Traynor decided it might help to have someone talk to Isobel personally, and convince her to break up with Jamison.'

'Convince her like how? Offer her something? Slap her around?'

'Well . . .'

'Anyway, why threaten to deport a person's little sister to get her to do something, and then . . . before the person's had time to prove whether she'll do it or not . . . go after her personally?'

'I think what you're saying,' Dugan said, 'is that there's more here than meets the eye.'

'Just the cliché I had in mind.' Kirsten got first to her knees, then stood. 'But we won't solve anything tonight.' She yawned and stretched her arms up toward the sky. 'By the way, who's your "reliable source"? I mean about those vice-presidential rumors?'

'Larry Candle.'

She lowered her arms and stared at him. 'You're kidding.'

'No, really. He wants to help us out, on our Isobel Cho case. I told him, of course, that we don't *have* an Isobel Cho case.'

'Which *we* don't,' Kirsten said. '*I* do. Larry's not your partner in the law firm; and you're not my partner in Wild Onion, Ltd.'

'Of course not. Not technically. But remember what you told Isobel this morning? "With Dugan," you said, "you also get me." That may not be a legal *partnership*, but it's sure gotta be a joint venture.'

'Lawyers, Jesus.' She sat back down on the blankets, reached for her glass, and held it out. 'More, please.'

'I thought you were bubbled out.'

'That was *then*. I've got my second wind now. Besides, we don't want it to go to waste.'

'No, we don't.' He picked up the bottle and tilted it. 'And when it's gone,' he said, 'we'll go downstairs, do what we do, and leave the big decisions to God. Or . . . you know . . . whoever.'

'Actually, not a bad plan.' She ran the palm of her free hand across the blanketed surface around her. 'But I'm thinking . . . why go downstairs?'

TWENTY

'Yeah,' Dugan said. 'I understand. Just see what you can do, OK?' He hung up the phone.

It was nine thirty Wednesday morning and he'd been talking to his lawyer, Renata Carroway. He stared down at the open file on his desk, his mind a million miles away from the case in front of him. Renata was to meet with the lawyer at the Attorney Registration and Disciplinary Commission that afternoon. She'd been trying to get him a private reprimand, with neither an admission nor a denial of guilt from Dugan, but the ARDC wouldn't go for it. Now she'd try to hammer out a deal for a public censure, and no suspension of his license.

Dugan wasn't optimistic about his chances for that, either. Renata was good, but she did mostly criminal defense work and wasn't used to dealing with those ARDC people. He'd asked around among friends who'd had ARDC problems, and the word was that the lawyers there were polite and friendly, and didn't come across with that typical prosecutorial attitude. But in their hearts they knew they were on the side of God, and justice, and the American Way. He just hoped Renata could keep his suspension short.

Dugan didn't know how long he'd been sitting there before he finally shook his head and picked up the phone again and buzzed Mollie. 'Get that new guy at the bank for me, would—'

'Hey, hey, whaddaya say!' Larry Candle burst through the door. 'Everyone ready for Hump Day?'

'Cancel that, Mollie,' Dugan said, and hung up.

'Hate to interrupt, Doogie boy,' Larry said – an obvious untruth, since interrupting was something Larry loved to do – and dropped himself into one of Dugan's client's chairs. 'But I knew you'd want my report a.s.a.p.'

'Report?' Dugan was caught off guard.

'Yeah, my report on rumors running around about Senator Eleanor Traynor being vetted for a vice-presidential run.' Larry shook his head. 'As me poooor old mither would've said, Lord rest her beloved soul, "Saint Patrick preserve us from such a fate."' His brogue wasn't any better than his Spanish.

'Your mother's Jewish,' Dugan said, 'and living in Scottsdale.'

'Yeah, but I was watching *Angela's Ashes* on DVD last night, and—'

'Uh-huh. What's your report?'

'OK . . . well . . . first of all, I couldn't find that blog comment I told you about. Second, I couldn't find one damn reference to Traynor and the vice-presidency. No rumors, no denials, nothing. Period. You know what that means, right?'

'It means you couldn't find the site where you saw it.'

'No way. It means somebody caught that comment and was able to get it removed. Like I told you, whoever talked about that rumor said it was all very hush-hush.'

'But you also said you couldn't remember where you'd seen it.'

'I know, but it hadda be on some site I usually look at. And wherever it was, it oughta be still there, but it isn't.' Larry looked at his watch and stood up. 'Gotta run. I have a case on the nine thirty call.'

Dugan checked his own watch. It was nine thirty-one.

TWENTY-ONE

Gillem & Cox had five floors of offices in the building on Wacker Drive, and on Wednesday morning, when Kirsten walked into the firm's main reception area, it suddenly struck her that through the years she'd had more than her fill of the elegant facades that these high-priced law firms favored. This was just one more, and boringly typical: teak flooring, oriental rugs, and upholstered furniture in three shades of gray – all served up on about a half-acre of space, with generous side dishes of mahogany and potted foliage.

Two middle-aged men in matching navy business suits sat side-by-side in matching ash-gray chairs. One stared straight ahead, motionless, somehow exuding prosperity and anxiety at the same time; the other fiddled nervously with some sort of hand-held electronic device. Kirsten imagined they were hedge fund managers . . . hopefully under indictment.

The firm had the apparently obligatory African-American receptionist, looking like she'd stepped out of *Sports Illustrated*, then stopped off at *Vogue* on the way to work. 'Good morning,' the woman said, with practiced hospitality. 'May I help you?'

'I'm here to see Jamison Traynor,' Kirsten said, 'and I don't have time to waste.'

That changed the woman's attitude considerably. 'Ex*cuse* me?' she said, managing to speak and purse her lips at the same time.

'You're excused. Which part didn't you catch?'

'Mr Traynor is at a meeting. I don't believe you have an appointment.'

'I don't . . . not yet. But I will shortly, once you get him on the phone.'

'I'm sorry, but—'

'No offense taken. Get Jamison Traynor on the phone and tell him there's a detective out here who has information about Isobel Cho.'

Kirsten went and sat on a sofa as far from the receptionist and as close to the door as possible, and called Cuffs to verify that he had Isobel available and ready to call Jamison right away if necessary.

A few minutes later a young man strode into the reception area. He spoke with the woman at the desk, who rolled her eyes and nodded toward Kirsten. He was tall, with angular, chiseled features, and dark hair, tanned skin, and very white teeth. He wore a well-tailored charcoal suit and – for reasons a psychologist might play with forever – buttoned his jacket as he glanced around the room. He'd look great in a society-page photo with Isobel at his side. Kirsten decided the guy couldn't help it if he'd been spoiled rotten by a mother who'd married well, and whose deceased husband left her wealthy enough to buy a senate seat. OK, so she'd withhold judgment on Jamison for awhile.

She stood, but stayed put and made him come over to her. He looked relieved to see her, and worried at the same time. 'I'm Jamison Traynor, officer,' he said. 'What is it? Is Isobel—'

'Is there a restaurant, or a coffee shop in the building, where we can talk? This place—' She almost said *creeps me out*, but caught herself. 'I'd prefer a little more privacy.'

'Yes . . . of course. But is everything . . . is Isobel OK?'

'Isobel's fine. I spoke with her yesterday.'

'But where—'

'I just have a few questions to ask. Let's take the elevator.'

He went with her, without bothering to explain to anyone where he was going, which she considered a plus. On the ride down there were others in the car, and he had enough sense to keep quiet. They went to one level below the lobby, and then to a restaurant with a coffee bar. They picked up coffee in paper cups and went through the doors to an outdoor patio, with wrought iron tables and chairs that looked out across the Chicago River some ten feet below them. When they were seated, Jamison said, 'The last detective I spoke with said they'd talked to Isobel's father . . . and that it wasn't a police matter.'

'Did he?'

'So is there some new . . .' Jamison paused, stared at her. 'I don't think you're really a police officer.'

'Did someone say I was?'

'I got that impression from Jocelyn, the receptionist, but I wouldn't swear that's what she said.'

'Well, I didn't tell her I was, and I *would* swear to that.' She handed him one of her cards.

He frowned. 'Another private detective?'

'By "another," I take it you mean in addition to Tyrone Beale.'

'Yes. And you're working for . . . ?'

'For Isobel.'

'You mean . . . for her father?'

'For Isobel.'

'But . . . that is . . . I *know* how much private detectives charge, and . . .'

'And Isobel has very little money, is that what you mean?'

'Yes.'

'And you can't *imagine* anybody working for a client unless it's in return for a substantial amount of money, right?'

'Well, we all have to make a living.'

'I make a very fine living, thanks. Would you like to discuss my last year's IRS return? Or shall we talk about Isobel?'

Anger flared in his eyes, which she took as another good sign. 'How can I be sure,' he said, 'that Isobel even knows you.'

She took out her cellphone and called Cuffs.

Like Juan Cho, Jamison stepped out of earshot when Isobel called him back, and while he was away, Kirsten called Cuffs again. 'You never told me where you'd stash Isobel.'

'No, I didn't.'

'But she's not at *your* place, right?'

'Jesus, are you out of your damn mind?'

'I'm not so sure. But anyway, I don't know where you are.'

'No, you don't.'

'What about Isobel? She happy?'

'She's not tied down, and she hasn't run off. I think she's got the picture, and she's got things to keep her busy and— Oh, she just ended her call with that guy.'

'OK. Well, then, bye.'

'Yeah, have a nice chat with the boyfriend.'

When Jamison was back and sitting down again, Kirsten asked, 'Did she tell you where she was?'

'No, and I can't stand not knowing. Do *you* know?'

'No. She obviously doesn't want us to know.'

'She said don't bother calling or texting. She's not answering, and not checking messages. I mean . . . I don't get it. This is crazy.'

'No, it's not crazy. She just doesn't want you to have to lie if anyone asks you where she is.' She paused, then said, 'I guess Tyrone Beale hasn't spoken to you about me.'

'That's right, but I haven't talked to him in a couple of days. Why? Did he say he would?'

'No, I just . . . thought he might.'

Jamison waved off some small birds that fluttered about, looking for handouts. 'Anyway, what about Isobel? Is her father telling the truth? No one's seen her since Friday night. Why is she—'

'As to her father telling the truth, it's true that she stayed at his house over the weekend and left on Monday. Beale and I both saw her yesterday morning, at Beale's office.'

'And . . . ?'

'And we talked for a while and she left his office. I don't know where she went, but as you can see, I do know someone who is able to reach her quickly. Keep that to yourself, for Isobel's sake. She seems to know what she's doing, how to stay safe.'

'Safe from whom? Is she hiding from someone? Why doesn't she just go back to her apartment?'

'I can only tell you what I know. And not *everything* I know, at that. Some things I promised her I wouldn't tell anyone, and I'll keep that promise. In turn, you have to promise me that you won't tell anyone what I tell you.'

'Yes, of course, I promise.' His response was quick, automatic, as though there was no need for consideration.

'First,' Kirsten said, 'if Isobel reappears, she'll have to make it clear right away that she's breaking up with you, for good.'

'*What?* I don't believe you. I mean, we're not . . . engaged . . . exactly. But we—'

'I didn't say she *wanted* to break up with you. I said she'd *have* to, if she reappears.' Kirsten briefly outlined Isobel's dilemma, including a threat if she didn't break up with him.

'That's crazy,' he said. 'What kind of threat? And who would do such a thing?'

'The people I think are most likely to try to keep two young people apart are either jealous ex-lovers, or their parents.'

'Neither one of us has an ex-lover like that. I'm sure of it.'

'Which leaves parents . . . either Isobel's father, or your mother.'

'Then it must be her father. That's why he had her dragged in Friday night.'

'Maybe,' she said, 'but what about your mother?'

'That's absurd. I mean, my mother isn't crazy about Isobel, or about Isobel's father. But she would never dream of coming between us. And she certainly wouldn't threaten Isobel in any way.'

'I'm sure you're right,' Kirsten said, although she wasn't sure at all. 'Still, I promised Isobel I'd try to get this resolved, and I have to cover all the bases. I need to talk to your mother. For one thing, people sometimes do things on behalf of politicians, when the politicians themselves don't even know the things are being done.'

'I suppose that's true,' Jamison said. 'But the whole idea of a threat is bizarre, anyway. What is it? What are they threatening to do?'

'I'm sorry, but that's something I promised Isobel I wouldn't tell.'

'That's ridiculous. I don't care what you promised. You *have* to tell. If you don't, how can we stop whoever it is from doing . . . whatever it is?'

'I really don't know yet. But if my giving *my* word means so little to you, I can't trust you to keep *your* word, and I can't use your help.' She stood. 'Go on back up to the Taj Mahal, and your desk full of papers.' She grabbed her coffee and left.

The patio opened directly on to a walkway along the river, so she didn't have to go back through the restaurant. She headed north, not looking back, but not walking very fast, either. And she didn't get far before she heard steps behind her.

'Wait,' he called.

She stopped and turned. Maybe he *did* love Isobel. He certainly looked desperate enough. 'What is it?' she asked.

'I wasn't thinking. But I can keep a promise, and I will. I want to help Isobel. What can I do?'

Sometimes all it takes is a little drama, she thought, to get people to commit themselves.

The odds were against anyone without a briefcase full of campaign cash getting a same-day appointment with a US senator. But Jamison made a call right there from their wrought iron table, and with the help of a little obviously well-practiced wheedling, he managed to set it up. He told his mother that it had to do with Isobel, and that he'd rather not go into any further details on the phone. In the end she agreed to meet with Kirsten that very evening. Now all Kirsten had to do was get herself to Washington, DC.

Jamison was certain that wouldn't be a problem, and he took her back upstairs to the Gillem & Cox suite and to the firm's travel person, who was obviously used to making last minute arrangements. 'Not a problem,' she said, 'and I can put it on your credit card.'

'Uh, sure.' Kirsten was certain that a ticket to DC for a flight that same day, and back home the next, would cost a minor fortune. So she was surprised when it didn't cost a whole lot more than her recent round trip to Seattle. A hotel room proved to be another story. There weren't many available, except out beyond the beltway. The travel person, though, recognized the restaurant where Kirsten was to meet the senator as being in a small luxury hotel near The Watergate, and she was able to book a room there. The room cost more than the round-trip flight.

Jamison offered to reimburse her for her expenses. 'After all,' he said, 'it's for Isobel.'

'No thanks,' she said, recalling how she'd just told him what a great living she made, and not wanting him to think he had any control over her. She glanced at her watch. She had another errand to perform, and then she had to get home, pack a bag, and get to O'Hare for her afternoon flight.

As she was leaving Gillem & Cox she stopped and spoke to the receptionist. 'Sorry about that rudeness earlier,' she said, with a genuine smile. 'I just needed to get your attention.'

The receptionist seemed truly surprised by the apology, even grateful. She smiled back. 'Whatever works, honey,' she said. 'Besides, you don't get the prize. You weren't the rudest person to pop in this morning.'

TWENTY-TWO

Kirsten rode the elevator down from Gillem & Cox and when she got to the lobby she called Wancho's Towing. She was surprised at how easily she got through to Juan Cho, and surprised again when he agreed to see her without objection. He said it had to be right away, though, because he wouldn't be there long.

When she got to Wancho's she got yet another surprise. Folding security gates were stretched across the plate glass windows and a grate covered the door. A sign taped to the window said: THIS SITE CLOSED FOR RENOVATION. The sign went on to say that towed cars awaiting pick-up had been moved to the lot of another towing company, Donahue's, about a half-mile away, and should be picked up there.

The door was locked. She rang the bell. She peered through the glass and saw that the ATM machine was gone. She waited, and a minute later saw the door beside the darkened cashier's window open and a very large man appear. He was probably the man who Dugan said had a fist 'like one of those iron shot-put balls.'

The man turned a deadbolt key on the door and let her inside, and then ushered her back to Cho's office. '*Señor* Cho will join you soon,' he said.

She sat down, and a few moments later Cho came in, with two paper cups of coffee. He wore gray pants and a white dress shirt with no tie, and the worn, tired look on his face made it clear that he needed the coffee. She'd already had way too much, but took the cup and thanked him for it.

'I don't have a lot of time,' he said, as he dropped into the chair behind his desk. 'Is it Isobel? Is there a problem? Where is she?'

'Isobel's fine. She's safe, and I still honestly don't know where she is.'

'Well then, how do you know she's—' He stopped, sipped some coffee, then set down the cup. 'If you don't know where she is, you can't tell anyone. But who would be asking you about her?'

'No one's asked me yet, other than Jamison Traynor, and I couldn't tell him either. But someone else might be asking me any day now, because I'm positive someone's looking for her, and I don't know that it's someone who has her best interests in mind.'

He'd lifted his cup again, but stopped midway to his mouth. 'What do you mean? I know you don't mean *me*, dammit.'

'No. We've been through that. I don't know who it is.' She shrugged. 'Isobel's life isn't going the way she expected it would. She falls in love, but the young man's mother doesn't approve of his choice. She graduates with honors from a very prestigious school, but comes home to learn that someone – is it the young man's mother? – is threatening to have her baby sister deported if she doesn't break up with him. Her apartment is broken into, and—'

'What? I heard nothing about a break-in.'

'I guess she didn't want you to worry. No one was home at the time. One of her roommates had an iPod taken. They changed the locks and that was it. But shortly after that, coincidentally or not, she began to feel as though someone was stalking her. She told Jamison and he hired Tyrone Beale. Then yesterday she's with me, at Beale's office, and two men, acting like police, come knocking on the door.'

'Police? What did *they* want?'

'They may not have been police, or at least not on official police business. I don't think they were there for Beale, or for me, but I don't know what they wanted because they didn't get in. And they left when my husband . . . who was also there . . . challenged them.'

'So . . .' Cho seemed to be thinking, 'does this Beale person know where Isobel is?'

'No. No one knows.'

'And still, you're sure she's OK?'

'As sure as anyone can be of anything in this life.'

Cho drank the last of his coffee. 'OK, and you have come here why? What do you want from me?'

'I don't know yet. Not exactly. But if we work together, the two of us, we should be able to—'

'Not me. Not now. I'm leaving this afternoon . . . for China. As you know, I have business there.'

'Business? You're going on a goddamn *business* trip? This is your *daughter* we're talking about. In fact, *both* your daughters may be in jeopardy.'

'My plans are already made. I am closing my business here temporarily, until I return.'

'I saw the sign. Do you always do that when you leave the country?'

'No, but this time I must. I trust Luis, my manager, but I do not wish to leave him responsible for my towing crews for more than a few days, and this time I may be away longer than that. Luis and his wife have agreed to care for Luisa, and that's responsibility enough for him. It's arranged. I will go.'

'Jesus! What kind of father are you? Business can *always* wait.'

'No, not always.' Cho stood and went to the door, and opened it. '*Luis! Ven aquí!*' he called, and then returned to his desk.

The large man who'd let Kirsten in stepped into the office, closed the door behind him, and stood in silence.

'This is Luis,' Cho said. 'He will be seeing to Luisa's welfare, in a place known to no one –' nodding at Kirsten – 'including you. And including Isobel.'

'And you're leaving town.'

'Leaving town, and leaving the country,' Cho said. 'I will be in a remote area and it will be difficult . . . in fact, impossible . . . to reach me. Meanwhile, I want you to see that Isobel remains hidden, and safe. From everyone. You will be well paid.'

She was already committed to helping Isobel, and she wanted to tell this bastard she didn't take orders from him and he could go to hell, but instead she said, 'I can't believe that you'd run off and leave both your daughters just now. It's . . . it's disgusting, and cowardly.'

'Your opinions mean nothing to me. You will see that Isobel is safe?'

'Yes, on two conditions, and neither of them is money.'

'Name them.'

'Luis understands English pretty well, right?'

'Well enough.'

'I want a phone number where I can reach Luis if I have to, day or night; and I want him to have my number.'

Cho nodded to Luis and Luis gave her his cell number and she gave him one of her cards. 'So,' Cho said, 'you have your two things. Do you—'

'No,' she said. 'The exchange of phone numbers was only one thing. There's something else I want. Something I might or might not use.'

TWENTY-THREE

At noon Mollie buzzed Dugan. 'Phone call,' she said. 'Tyrone Beale.'

Dugan picked up and said, 'Using the phone again? What happened to your "light footprint" routine?'

'I got a new cellphone this morning. I tossed the old one. You know where the Temple Building is?'

'Clark and Washington.'

'Right,' Beale said. 'Can you meet me there in, say, fifteen minutes? I got something to show you.'

'I can manage that.' Actually, a good excuse to get out of the office. 'They have a chapel there, right? Way up at the top?'

'That's the Sky Chapel, and it's usually not open. But the main church, on the first floor, that's open every day. We can talk there.'

Although it was only about a five-minute walk from his office, Dugan had never had any reason to go inside the Temple Building. It was a skyscraper built in the gothic style, with steeples and gargoyles and the whole business – mostly up at the top, not very noticeable from street level – and was home to a Methodist church. Dugan didn't know how many of the twenty or so floors were used by the church, but he knew the building was mostly commercial office space, and lots of lawyers had offices there, including, about a hundred years ago, Clarence Darrow.

The entrance was on Washington Street and the tiny lobby, with its ATM machines, didn't look much like the entrance to a church. But beyond that was another entrance – the plaque on the door said SANCTUARY – and he went through into a dimly lit, surprisingly large church, complete with altar, pews, high ceiling, and stained-glass windows. He guessed the place sat at least a thousand people. Once in a while he went to his office on Sunday mornings, and he'd see people headed there for church services. Never seemed like very many people, though, so he was surprised to see, just inside the door, a bulletin board overflowing with notices of events and activities.

There was some sort of noon service going on, but only about twenty people there, all up at the front, so he figured he and Beale could sit near the rear and talk, and not bother anyone. He didn't see Beale, though, so he took a seat near the wall to his right, put his phone on vibrate so as not to disturb anyone, and waited.

Hardly a minute later Beale showed up. He sat in the pew in front of Dugan, which seemed strange until Beale turned and faced him, and he realized Beale could talk to him and keep an eye on the church entrance behind them at the same time.

'Your face is looking better already,' Dugan said.

'I'm a quick healer.' Beale glanced around the church. 'I followed you here,' he said, 'and I don't think anyone else did. And no one followed me, either. I don't know if I'm being paranoid, but I didn't like those two guys showing up at my place yesterday.'

'Did they come back again?'

'I don't know.' Like Dugan, Beale was keeping his voice down almost to a whisper. 'I left not long after your wife left with Isobel, and I haven't been back. I'd like to know who those guys are. You saw 'em, right?'

'Yeah, and they acted like cops, but they didn't identify themselves.' He told of his brief encounter with the men, and how they drove away in a hurry, but he didn't mention the stolen plate. 'Any reason why law enforcement should be showing up at your door?'

'No way,' Beale said. 'Besides, if that's who they were, why'd they run when they thought you were calling the cops?'

'Cops or not, whoever they are, they must have been looking for Isobel.'

'Yeah, but why? The cops say they don't consider her a missing person.'

'Right,' Dugan said, 'but maybe there's something else. You've had more contact with her. Any sign of her being into anything dishonest? Or hanging with people who might . . . I don't know . . . be into something.'

'Are you kidding? I mean, she's independent and hard-headed and drove me nuts. But anything shady? No sign of it. Girl just graduated from a high-tone university on the east coast with great grades. Said she's taking some time off, to decide what to do with her life. We didn't talk a lot, but she told me she planned to spend part of this year in . . . I don't know . . . South America somewhere . . . volunteering with some do-gooder group, getting fresh water to villages in the boonies. That's the kind of people she hangs with.'

'South America? Maybe that'd be a good way to get her out of—'

'Nope. The whole program's on hold. The guy who ran it, and recruited her . . . it was during the school year, on campus . . . was a minister I think, or at least connected with a church. But he's dead. Got himself gunned down in Washington, DC. Armed robbery, or carjacking or something. That hit her pretty hard.'

'Jesus, a tough year for her.'

'She's a tough girl.' Beale's eyes switched to the door as

someone came inside. Dugan turned to look, too, but it was just a woman who headed up the aisle toward the altar. 'Anyway,' Beale said, 'I don't see Isobel as someone law enforcement's interested in.'

'Maybe the cops changed their mind about her being missing. Have you talked to Jamison?'

'No. Problem is, I'm not sure what I'd tell him. Your wife wanted me to help get his cooperation with her. She and I had a little . . . disagreement about that, but my brother said . . . well, no . . . skip him. Thing is, I asked around about Kirsten, and she's . . . there's no reason for me to screw up whatever she's got in mind.'

'I'm sure she'll be glad to hear that.'

'Anyway, those two guys,' Beale said. 'You saw their faces, right?'

'I did, and I'd recognize them if I saw them again. But a verbal description's not much help in identifying unknown persons. I even worked with a sketch artist once, trying to make a drawing of someone I'd seen. That wasn't very successful, either.'

'Uh-huh.' Beale reached inside his jacket. 'But these might help.' He came out with a manila envelope, about five by eight inches. He took two photos from the envelope and handed them to Dugan.

Both were grainy black-and-whites, as though taken by a security camera, but both showed clearly the two men Dugan had seen the previous day. They were in the hallway leading to Beale's place, walking toward the camera.

'These are stills from a surveillance video?' Dugan asked.

'Right. The camera's hidden in a picture at the end of the hallway, and transmits to my laptop. My apartment's behind that wall. A motion sensor starts the camera, and you can either watch whoever's coming in real time, or you can play it back and watch later. I tried to pick out the clearest shot I could get of each of them. Those are copies for you to keep.'

'Thanks, I guess, but these photos—' Dugan stopped when he noticed some of the people up in the front pews getting to their feet. He thought the service must be over, but then the people started walking up toward the altar. 'Damn,' he said, 'I didn't even know Methodists *had* communion.'

Beale shrugged. 'Methodists? What's that got to do with anything?'

'Nothing,' Dugan said. 'Anyway, these photos are great, but they still don't get the guys identified.'

'They get us a step closer.'

'Maybe, but what's with the *us*?' Dugan asked. 'Not screwing up what Kirsten's got going is one thing. Working together is something else. She said you didn't like the way she was playing, told me you bowed out.'

'Maybe she sees it that way, but I say she's the one cut me outta the loop. Anyway, those guys came banging on *my* door, and I wanna know who they are. You can help with that, and now you got some pictures to make it easier.'

'So . . . let me see. You wouldn't help Kirsten with Isobel's problem, but you want me to help you with yours.'

'Sure, but like you said, those two guys must have come looking for Isobel, so they're *her* problem as much as mine. In fact, *more* than mine. And they're *your* problem, too. They saw you, and they'll be trying to find out who you are. So we all wanna know the same thing: who are they and what do they want? And we all benefit by helping each other find out.'

Dugan couldn't argue with that, and he and Beale both promised to share anything they learned. By that time the noon service was over and Dugan took the photographs and joined the worshippers as they filed out, past the ATM machines and into the sunshine.

Who are those guys, and what do they want? Who are those guys, and what do they want?

That refrain played over and over again in Dugan's head, like a line from an old movie. *Ah yes*, he thought, *Butch Cassidy*. He walked south on Clark Street, intending to go back to his office. But when he reached his building he kept right on walking, bound for nowhere in particular.

The simple answer to what was happening with Isobel was that she fell for a guy whose mother didn't want her son getting mixed up with a family headed by someone like Juan Cho. Not that Cho was an outright crook, at least not as far as Dugan knew. But everyone loved to hate Wancho's Towing, and Cho's heavy-handed crews were notorious. Cho simply wasn't the kind of popular all-American guy you picture jumping up on to the platform with your family when you accept a vice-presidential nomination.

If the rumor Larry said he read about was true, it was easy to imagine Eleanor Traynor's people looking to put an end to Isobel's relationship with Jamison. And if the way they chose was to threaten to have a little girl taken away from her father and shipped to the other side of the world? Maybe not so inconceivable. Couldn't political crews be as heavy-handed as tow truck crews?

But the two guys at Tyrone Beale's door didn't fit into that scenario. Beale *might* be mixed up in things he wasn't talking about. And the men *could* have been looking for Beale, and just *happened* to show up when Isobel just *happened* to be there. But a coincidence like that? Not a chance. Those guys were there for Isobel.

Could she be into something Beale didn't pick up on? Criminal involvement seemed pretty far-fetched. Still, anything was possible. And with Juan Cho as a father . . .

Who are those guys, and what do they want?

And these photos? How useful were they, really? Kirsten might know how best to use them. All he could do was imagine himself getting the Chicago police department to let him sit down and page through books of photos of . . . what? . . . twelve or thirteen thousand Chicago police officers? . . . and trying to match two of them with pictures of these two guys who *might* be cops. Then maybe he could try the State Police. Or the FBI. Or . . . what the hell . . . Homeland Security?

On the other hand, as Beale pointed out, the men had also seen him and they might be busily trying to identify him. In fact, maybe they already knew who he was. And maybe Beale *wasn't* paranoid. Maybe they were all under surveillance. In fact, he had the feeling right now that—

No, that's ridiculous.

But he couldn't help it. He caught himself looking around.

TWENTY-FOUR

The afternoon flight to DC was uneventful, and Kirsten had no baggage to pick up. She was so hungry when the plane landed that she grabbed a Coke and a very unsatisfactory slice of pizza, and ate the pizza on her way through the terminal.

When she stepped outside she was almost knocked down by what felt like ninety-five degree heat, and ninety percent humidity. By the time she closed herself into an air-conditioned cab she was already soaked with perspiration, and was glad she hadn't finished her drink.

At seven o'clock, Eastern Daylight Time, fresh from the shower and wearing what she thought of as her Kinsey Millhone outfit – a plain, wrinkle-free black dress, great for traveling – she stood in the entrance to the hotel restaurant's bar.

The room was crowded with thirty-somethings, and upbeat music floated gently through the air, along with the smells of liquor and expensive cologne, and fresh money. Eleanor Traynor had said to come to the bar, and promised they'd have no trouble finding each other. Kirsten wasn't so sure. There was no one old enough to be Jamison's mother, unless they were tucked inside one of those tall padded booths along the wall to her right.

'Follow me, please.'

Kirsten jumped. The man was so close she could feel his breath on the back of her ear.

'The senator is waiting,' he said. 'She has a very heavy schedule.'

Kirsten spun around. 'Who *are* you? *What* senator is waiting?' He stayed too close to her. She didn't step back.

The surprise that flashed across his face at her reaction was gone at once, replaced by no expression at all. 'My name is Erik Decker. I am Senator Eleanor Traynor's executive assistant. Why? Were you waiting for some other senator?' He still didn't move.

'Please step away from me, Mr Decker.'

Decker stared back at her, not smiling, not frowning, not moving. He was of medium height and build, plain-featured, balding, with a strong, wide mouth and a square chin. His eyes were shrewd, and hard, and he was clearly used to having his way. He wore a well-tailored gray suit and a striped tie, and held his hands deep in his jacket pockets. 'You seem to be feeling rather hostile,' he said.

'What I'm feeling is crowded. So unless you want a scene, one that will draw an *awful* lot of attention . . .'

He nodded, just slightly, and moved backwards, smoothly. 'Shall I inform the senator that you no longer wish to talk to her?'

'Why not just take me to your boss, and then slither away?'
'As you wish.' And finally he smiled. 'My pleasure,' he said.

The booths were all empty, but past them, in a secluded alcove
at the far end of the bar and just around to the right, was Eleanor
Traynor's table. Decker introduced them and disappeared back
around the corner.

'I appreciate your seeing me on such short notice,' Kirsten
said, when they were both seated.

'I see it as my responsibility to communicate with my constituents
whenever and wherever possible. It's how a legislator stays in
touch.' She said those practiced words as if for the ten thousandth
time.

'Do they all have to be screened by Erik Decker first?'

'Ah, you've had words with Erik.'

'A few.'

'He's very faithful. He's been with me a long time.' Then she
looked past Kirsten. 'But here comes Anthony. They serve an
excellent Sauvignon Blanc here. You should give it a try.'

'Thank you. I'll do that.' Best to get the conversation off on
a friendly note, although how it would end was anyone's guess.

Anthony arrived, and Traynor ordered two glasses of wine.
'Well,' she said, 'when Jamison asked me to see you, I couldn't
say no. But I have to tell you what I told him, it's a waste of
money, his paying you to help him find that . . . that girl.'

'You mean Isobel Cho?'

'Of course, who else would I mean?' Traynor took a substantial
hit from her Sauvignon.

'Your son is very fond of her, and—'

'Oh, don't mince words. Jamison's entirely lost his mind over
that girl.'

'You mean Isobel Cho,' Kirsten said. 'She has a name, you
know.'

Eleanor lifted her glass, then put it down and leaned slightly
toward Kirsten. 'Jamison practically begged me to see you, so
here you are. But if what you want is to play games, then I assure
you, it will be a very short conversation.'

'What I want is to find out what's happened to Isobel.'

'That may be what you're supposedly doing, but as far as I
know, there's no sign at all that anything's *happened* to her.'

'No one seems to know where she is.'

'Which means nothing. She's probably run off somewhere. She realizes she's out of her element with someone like Jamison, and she's afraid to tell him it's over.' She sighed. More a sigh of relief, it seemed, than of sympathy for her son. 'Jamison's a bright boy, but honestly . . .'

'There's some evidence,' Kirsten said, 'that her disappearance didn't begin with her running away, but that her father kidnapped her.'

'What sort of evidence?'

'I'm not at liberty to say.'

'Well, *that's* certainly a handy answer. Anyway, people like her father . . . who knows *what* they do? The man's a thug, but I understand the police have talked to him and his explanation satisfied them. So, whatever it was, it satisfies me.'

'If he kidnapped her,' Kirsten said, 'I'm going to find out why, and whether it was his own idea or somebody else's. What's clear now,' she went on, 'is that she's no longer with her father. What's not clear is where she is. Jamison doesn't know. Her father and her friends all say they don't know. People don't often simply vanish, whatever their reasons.'

Eleanor finished her wine and looked at her watch. 'I have a limited amount of time,' she said, 'and unless you can explain just what you want from me, I'll be on my way.'

'I keep looking around for someone who has a motive for moving Isobel out of the picture, and I keep coming up with the same answer: You.'

'Really.' Eleanor didn't look at all startled at this. 'Well, I have to say you're right about one thing. I'd be thrilled to have that girl out of my son's life . . . for good. How many parents would love to have their son or daughter stop seeing whoever they're seeing? But they don't go around making people "disappear". And I don't either.' She leaned toward Kirsten. 'Also,' she said, 'I don't take accusations lightly.' The woman wasn't famous for deep thinking, but she had a flair for drama.

'I should hope not,' Kirsten said. 'And so far I'm not accusing anyone of anything. But I'm going to find out whether someone wants Isobel out of the way, and who it is, and what they're doing about it. Right now I'm simply inviting you to give me some reason why I shouldn't stay focused on you.'

'That's about the most bizarre thing I've ever heard. Why in God's name should I care whether you "focus" on me or not?'

'You should care because I'm very good at what I do,' which was true, if a bit self-congratulatory. 'And I assure you, my methods are absolutely and entirely legal and non-intrusive,' which was a bit of a stretch, and meant mostly for anyone else who might be listening in, or making a recording. 'Even so, it's very possible I'll find things you don't want most people to know.'

Eleanor reached down beside her for her handbag and set it on the table. 'You,' she said, 'are a very strange woman.'

The handbag may have been a signal because, even before Kirsten could answer, Erik Decker appeared out of nowhere. Eleanor stood and the two of them left without another word.

Eleanor hadn't finished her drink, but Kirsten was in no hurry, and finished hers. It *was* a very good Sauvignon Blanc. Anthony returned and she asked him if she owed anything.

'Oh no, miss,' he said. 'The evening will all be added to the senator's account.'

'Good.' Kirsten smiled. 'Then why not bring me a dinner menu?'

TWENTY-FIVE

At a little before nine o'clock Kirsten rode the elevator up to her hotel room, thinking that this little whirlwind trip to Washington was costing her a bundle, despite having dinner on Eleanor Traynor . . . or maybe on the tax-paying public. Still, she knew she'd accomplished what she'd intended, which was to convince the junior senator from Illinois – and, as a bonus, the senator's well-dressed, highly-refined goon – that they weren't dealing with some easily-intimidated person, and to stir up some trouble . . . if there was any trouble to stir up.

When she got to her room she checked carefully to see whether everything was as she'd left it. She discovered everything wasn't . . . not quite. So she turned on the TV, scanned the available pay-per-view movies, and ordered a nice romantic comedy. When it started up she changed into her only other outfit, tan pants and a blue tailored blouse, and left the room . . . very quietly. Her large shoulder bag was her only luggage, and she took it with her.

She rode the elevator down and walked to the lobby, where she found a surprising amount of hustle and bustle. Perfectly-coiffed people – nearly all of them, men and women alike, in business suits – moved smoothly through a hushed atmosphere that seemed subdued and somehow hyperactive at the same time.

There were a few guests still at the desk checking in, and others striding toward the elevators, pulling wheeled luggage behind them. Most people, though, were gathering in small groups and heading out. Lobbyists, she thought, in their native habitat, ready for drinks and dinner, and plotting out the next day's palm-greasing. There were plenty of comfortable-looking sofas and armchairs available, but not a soul sitting on any of them. Virtually everyone was engaged in conversation, either with the live bodies around them, or on cellphones or texting devices.

She went out the entrance and was stunned at the immediate slap of heat and humidity she'd forgotten about. Exhaust fumes, too, from the constant flow of cabs and limos, trolling for passengers. There were benches where people could wait for their transportation of choice, but every one of them was empty. Sitting down was apparently a sign of weakness around here.

She sat on a bench and called Dugan.

'Hey,' he said, 'you missed supper.'

'I'm in Washington.'

'Not Seattle again, I hope.'

'No, DC.'

'Sounds like you're outside somewhere. You on your way home now?'

'In the morning,' she said. 'Meanwhile, while I was meeting with a senator and having a bite to eat, someone went through my hotel room.'

'Jesus. Are you . . . all right?'

'Yes.'

'Anything taken?'

'There was nothing to take, but they might have planted a bug.'

'Better behave yourself.'

'I wasn't planning anything more clandestine than this call.'

'That's a relief. But look, you should get a different room.'

'I'm checking out and going to a hotel near the airport. I should be home by noon. I'll drop by your office and we can talk.'

TWENTY-SIX

K irsten called Dugan at eleven thirty from O'Hare, as soon as she got off the plane. To her surprise he suggested they meet somewhere besides his office. 'How about lunch at the Ogilvie Center?' he asked.

She agreed and took the CTA Blue Line downtown. The ride was fine, especially with no luggage but the shoulder bag. Not as cozy and comfortable as having Dugan pick her up in her own car, but better than a taxi.

She walked to the Ogilvie Transportation Center, just west of the Loop. The food court there, which served not only the station for commuter trains to the north suburbs, but also forty stories of offices rising above the station, was noisy and jammed with the lunch crowd. She circled the area twice, watching for anyone observing either her or Dugan, whom she'd already spotted, nursing a cup of coffee at a tiny table far from the entrance. Seeing no one suspicious, she picked up a couple of chicken wraps and one Diet Coke – they'd agreed to watch their calories – and by twelve forty-five she was standing beside him. He was talking on his cell . . . or at least listening.

She leaned and gave him a kiss on the back of his neck, and he kept his phone to his ear and didn't even look up, but put his free hand on her thigh . . . pretty high up, actually. She stepped away before they got arrested, and sat down across from him.

'OK, Mollie, have a nice time,' he said, and put the phone in his pocket. 'I've been out of the office about half an hour and that was Mollie calling to see if I was still alive, and to tell me she's going out for lunch.'

'Out for lunch?' Kirsten knew Mollie never went out for lunch, hardly ever left the office all day, for anything.

'A new development. Three times last week and so far twice this week. Larry Candle told me she's found a lunch-mate. Larry pays attention to those sorts of things.'

'A *lunch*-mate?'

'Yeah, a guy. But when you see her don't say anything about it. She's very touchy. I mean, I happened to mention it and . . .' He lifted his hands and shrugged.

'So . . . you just "mentioned" it, right?

'Well, maybe I teased her . . . a little. But Jesus, if I weren't her boss she'd have fired me.' He shook his head. 'Anyway, someone got into your hotel room, but you didn't seem very upset about it. What happened? I guess they didn't steal anything.'

'I'm sure they were looking, not stealing. When I went down to see Eleanor Traynor I took a little clutch bag and my phone with me. Everything else was in the room. In here.' She patted her shoulder bag. 'But there was nothing to find. After I talked to you I took a cab to a hotel near the airport. End of story. Your turn. Anything new?'

'First, Larry Candle can't find that reference he saw on the Internet about Traynor and a vice-presidential run. He insists someone got it removed from the Net.'

'It's hard to kill an Internet rumor,' Kirsten said. 'But I wouldn't be surprised if she *were* being considered by someone. Think about it. She's a woman. Not much of a thinker, but shrewd enough; and not unattractive. Plus she's one of those megabucks people who are good at that "just-one-of-us-folks" scam. What else could you ask for?'

'I could ask for a rudimentary awareness of the international geopolitical scene, a willingness to speak rationally about complex—'

'My question was rhetorical. But anyway, the loftier her ambitions, the bigger motive she has to distance the Traynor family from the Cho family. And she's got a right-hand man who belongs in a vampire novel.' She paused. 'So? What else is new?'

'Before I get to that, there's something I've been wondering. Without Jamison Traynor you'd never have gotten that appointment with the senator, right?'

'Well . . . I'd have gotten to her somehow, but certainly not that quickly and easily. He even offered to pay the expenses of my Washington trip.'

'So,' Dugan frowned, 'he *does* seem to love Isobel, right?'

'I think so, yes.'

'And he's willing to do what he can to help her?'

'Yes,' Kirsten said, 'and I think I know where you're going with this. I've been asking myself the same thing.'

'Asking yourself what?'

'Asking myself why Isobel . . . who has a handsome young man who loves her and who not only wants to help her, but also has what it takes – in the way of very deep pockets – to get things done . . . why Isobel doesn't turn to him for help.'

'Exactly. And what sort of answer has yourself been giving you?'

'None at all, until yesterday, when Jamison offered to pay my way to DC, and I turned him down. I didn't want him to think he had any control over me.'

'And you think that's why Isobel hasn't gone running to him, because she doesn't want him thinking he can control her?'

'Maybe not that exactly, but maybe something along those lines.' Kirsten sipped some Diet Coke. 'Anyway, you were about to tell me what else is new.'

'OK. I went to church yesterday.'

'That's certainly new.'

'Yes, and while I was there I picked up some photographs. Then I went for a walk, and met some really interesting people.'

'Church is a strange place to pick up photographs.'

'The whole afternoon was strange.'

Dugan gave her a rundown on his meeting with Tyrone Beale at the Temple Building, and Beale's giving him the photographs of the two men. 'I thought they looked like cops, but I could be wrong. Anyway, Beale doesn't think Isobel's mixed up in anything criminal. She graduated with honors from some university out east, and—'

'Tufts,' Kirsten said. 'Near Boston.'

'Yeah, whatever. But Beale says she's not just bright, but also idealistic. By now she planned to have been down in South America, helping some church group get water delivered to mountain villages.'

'But she's not. So what happened?'

'The whole project got put on hold after the guy who ran it, and who recruited her . . . a minister, I guess . . . was killed in a robbery in our nation's capital, where he was doing some fund-raising. The DC cops think it was a botched carjacking.'

'Damn, is anything going right for Isobel these days? But the photographs. Was that the reason Beale wanted to meet? To give them to you?'

'Right, and also to make sure we both agreed that we wanted to know who it was who came knocking on his door, and that we'd share anything we found out.'

'Fair enough.' She'd finished her chicken wrap and noticed that his was still sitting there, untouched. 'You gonna eat that?'

He looked down at it. 'I don't think so,' he said. 'I got here a little early and had two chili dogs with fries while I waited.'

'Fine.' She snatched up the wrap. 'So . . . let's get to those "really interesting people" you met on your walk.'

'OK, but first . . . something else Beale said. Or something he *didn't* say.'

'Mmm-hmm,' she said, through a tasty mouthful of chicken, tomatoes, and green peppers.

'I guess he had negative feelings about you after your disagreement about him helping you get Jamison Traynor's cooperation. But that changed. He started to say he talked to his brother about you, but then he said, "Well no, skip him" – meaning his brother – and that he'd talked to some people who changed his mind about you.'

'His *brother*? Who's his brother?'

'I thought maybe *you* knew. I got the impression he wished he hadn't mentioned the guy in the first place.'

'Really.' She sipped her drink, recalling the limo driver who picked Beale up after he left the zoo. Andrew was back in town, and maybe she *did* know who Beale's brother was. 'I'll have to think about that,' she said. 'Let's get to the interesting people.'

'Right. Well, to begin with, Beale told me he'd been watching me while I walked from my office to the Temple Building, and he was sure no one was following me. Then, when I left the Temple Building, I mixed in with the people who'd been there for a noon service and—' He stopped. 'Did you know Methodists go to communion? I mean, with little wafers and—'

'Dugan . . . just get on with it.' She waved what was left of the wrap at him.

'OK. When I left there I was thinking about Isobel and all, and I had walked about a half-block past my building when I suddenly got this *weird* feeling.' He stretched out the *weeeird*. 'So I spun around . . .' He paused, obviously enjoying the drama.

'And saw two guys following you.'

'Damn, you knew already?'

'Just a guess, Dugan. I mean . . . all that build-up had to lead some*where. Were they the same two guys from Beale's place?'

'No such luck. Anyway, long story short, they were FBI. And you know what? I hate talking to federal guys. You have to be careful not to say too much, and at the same time not appear to be hiding anything. And on top of all that you have to stick to the truth, because a year or two later, when they haven't been able to prove a damn thing about whoever or whatever they're looking at, they go for the consolation prize . . . and get the people they questioned sent away for lying to federal agents.'

'You were keeping it short,' she said. 'What did they ask and what did you say?'

'They asked about you, where you were, and I said I had no idea. They asked if you were working on a case, and I said if I didn't even know where you were, how could I know what you were doing. They said not to get smart with them, that they meant did I know of anything you were working on these days.'

'And you said?'

'I said I thought you were working on something having to do with Isobel Cho, but I couldn't be sure. They asked if I knew where Isobel is, and I said no. They asked if *you* knew, and I said I couldn't speak for you. And that was it.'

'Did they tell you to tell me to contact them?'

'They did, actually, and I said I'd do my best to remember. They didn't like that. They take themselves kind of seriously.'

'How do you know they were really FBI?'

'Their IDs looked authentic to me. One guy was Karl Schell, with a "K" and an "Sch." The other was Ronald Ragan . . . without the "e," but pronounced just like the Great Nodder-Offer. I asked him. Later, Mollie told me they'd shown up at the office after I left to meet Beale. They introduced themselves as FBI, and sat there until they got tired of waited for me. I think they came out of my building just after I passed, and saw me.'

'They would have had to know what you look like.'

'Yeah, but my picture's on my website. Nice shot, too. Anyway, whoever they were, I didn't tell them much of anything.'

'And this was early afternoon, right?'

'Yeah, maybe one o'clock.'

'Before I even left for Washington.' She downed the last bite of her lunch.

'True,' he said, 'but what time did you make the appointment with Traynor?'

'Eleven maybe, but how many senators can order up an immediate FBI interview of someone on the basis that the person asks for a meeting?'

'A handful, if that, and Traynor's only been in the club a few years.'

'So I doubt that the FBI's wanting to talk to me had anything to do with my meeting with Traynor.' Kirsten finished her Diet Coke and set the cup down. 'I hate talking to the Feds as much as you do, but . . .' She dug her cellphone from her bag.

'What the hell? Let *them* find *you*. That's their job.'

'They gave you a card, right?'

'Two of them,' he said. 'One each.' He handed her both business cards. 'Ever notice how those guys *love* to give out their cards?'

Fifteen minutes later, Kirsten was listening patiently to Dugan. 'You know as well as I do,' he said, 'that no one should ever talk to FBI agents without a lawyer. Especially to pompous idiots like those two. I'm going with you.'

'No.' She looked at her watch. 'I said I'd be at the Dirksen Building at two. I can make it in plenty of time on foot. You go back to your office. You'd only antagonize them.'

'*Antagonize* someone? Me?'

'Anyway, it's not about me. It's about Isobel. They're looking for her, and without a lawyer getting in the way, I'm more likely to find out why.'

'I won't be "getting in the way." I'll be absolutely quiet. I mean, you know, unless they start acting like real ass—'

'Right. That's why I'm going alone. Period.'

TWENTY-SEVEN

'**A**s I said before,' Kirsten said, struggling to stay patient, 'I consider the identities of my clients confidential.'

It was three o'clock and she and the two FBI agents, Schell and Ragan, were crammed into an interview room about thirty stories up in the Dirksen Federal Court Building, at the south end of the Loop. She'd been glad they'd agreed to meet with her here, and hadn't made her fight her way through traffic all the way out to the Bureau's Chicago headquarters, three or four miles south-west of the Loop. Now, though, she wasn't so sure. They were stuck in a warm, drab, windowless room, with barely enough space for a table and three chairs.

'Your husband says you're working on something related to Isobel Cho.'

'That's right.'

'Have you spoke to Jamison Traynor?'

'About what?'

'About this matter related to Isobel Cho.'

'Yes.'

'Is Jamison Traynor your client?' Schell was asking the questions, while Ragan took notes that seemed far more voluminous than Kirsten's answers. They both wore gray suits and blue ties, and at least one of them smoked cigars. Maybe both. She hated that smell.

'I'm not going to start eliminating candidates. The identity of my client is confidential.'

'That's not the law,' Schell said.

'It's my belief, and my position. I'm not a lawyer and I'm not represented by counsel. If a judge decides that I'm legally required to reveal my client's identity, I will.'

'Are you looking for Isobel Cho?'

'Not actively.'

'What does that mean?'

'It means I don't know where she is and I'm not trying to find her. I have no evidence to suggest that she's been the victim of foul play. It's quite likely that she doesn't *want* to be found.'

'So,' Schell said, referring to some notes in front of him, 'in regard to this matter "related to Isobel Cho," have you spoken with anyone at Tufts University?'

'No.'

'Anyone at the daycare center where she volunteers?'

'No.'

'What about hit the rock?'

'Hit the rock?' She shook her head. 'I don't get it.'

'Is your answer "no"?'

'I guess it must be.'

'Have you spoken to any of her girlfriends, or roommates?'

'No.'

'Have you spoken to Juan Cho?'

'Yes.'

'Is he your client?'

'The identity of my client is confidential.'

'Does he know where Isobel is?'

'I don't know. He told me he didn't.'

'What were you retained to do?'

'I don't see how that would help you find Isobel.'

'You don't have to see things. Just answer the questions.'

'Could we hold on a minute here?' Kirsten smiled, still fighting to keep things on a friendly basis. 'If I'm face-to-face with a federal investigation of some criminal activity I'll cooperate as much as I can. But from what I've learned about Isobel I find it highly unlikely that she's been involved in any crime. So before I answer more questions I really need a little explanation as to why you're asking them.'

'We're conducting an investigation on behalf of the United States government,' Schell said, reminding Kirsten of Dugan's 'pompous idiots' comment. 'What were you retained to do for Isobel Cho?'

'I haven't said I was doing anything *for* her. I said I was working on a case *involving* her.' She paused, and the two agents just stared at her until she asked, 'Why in the world is the FBI looking for Isobel?'

'We have reason to believe,' Schell said, 'that Ms Cho may have information relevant to a criminal enterprise.'

'What sort of criminal enterprise?'

'That's our business.'

'I agree, but that's no reason not to tell me. What crime? Is she a suspect? A witness? A victim? A little information from you would help me decide how to proceed.'

Schell looked at Ragan, who shrugged. Schell turned back to Kirsten. 'We might be more inclined to tell you if we got a little cooperation from you.'

'Good point.' She'd held out long enough, and they could learn it soon enough from Juan Cho, or from Jamison. 'My client is Isobel Cho.' She raised a hand to stop Schell when he opened his mouth to speak. 'I don't know where she is. My job is . . . well . . . to try to figure out why everyone's taken such an interest in her.'

'Everyone? Like who?'

'My understanding is that Isobel's father had her picked up on the street and brought to him early last Saturday morning. There were witnesses to that, including a man named Tyrone Beale who was apparently acting as her bodyguard, and another man who—'

'Another man who's your husband. We know that. Get to the point.'

'I don't have a "point." I'm being cooperative.'

'Alright, then, go ahead.'

'There may be some dispute as to whether Isobel's father had her brought to him against her will or not, but at any rate both he and she agree that she left his home freely early Monday. The Chicago police don't appear to be looking for her, and until now I wasn't aware that anyone else in law enforcement was, either.'

'You were going to tell us about this "everyone" who's taken an interest in Isobel.'

'And that's what I'm doing. I began with her father, who seems to have felt a sudden urgent need to see her. Then, at about sunup Monday morning, two men were seen sitting in a car outside her father's home, apparently watching the house.'

'Who told you that?'

'She did.'

'When and where did you talk to her?'

'Two days ago, Tuesday morning, at Tyrone's Beale's office. I'll get to that.' She raised a hand again to stop Schell from objecting. 'Let me take this in order. Isobel was frightened when she was told there were men watching the house, and she left by a back way.'

'Who were the two men? What did they want?'

'Those are among the questions I'm trying to answer. When my husband told me you two stopped him on the street, I thought maybe it was you who'd been watching Cho's house. Now . . . I think probably not.' She wasn't at all sure, but no need to say that.

'You said "everyone." Who else?'

'Tuesday morning I went to Beale's office to try to find out more about what happened when my husband ran into him at Wancho's Towing. Beale's place is on the third floor and a woman buzzed me in. I was surprised to discover the woman was Isobel Cho herself. Beale wasn't there, but he came in just after I arrived. It turns out Isobel had shown up there a little earlier and asked him to go get my husband, which he did.'

'And you knew nothing of that?'

'Nope. It was all a surprise. That's the first time I'd ever met Isobel. But she was clearly afraid. It appeared that someone may have been following her, stalking her. I didn't know what was going on . . . and I still don't . . . but I liked her and I promised I'd help her.'

'Did your husband hear that?'

'I don't know what he heard. He was wandering around the room. She and I were talking informally. I didn't even quote her a fee. We were interrupted when two men knocked on Beale's door. You have to be buzzed into the building, but they'd gotten in somehow.'

'The same two men?'

'I don't know. I didn't see them, either at Isobel's father's house, or at Beale's office.'

'What happened when the two men knocked on the door?'

'Mr Beale wasn't expecting anyone, and he decided not to respond to the knock. Isobel left, down the back stairs.'

'Did you try to stop her?'

'No.'

'Did you call the police?'

'No. The men left. There didn't seem to have been any crime committed.'

'Why did Isobel run?'

'I didn't say she *ran*. I said she left. Although she obviously didn't see the men at the door, she may have assumed they were the same men who were watching her father's house.'

'And do you still say you don't know where she went, or where she is?'

'No . . . or yes. That is, yes, I still say I don't know where she is. Because I don't.'

'And yet you consider her your client?'

'Yes. I mean, nothing was formalized, but I made a promise. Before we were interrupted.'

'And that's enough to make her your "client"?'

'It is for me. In this case, anyway. I keep my promises.'

'OK. So . . . who else?'

'Who else what?'

'You said "everyone" was taking an interest in Isobel.'

'Oh. Well, there's . . . you know . . .' She spread her hands out, indicating the two of them.

'Anyone else?'

'Not that I know of. But now it's your turn. What's the nature of this "criminal enterprise" you think Isobel may have information about?'

'As I said earlier, that's our business.'

'So . . . I get nothing in return for my cooperation?'

'If you cooperate fully you'll have the gratitude of your country. But more importantly, as a citizen you're expected to answer truthfully any and all questions put to you by federal agents in the course of their investigation.'

'Yeah, well, as a citizen, I'm about answered out.' She hadn't told them anything they couldn't learn from Jamison, or Cho, or Beale, or even Dugan. But she hadn't learned much, either. And she wasn't going to. 'It's been fun,' she said, and stood up.

'Sit down.' Schell's voice held a new bullying tone. 'We're not finished here.'

'Maybe *you're* not finished, but I'm leaving.'

'What did you do after Isobel left Mr Beale's office?'

'What I did is my business.' She stepped to the door and opened it, and neither of them made a move to stop her.

'If you come across any information regarding the location of Isobel Cho,' Schell said, 'we expect you to contact us.'

'Uh-huh,' she said, over her shoulder.

'Excuse me, ma'am.' Those were Ragan's first words. His voice was thin and nasal . . . and unpleasant. She stopped, and he said, 'I trust you understand, and appreciate, Agent Schell's statement.'

She turned and stared at him, then turned away again and left, pulling the door closed behind her.

TWENTY-EIGHT

'So,' Dugan said, 'not much help talking to the Feds this afternoon, huh?'

'Not really.' Kirsten sipped her wine, and it appeared to Dugan that her mind was somewhere else.

They were eating pulled pork sandwiches at Twin Anchors; she sipping Sauvignon Blanc and he drinking Moose Drool – the brew Larry had put him on to – from a glass. It was eight o'clock and Sinatra was on the jukebox, just like he'd been the previous Friday, when Dugan was there with Larry Candle. But this was a Thursday, and the crowd was much younger and noisier, and as far as Dugan could tell nobody was listening.

'You think anybody in this place is over thirty-five?' he asked. 'I mean, besides you and me.'

'Let's not go there,' she said. 'You ever hear of something called "hit the rock"?'

'Sure. When you "hit the rock" you do a fist bump. Like what set off the crazies when the Obamas did it.'

'If you say so,' she said, 'but it's something else, too. Your government friends were asking me who I'd talked to about Isobel, and said "What about hit the rock?" I didn't get it, but later I thought maybe it was the name of a company, or a music group or something.'

'And you did a computer search.'

'Yep.' She downed a forkful of coleslaw. 'Didn't Beale say Isobel was supposed to spend time working on a water project in South America with some church group?'

'He said a non-profit, and the guy on the ground was a minister. But yeah, South America.'

'If I'm right, then he was wrong . . . a little. There's a church

. . . one of those mega-churches, I think . . . out in Kane County that has a project called Hit the Rock, and they've been working in *Central* America, not South. They set up water collection and delivery systems for remote mountain villages in Guatemala.'

'And they call the project "Hit the Rock"?'

'Yeah,' she said. 'Church . . . mountains . . . water. Get it?'

'Ummm . . .' He caught the waitress's eye. She was cute as hell . . . but could she possibly be old enough to serve liquor? He raised his empty glass and tapped on the side of it to signal his need for another beer. And maybe that's what triggered his train of thought.

'Dugan? Are you leering?'

'No, I'm thinking,' he said. 'So . . . the people are wandering around in the wilderness and they're getting pissed off because they're dying of thirst, and God tells Moses, "Hit the rock." And he does. And water comes out.'

'Jesus,' Kirsten said, clearly impressed.

'No, no, no,' he said, and watched the waitress set a new bottle of Moose Drool beside his glass. 'That was *way* before Jesus.'

'And you,' Kirsten said, 'are *way* beyond hopeless.'

'Shows you what a Catholic education will do for you. Anyway, what's the relevance?'

'It's just interesting. I mean, the guy who was running it was murdered.'

'Right. In DC. They say it happens there with some frequency, sadly.'

Her cellphone buzzed, and she took it out of her purse. She flipped it open and looked at the screen, but it was obvious that she couldn't tell who was calling. 'Hello?' she said, and as she listened he saw her eyes widen. 'Yes, of *course* I remember. But you don't sound so good. Are you OK?'

'Who is it?' he asked. 'What—'

She stopped him with a wave of her hand, saying, 'Well, yes, if it's important. I can—' She folded the phone and stared at it. 'He hung up,' she said. 'Sounds like he's stoned.'

'Who was it?' Dugan asked. 'Wasn't Cuffs, was it?'

'No. It was Andrew.'

'Andrew? Who's Andrew?'

'I should call him back.' She flipped the phone open again,

tapped out a couple of numbers, and put it to her ear . . . and waited. 'Damn,' she finally said, 'he must have turned it off.'

'Who the hell is Andrew?'

'Tyrone Beale's brother.' She slid the phone into her purse. 'He's at Beale's place. They're both there. They've run into some kind of problem, and he asked me to come.' She stood. 'I'll see you later at home.'

'Bullshit.' He stood, too, and dropped a couple of bills on the table. 'I'm coming with you.'

'No, there's—' She stopped, and then, to his surprise, she said, 'Sure, why not? You'll recognize Andrew when you see him.'

'Up there, at the White Hen,' Dugan told the driver, as they rounded the corner on to Beale's block.

During the brief cab ride Kirsten had told him how she'd recognized the man driving the Cadillac that picked up Tyrone Beale on the day Beale met Dugan for lunch at the zoo. He'd been one of two men she and Dugan had seen one dismal rainy day some years earlier, going into, then coming out of, an adult book store, leaving behind a store clerk with a broken neck. Kirsten learned later that the man's name was Andrew and that, while his resume wasn't spotless, he was definitely no killer. Later, he'd saved her life; and Dugan's, too.

It was just past nine o'clock when the cab pulled to a stop, and the street was dark and quiet. Parked cars lined the curbs along both sides, but there weren't many people around. The bars at each end of the block, and the White Hen Pantry, were the only businesses open.

Dugan paid the driver and when he climbed out Kirsten was already going into the building, using the door between the cleaners and the White Hen. When he caught up with her she was in the small vestibule, yanking impatiently on the locked glass door into the inner lobby and the stairs. 'They don't answer my buzz,' she said, and then started pressing all the buttons for both the second and third floors, and still getting no answers.

'Most of the units aren't even leased out yet,' Dugan said. 'And the ones that are, except for Beale, are businesses. They're probably all closed.'

'I *know* that, dammit. I'm just—' She stopped. 'I'll try Andrew again.' She dug out her cell, but again got nowhere. 'What is *wrong* with him?'

'Let's try the back way,' Dugan said. He went out to the sidewalk and into the White Hen, Kirsten on his heels.

An Asian man in his thirties was behind the counter, and was busy waiting on a customer, but Dugan spotted one of the women from Lo-Kee cleaners, the younger one. She was off to the side pouring water into the store's coffee maker, and he remembered that one family owned the building and ran both businesses. He approached the woman. 'Remember me from a few days ago? I came into the cleaners with Mr Beale and we went up to his place. Then I came back down and—'

'I remember,' she said. 'Beale leave message about women gone somewhere and you look unhappy.'

'Right. And this is one of the women.' Nodding at Kirsten. 'So now we're trying to reach Mr Beale and his brother, Andrew.' He stopped. 'Do you know Andrew?'

'Yes. Andrew.'

'Well, Andrew said he was . . . *they* were . . . here, upstairs. But they don't answer the bell. Do you—'

'Andrew call.' This came from the man behind the counter, and Dugan turned. 'Five . . . maybe ten . . . minute ago. He say *woman* coming.' He looked at Kirsten. 'What is your name?'

'Kirsten. But where—'

'Ah.' The man nodded. 'Andrew say cannot work buzzer. He say please to let you in. He say back upstairs door not locked.' A black kid in camo pants and a baseball jersey approached the counter with a bottle of orange soda and a package of doughnuts. The man said, 'My wife unlock door,' and turned to ring up the purchase.

The woman led them to the rear of the store and into the little hall by the alley door, the same hall Beale and Dugan had entered by way of the cleaners, and unlocked the stairway door. She smiled and left them, and they went up.

The third floor door was unlocked and Dugan pushed it open and they went into Beale's kitchen. There was a definite bathroom odor, as though a toilet had overflowed somewhere in the apartment.

'Andrew?' Kirsten said. 'What's wrong?'

When they entered, the man sitting at the kitchen table had lifted his head from where it rested on his arms, folded on the table. He stared at Kirsten, but didn't answer her, and Dugan wondered whether he could even see anything out of those glassy eyes. *Jesus, 'stoned' is right*. His expression was so blank that Dugan wondered whether he'd even have recognized this guy as the man whose face he'd seen just that one time, outside the porno store.

'Andrew,' Kirsten said again, 'what is it? Where's Beale? I mean . . . Tyrone . . . your brother?'

Andrew still just stared at her, but then he raised his arm – slowly, as though its weight were almost too much for him – and waved a hand toward the doorway into the hall leading to the rest of the apartment. Finally he opened his mouth. 'Too hard,' he said. 'Can't go up there.'

His voice was deep, but at the same time empty, hollow, and Dugan suddenly knew – and knew that Kirsten knew, too – why it was that Andrew couldn't leave the kitchen, couldn't make himself go down that hall, even to buzz them in.

They went through the doorway and into the hall, and looked into each room. The smell grew stronger as they went, and it didn't come from the bathroom, or the bedroom, or the room set up with a TV, a couch and a weight machine. Lights were on throughout the apartment and the rooms were all in disarray. But it was only when they got to the front, to the room furnished as an office, that they found what they both knew they'd find.

TWENTY-NINE

Although one would have been more than enough, Tyrone Beale had clearly taken at least two rounds to the back of his head. Kirsten was certain the bullets had been hollow points, designed to expand on contact. This meant they'd wreak maximum internal havoc, but have less chance of passing through their target and striking unintended bystanders. In Beale's case, however, the slugs had exited, taking a substantial amount of blood, brain matter and facial tissue with them, splattering most of it on the wall above where he lay on his side on the floor.

She had her cell in her hand, but turned first to Dugan. 'You better go back and stay with Andrew. Don't let him leave before the cops get here.'

He was staring down at the body, all the color gone from his face. 'You don't . . . don't think Andrew's the one who . . . killed him.' He seemed to be fighting hard to get his breath.

'No, but the cops'll be suspicious if he's gone. Plus, they might want to do gunshot residue tests on him. And maybe us, too.'

'But who do you—'

'Dammit, Dugan, would you get going? The guy's in shock, out of his mind, and probably doesn't trust police. He might just pick up and run.'

'OK, OK. I'm gone.'

Her concern about what Andrew might do was genuine, but in addition she didn't want Dugan getting sick. She'd been a violent crimes and homicide detective and was more familiar with gruesome death scenes than Dugan was. During his years as an assistant state's attorney he had prosecuted homicide cases, and had necessarily seen numerous crime scene photos, but the real thing was much worse. Photographs are cold, two-dimensional . . . and photographs don't stink.

She felt a little queasy herself.

She wished she had time to talk at length with Andrew, but the people in the White Hen might be able to pinpoint the time when she and Dugan came upstairs, and too much time passing before she made the 911 call was likely to make the cops suspicious. So she called. And waited.

She was careful not to touch anything, including the body. She knew that was about the first thing the cops would ask her. It seemed to her from the blood coagulation that Beale had been dead about an hour, probably no longer than two. He'd obviously been sitting in one of his two client's chairs, with his hands pulled behind the back of the chair and his wrists bound with plastic restraints. Both he and the chair had fallen, or been pushed, sideways on to the floor. From the splatter pattern on the wall, she knew that he'd been shot first, and then been knocked over . . . probably out of anger or frustration on the shooter's part.

He wore brown loafers and no socks, tan pants and a blue shirt. Without moving his arms, she could see only one of his hands, but the knuckles were scraped and swollen. She squatted and forced herself to take a closer look at what was left of his face. She couldn't be sure because so much of the skin had been blown away, but it looked to her as though he'd been beaten, badly, before he was shot.

She stood up and surveyed the room. Tyrone Beale's brand new office was the front room of what was intended as a suite of offices. His private detective's license, issued by the state of Illinois, was hanging on the wall behind his desk. She moved closer and stared at the license, and suddenly a sadness swept through her and she shuddered. Beale hadn't been a friend. There hadn't been time for that, and friendship may never have happened anyway. But the man had been a living human being. The man had talked his landlady into letting him turn an office suite into living quarters. The man had framed his license and hung it up, and had hopes and dreams about the future, and what he'd make of it, and . . .

She shook her head. *No time for that, dammit.*

Except for the license the walls were empty, and the desk – not a scratch on its golden oak finish – along with the two client's chairs and an imitation-leather desk chair, were it for furnishings. No file cabinet. No bookcase. No clothes rack. No computer. Not even a landline phone. Closed mini-blinds on the one window. Beale's operation was . . . had been . . . even more bare bones than her own.

There was no sign of forced entry, and she assumed they'd caught him somewhere else and made him let them in. The desktop was bare and the drawers had been pulled out and emptied on to the floor. Either there'd been little in them, or else most of the contents had been carried away. She guessed the former was true. There were no spent shell casings lying around. Not to mention no cigarette butts, no used coffee cups or whiskey glasses, and – she'd have bet on this – not a fingerprint, speck of blood or spittle, fleck of dandruff or strand of hair that didn't come from Tyrone Beale . . . or maybe from her or Dugan or Andrew.

There was little use searching through the apartment. She'd have to admit it to the cops if she touched anything, and from the looks of it a search had already been performed by the killers. Whoever they were – and it had to be *they*, since she couldn't imagine anyone sending just one man to deal with the likes of Tyrone Beale – she was afraid she knew what they were looking for. Or, more accurately, *who*. It was Isobel they were after. Kirsten could *feel* that to be the case. And, if she was right about the marks on Beale's face, they did more than simply search the premises.

They couldn't have learned from Beale where Isobel was, because he didn't know. But he might very well have blurted out the names of the last persons he knew who'd seen her. And whatever he said or didn't say, they'd shot him, which obviously kept him from identifying his attackers. But it also, she thought, sent a message. A message she wasn't about to ignore.

She hurried back to the kitchen. 'The cops will be here any minute,' she said, 'and all of us will have to answer a lot of questions. But . . . Andrew?' He looked up at her. 'I do *not* intend to tell them that I know you . . . which I don't . . . or that I've ever seen you before last Monday, when you picked up your brother after he left the zoo.' When he just stared at her, still looking dazed, she said, 'Do you understand?'

'Yeah,' he said. He seemed several years younger than his brother, not quite as tall or as wide, but with the same muscular build, the same dark skin tone. He was wearing what might have been a work uniform, blue pants and a blue long-sleeved shirt. Unlike his brother, who'd kept his scalp smoothly shaven, Andrew had a full head of hair, although cropped closed to his head.

'Was your brother dead when you got here tonight?'

'Yeah.'

'And you were alone?'

'Yeah.'

'OK, they're going to ask you why you called *me*, and not the police,' she said. 'So . . . ? Why?'

For the first time, feeling flashed in his eyes. 'What, you don't *know*?'

'I think I *do* know, but what will you tell *them*?'

'Yeah, well, I'll tell 'em . . . I'll tell 'em I didn't know what I was doin'. That Tyrone had told me he been talking to you. Tell 'em I guess I wasn't thinking straight, and—'

A loud buzz interrupted him.

'No time now,' she said, and ran back to Beale's office, where she hit the intercom button. 'Yes? Who's—'

'*Police!* Open the door!'

At once she hit the button that unlocked the downstairs door, hoping to save Mrs Kee the expense of a smashed lock . . . or an entire door.

She went across and stood in the open doorway to Beale's

office, until the first cops appeared at the head of the stairs and
came toward her along the hallway. The two in the lead held
guns in their hands, pointed down at the floor beside their legs.

She held nothing in her hands, and she kept them clearly in sight.

THIRTY

'Tell me again what brought you here,' Smits said. They
were sitting in Beale's apartment, in the room with the
TV and the weightlifting equipment. Smits was polite
and seemed a competent enough homicide investigator. But he was
young and – to Kirsten's mind, anyway – a little too worried he
might miss something. He kept repeating the same questions.

She'd barely known Tyrone Beale, and when she'd asked for
his help he'd walked away. Still, though, he hadn't deserved to
be savagely beaten, and to have his brains splattered around the
room. She wanted whoever did this identified, and punished . . .
and she wondered whether Smits and his partner, who just then
was interviewing Dugan, were up to the task.

'Excuse me,' Smits said, 'but would you answer the
question?'

'Oh, sorry. Um . . . like I already said, I received a phone call
from Mr Beale's brother,' she said, 'and my husband and I left
the restaurant and took a cab here at once.' She paused. 'When
we got here we—'

'Why did the victim's brother call *you*, specifically? And not,
say, the police?' This, finally, was a new turn.

'To be sure about that, you'd have to ask *him*,' she said. 'But
when we got here he appeared badly shaken, almost catatonic.
I don't believe he was thinking clearly. I guess he knew that his
brother and I had recently met, and that we'd both been involved
in matters related to the same person.'

'Matters related to who?'

'They had to do with a young woman named Isobel Cho.
Maybe you're aware that Mr Beale had been hired some time
ago to protect Ms Cho, and that he and my husband . . . well
. . . they ran into each other at—'

'I know about that. So what's your involvement with Ms Cho?'

'I spoke with her last Tuesday. Right here, in fact. That is, in Mr Beale's kitchen. She was looking for help and I agreed to help her.'

'What sort of help?'

'Sorry, but that's between her and me.'

'Between you and her and the victim, you mean, since you already said that you and the victim were both working for her.'

'No, I said we'd both been working on matters *related* to her. As I said, he had previously been hired by Isobel's friend, Jamison Traynor, to . . . well . . . you already know that. Anyway, that job ended, as far as I know, early last Saturday morning, at Wancho's Towing. It was on Tuesday morning that I agreed to help Isobel. Mr Beale and I were *not* working together . . . or even simultaneously, as far as I know.' She paused. 'Does all that make sense?'

Smits stared at her. 'Where is Ms Cho now?'

'I don't know. After we spoke last Tuesday she went her way and I went mine. I assume she'll contact me if and when she wants to. She has my number. I don't have hers.' *Walking a thin line here,* she thought.

'And are you . . . worried about her? Concerned about her safety?'

'You know, I want to cooperate, but I don't see that my mental state has anything to do with your murder investigation.'

'You don't have to "see" anything. I asked you a question.' That was the same thing the FBI agent had said.

'I *am* concerned about Isobel, yes. In fact, it looked to me like Mr Beale was severely beaten before he was shot. I have to wonder whether someone was trying to get information from him. I have no idea what he's been involved in, and it's possible that his murder had nothing to do with Isobel Cho. But it concerns me that the information the killer, or killers, wanted might have had to do with her, or her whereabouts.'

'Why would someone be looking for her?'

'I have no idea.'

'And is that what you're doing for Isobel? Trying to find out?'

'Again, I don't want to be difficult, but that's between her and me.' Kirsten saw no reason to drag Eleanor Traynor and her desire to get Isobel out of her son's life into this. She couldn't imagine any connection between that and Beale's murder.

'Did the victim . . . Mr Beale . . . did he know where she was?'

'I don't think so. The last time I spoke with him, on Tuesday afternoon, he asked whether I knew where she was, and I told him that I didn't. In fact, I think Isobel probably wants it that way.'

'Why would he want to know where she was, if he wasn't involved with her any longer?'

'I'm not certain. I believe Mr Traynor may have asked Mr Beale where she was, and Mr Beale asked me if I knew.'

'Alright, let's get back to your arrival here this evening. You say you rang the doorbell and no one answered.'

And so it went.

'Tell me what brought you here,' Romero said. He and Dugan were in Beale's bedroom, a large room, clean and neat, furnished with just a queen-sized bed, a chest of drawers, and one straight-back wooden chair, which Dugan was sitting on. Romero stayed on his feet and wrote in a notebook while Dugan talked.

Romero had to be close to retirement and, while he seemed competent enough, what he mostly seemed was bored and anxious to get things over with. The guy's just-another-case attitude pissed Dugan off, and that very anger, focused on the detective, somehow helped him stop shaking, helped him push the picture of blood and brain matter from his mind.

'It was a phone call from Mr Beale's brother to my wife,' Dugan said, 'asking her to come here. She and I left the restaurant where we were having dinner and got a cab right away.'

He went on to tell Romero everything that had happened from then until the police arrived. The detective seemed concerned about Andrew's having called Kirsten and not 911, and Dugan said he could only speculate, and that Andrew had seemed dazed and possibly not thinking straight. 'I'm pretty sure his brother was his only living relative. He's taking it pretty hard.'

'Still, though, why your wife?'

'Well, like I said, he has no relatives, and maybe he knew his brother and my wife were working on things related to a woman named Isobel Cho. He probably got my wife's name and number from his brother.'

'So . . . the victim and your wife, how long have they known each other?'

'They met for the first time last Tuesday. Right here. I was

here, too. But I think Tyrone had heard of her before that. She
has a pretty good reputation.'

'Was *Andrew* Beale here at that time, on Tuesday?'

'No, just myself, my wife, Tyrone Beale, and Isobel.' He went
on to answer Romero's questions about the meeting, how it
came to be, and what he heard up to the point he left. There
seemed to be no reason to hide anything. When it came to the
two men who knocked on Beale's door he said, 'I talked briefly
to them. They spoke and acted like police officers.'

Romero looked up from his notebook and frowned. 'And you
think all police officers speak and act alike?'

'Well . . . maybe not *all*.'

'Did they say they were police officers?'

'No. They *did* say, though, that I should leave, unless I wanted
to be arrested.'

'Did they say why they were at the door?'

'No.'

'Did they threaten you, or anyone else?'

'Other than saying I might be arrested? No.'

'Did they say *they* might arrest you?'

'No.'

'And you have no idea who they are.'

'No. But I have photographs of them.' He explained how Beale
had given him photos taken by his security camera. 'His own
copies are probably here somewhere.'

'Uh-huh,' Romero said, still writing. 'And you think that just
because two men knocked on Mr Beale's door on Tuesday
morning they're of interest in an investigation of a murder that
occurred on Thursday evening?'

'Jesus, there's a man *dead* in there. Don't you—' He stopped,
took a breath. 'They'd sure as hell be of interest to me. I think
they might be law enforcement officers. And I think they could
be the killers.'

'And is that because they . . .' Romero checked an earlier page
of his notes. 'Because they "spoke and acted" like killers?'

'No. But Beale certainly wasn't expecting visitors that morning.
And they found him even though he tries . . . tried . . . to keep his
address confidential. They got into the building by telling one of
the other tenants they were police off— Oh, I didn't mention that.
I rang another tenant's bell and asked to be let in, and he complained

and said he'd already let the police in. So they must have said that.'

'Anything else?'

'They absolutely were *not* here on legitimate business. As soon as I took out my phone and said I was calling 911 they left.'

'You saw them go?'

'Yes.' He described the car and stated the license number, and Romero wrote everything down.

'Did you go ahead and call 911?'

'No.'

'Why not?'

'Because they hadn't actually done anything, except come inside and knock on Beale's door.'

'Right.' Romero nodded. 'That's what I'm thinking, too.'

THIRTY-ONE

The three of them, she and Dugan and Andrew, spent over two hours with the cops, each of them being interviewed individually; and all of them, Kirsten thought, probably answering the same questions over and over again. The place was a madhouse – although a strangely hushed madhouse – with too many people crowding in and through too small a space. There were evidence techs and photographers, and uniformed patrol officers and brass from the district station and the area headquarters, but the interviews were conducted by the two homicide investigators, Smits and Romero. There was no mention of gunshot residue tests.

By about eleven thirty Beale's body had been bagged and taken away, and finally the three of them were told they were free to go, but to be available over the next few days for further interviewing if necessary.

'Let's head toward LaSalle Street,' Kirsten said, when they were together out on the sidewalk. 'At this time of night we should still be able to get a cab around there pretty easily.'

'Yeah,' Andrew said, 'well, I . . . uh . . . I gotta go.' His voice was flat and he still seemed to be in a daze. He turned and walked away.

'Hey,' Kirsten said, 'where you going?'

'Home,' he said, not turning back. 'On the El.'

'No way,' she said. 'Dugan?'

'Agreed,' Dugan said. He caught up with Andrew and took his arm. Andrew yanked his arm away without looking at Dugan and kept walking. Dugan moved in front of him and blocked his way. Andrew stepped to the side and Dugan did, too. 'Hold on a minute, please,' he said, and held up his hands. 'We need to stick together.'

'What're you talkin' about?'

Kirsten had caught up with them. 'Andrew, please, look at me.'

He turned around, but kept his head lowered, staring at the ground.

'No,' she said, '*look* at me.'

He raised his head. 'What?'

'If you go home, who'll be there?'

'No one. Just me.'

'You have any family?'

'Just . . . just Tyrone is all.'

'Let's go,' she said, and this time it was *she* who took his arm.

They walked, and he didn't pull away. 'Where we goin'?' he asked, his voice still flat, as though he didn't really care.

'To get a taxi. When's the last time you ate something?'

'I don't . . . I'm not hungry.'

'Of course not,' she said. 'So when's the last time you *ate*?'

They took him to their condo and sat around the table in the kitchen, and Andrew ate a grilled cheese sandwich – American cheese on whole wheat – and drank a mug of hot tea with lots of milk, and Kirsten and Dugan sipped white wine and Scotch whisky respectively.

His brother's death had hit Andrew very hard. No family. Back in town only a short time. Who the hell did he have to turn to? Kirsten wanted badly to tell him it would be OK if he broke down . . . even cried. But she thought his self image might not allow that, and he might not react well to such advice.

There wasn't a lot of conversation, but when Andrew finished his sandwich Kirsten finally asked if he had a job he was supposed to go to in the morning. 'We'll have to call and tell them you can't make it.'

'Workin' for Tyrone, part-time, is all I got since I came back. There *are* no jobs. Got laid off in Kansas City, which is why I left there. Without Tyrone I got nothin'. No job, no people, no nothin'.'

'And you live alone, right?' Dugan asked. 'In what? An apartment?'

'This older lady, used to be a friend of my mother? She got a basement apartment in her house. Not even really an apartment. Just a bed and a shower. But, you know, it's a place.'

'Yeah, well, for tonight you'll stay here.' Dugan stood. 'We have a room we can set you up in. You'll have to sleep on a sofa, but it's long and comfortable, and you'll have a bathroom to yourself.'

'I don't know. I don't wanna—'

'I'll get out some sheets and stuff,' Dugan said, and left the room.

'Just for tonight,' Kirsten said. 'The three of us have a whole lot of talking to do, and I'm just not up to it now. And I don't think you are, either. Try to get some sleep, and in the morning we'll talk. When we're all fresh. OK?'

'Yeah. Well, I guess . . .'

She showed him to their spare room, the one they'd been planning for over a year to turn into a nursery when the time came . . . if the time came.

Dugan was spreading a sheet out on the sofa, and Andrew didn't seem to have the energy for any more objections about where he should spend the night.

Kirsten didn't have the energy, either, to get into a prolonged discussion. Because if Beale's killers were looking for Isobel, then any discussion had to lead to the issue of their own vulnerability. And to the issue of where the three of them should spend the night *after* this one.

THIRTY-TWO

The next morning, Friday, Kirsten put some eggs on to boil and at seven thirty sent Dugan out to pick up a few bagels. 'Yeah, yeah. I'll be careful,' he promised, and headed out the back door.

Dugan hadn't been gone long when Andrew showed up in the

kitchen. The change in his appearance was slightly encouraging.
He still looked haggard, with dark rings around his eyes, and
she wondered how much sleep he'd actually gotten, but his
expression held genuine grief now, not the mere blank emptiness
of the night before. His eyes were red, and she was pretty sure
he'd been crying. She hoped so.

'Sorry 'bout all this trouble,' he said. 'I just sorta fell apart
last night.'

'I'd have been surprised if you didn't,' she said. 'I'm really
sorry about your brother. He and I . . . we disagreed about a few
things . . . but he was a man a person could trust.'

'Yeah, well . . .' He looked around the room, not at her.

'If you want coffee there's a fresh pot there, and some mugs
in the cabinet right above.' She pointed. 'And there's cream
and—'

'That's OK,' he said. 'Just black.' He poured himself some
coffee and sat down.

'You know,' she said, 'you and I were talking last night, when
the cops interrupted.'

He looked up at her. 'What was it? I don't remember.'

'I was asking what you were going to say when the cops asked
why you called *me*, and not them. They must have asked you
that, didn't they?'

'Yeah. They did.'

'So what did you tell them? I mean, you didn't say you knew
me from before, right?'

'No. I'm not stupid. I told 'em I just . . . you know . . . froze
up, couldn't think what to do. I told 'em Tyrone knew you, and
he had gave me your card a while ago and . . . and that I didn't
really know *why* I called you. I just did.'

'Did they seem to have any problem with that?'

'Yeah, they had a problem, I guess. But I told 'em I knew
you'd call them, anyway, soon as you got there. I really wasn't
caring about what they thought.'

'Uh-huh. But . . . is there anything more to it? I mean about
why you called me and not them?'

He stared at her for a few seconds. 'What do you *think*?' He
seemed upset, almost angry, as though *she* were the one whose
brain wasn't working. 'Look here, I told you last night, I got no
people, no money, no nothin'. I'm sittin' there in that kitchen

and the only person in the whole world ever cared whether I live or die is layin' up in the other room . . . *dead*. Goddamn blood and brains and shit all over the floor and the fuckin'—' He stopped. 'Sorry.'

'That's alright. I understand. Go ahead.'

'OK. Well . . . see, I got a juvenile record . . . some for violent stuff. No adult sheet, though. I been clean, mostly. And lucky. You know about that. But I'm sittin' alone in there with a man shot dead. You think I wanna bunch o' damn police up in my face all by myself? I would've run off, but them people in the White Hen seen me, 'cause I went in the back way.' He stopped and took a breath, and it was as though all the sudden this man, who'd been almost mute the night before, couldn't *stop* talking. 'Even if he *is* my brother, you think them cops wouldn't wanna stick it on *me*? Close their damn case? What do I know? They lock me up for a coupla days . . . keep after me . . . knock me around a little . . . pretty soon I'm confessin' I *did* it, for Chrissake.' He stopped, looking as surprised as she was at his tirade. 'Anyway,' he said, more softly now, 'it happens, you know?'

'Yes, I know. It happens. But damn, there was no gun there, and if the people saw you go in they'd say so, and it would be clear you got there long after he was shot. And what motive did you have?'

'That's what I'm *talkin'* about, dammit. All those facts, and prob'ly more. You can spell 'em out. I couldn't do that. How you think them cops treat me you weren't there?'

'Depends on the cops, I guess,' she said. 'But you know what? I was pretty sure that's why you called me. Thing is . . . why didn't you tell me on the phone your brother was dead?'

'Because . . . well . . . you did right by me before, but that was a long time ago. I thought you might not come. I thought you might tell me just to call the cops. Or you might call 'em yourself, and not come. I just didn't know.'

'OK, I get it.' She looked at her watch. 'I wonder where Dugan is.' Then she looked at her watch again. 'Damn!' She jumped up and turned the flame off under the eggs. 'I hope you like hard-boiled.' She heard steps on the back stairway. 'That's him,' she said, going to the door. 'I hope.'

It was Dugan. He came in with a white paper sack which he put on the table. 'Bagels twice in one week,' he said. 'But these are one hundred percent whole grain . . . allegedly. With low-fat cream cheese.'

'I take it you didn't see anyone out there.' Kirsten was running cold water over the eggs.

'Lots of people, but no one to worry about.'

'And you called Mollie? Told her you won't be in?'

'I did. And she didn't even freak out. Maybe she's sick.'

'Mollie's never sick,' Kirsten said. 'Maybe she's in love.'

Nobody said much of anything while they ate breakfast. When they were finished they washed the dishes and sat down again with more coffee.

'Another thing we should talk about, Andrew,' Kirsten said. 'Does your brother have anyone you should notify about his death? I know you said there's no other family, but maybe there's somebody else who should be told.'

'He got an ex-wife, but I don't know where she is and I don't think she cares. No kids. He had different lady friends on and off, but me being out of town all these years I don't know about that. Since I been back he ain't said nothin' 'bout no one special.'

'Other friends, maybe?' Dugan asked. 'You know . . . guys.'

'Yeah, well, I guess he got friends, but . . . Shoot.' He shook his head. 'You know, here's how it was. When I came back he told me I could stay at his place till I got on my feet. But I know he got his business to run and all, and I didn't wanna be no problem to him. So I found this other place to stay at. He'd hire me to help with the driving and stuff when he had people who could pay, and . . . and anyway . . . I don't know.'

'Hey, don't worry about it.' Dugan waved his hand, dismissing the matter. 'We're just trying to tag all the bases.'

'Besides,' Kirsten said, 'the important thing is: What do we do now?'

'I don't know. I guess I—' Andrew stopped, then stared at her. 'You sayin' *we*? You sayin' you gonna help me?'

'Of course. We're in this together. We all have the same problem.'

'I guess I'm not . . .' He paused. 'What problem, exactly? I mean, what do you know that I don't?'

'I'm not exactly sure how to put this, but . . . well . . . it looked to me like whoever shot your brother beat him up pretty bad first.'

Andrew stared at her, not saying anything.

'I guess it *could* have been just meanness, but I'm thinking they were looking for information they thought he had. What it was, I don't know. But if it was information about Isobel Cho, like where she is, he didn't have anything to tell them. Thing is, maybe they know he had a brother, and the brother worked for him sometimes, so the brother might know something.'

'I don't know a damn thing about Isobel Cho. And I sure don't know where she is.'

'That's not the point,' Dugan said. 'Your brother didn't know, either.'

'And the killers,' Kirsten said, 'they can't be sure what you know or don't know.'

'So they might come after *me*?'

'I think it's at least possible.'

'Shit,' Andrew said, 'I hope they *do*.' He stood up. 'Tyrone had a gun. It must be at his—'

'Hold on.' Dugan stood, too. 'Let's just *think* a little, before we start running around.'

'Your brother's place has already been combed through,' Kirsten said, 'twice. Once by the killers, once by the cops. If he had any weapons there, they're long gone.'

'Yeah, but I know—' He stopped, then sat down, and so did Dugan. 'I can get a gun,' Andrew said. 'Ain't no problem there.'

'Andrew,' she said, 'there *is* a problem. These people aren't some local gang-bangers who don't know what the hell they're doing. From what I can see, these are professionals.'

'I don't give a fuck who they are. I'm gonna be ready for 'em.'

'Not just you,' Dugan said. 'We *all* have to be ready.'

'I still don't get it. You said the killers might come after *me*.'

'Yes, they might,' Kirsten said. 'But they might also know that your brother was in touch with a private investigator . . . me . . . who signed on to help Isobel, and that I, as far as he knew, was the last person who saw her.'

'How they gonna know that?'

'Because . . . because maybe your brother told them.'

'Bullshit. Tyrone was a *man*. Nobody gonna beat nothin' outta Tyrone.'

'OK, you're probably right,' she said, although she thought there were very few people who wouldn't say just about anything

if subjected to enough pain. 'But if they've been watching Tyrone
. . . and he said he thought someone might be . . . then they'd
know not just about you, but about me, too. And Dugan. They'd
know both of us had been talking to your brother.'

'So,' Andrew said, 'do *you* two know where Isobel Cho is?'

'No,' Dugan said. 'But like I said, that's not the point. The
point is what these people *think* we know, or might know.'

'You keep sayin' "these people." Who *are* "these people"?'

'Yes,' Kirsten said. 'Exactly.'

THIRTY-THREE

In Kirsten's experience, without several well-trained people
on the job, it was very difficult to tail someone – and in this
case *three* someones – if the targets suspected they were under
observation, and used their heads. And she planned to make it
even more difficult. So she and Dugan made several phone calls,
to help set up their disappearing act, and then it was time to go.
They both grabbed several days' worth of clothes and necessities,
and they, and Andrew, were ready to go.

Dugan carried a gym bag and she the same large shoulder bag
she'd used on her trip to DC. They locked the front and back
doors to the condo and set the alarm – which they almost never
did – and took the back stairs down to the alley. Avoiding their
own street, they hurried through the rain and caught a cab a block
away and took it to the Fullerton El station, where they climbed
the stairs up to the southbound platform.

Kirsten watched as Dugan and Andrew boarded a Red Line
train, which in a few blocks would angle down into the subway,
headed south, through downtown and out to the south side. That
train pulled away, and she waited a few minutes and caught a
Brown Line train, which also went south, but stayed up on the
elevated tracks. This one would make a circle around the downtown area – hence, 'the Loop' – and then head back north.

She exited the train on the east edge of the Loop and walked
to One Prudential Plaza, on East Randolph, where the Attorney
Registration and Disciplinary Commission had its offices. In the

parking garage she found the two-year-old Chevy Malibu she was looking for. The driver's door was unlocked, and the keys were under the floor mat. The Malibu was owned by Parker Gillson, who was the chief investigator for the ARDC. A call to Park was one of the phone calls she'd made that morning. She'd had no doubt that he'd lend her his car. In fact, he would probably have transferred the title to her if she'd asked. And she'd do the same for him. It helps to have long-time friends you can count on, she thought, even if this particular friend worked for the people who were seeking to take away your husband's law license.

Dugan had gone to borrow a car, too – actually an SUV, a Subaru Tribeca – from Fred Schustein, one of the lawyers who worked for him. Then Dugan and Andrew were to drive out to Andrew's place and pick up his things, and after that they'd just have to kill time . . . and stay out of sight. Or, as Dugan had complained, he was stuck with 'babysitting Andrew.' The three of them would stay in touch and meet up again sometime that afternoon or evening. Where they'd spend the night they hadn't decided. She had a place in mind, but she wanted to take a closer look at it before making a decision.

But first she had to follow through on another call she'd made before they left the condo.

It was nearly ten o'clock when she got to Horner Park, where just a few days earlier she'd introduced Isobel to Cuffs Radovich. She didn't pull into the parking area, but drove by, looking for Cuffs' rose-colored Ford convertible. She didn't see it, so she drove into the lot, to park and wait for him. It was a beautiful morning, and they must have been having some sort of kids' baseball tournament. There were games going on in at least three baseball fields that she could see, and the parking lot was completely full. There would have been one empty space, except that an old Ford pickup truck was straddling the line between two spaces, taking up both of them. The driver was sitting in the truck behind the wheel, and she was about to tap the horn and ask him to move over, when she noticed that he seemed to be a very big man, and that a woman was in the seat beside him.

It was Cuffs, of course, with Isobel; and before long Kirsten's borrowed Malibu and the battered pickup were sitting beside each other in the two spaces. He said the convertible drew too much attention. Kirsten suggested they sit in the Malibu and talk.

'Too damn stuffy in the car,' Cuffs said. 'I got some lawn chairs. We can watch the game.'

Kirsten couldn't believe anyone made lawn chairs big enough for a guy like Cuffs, but she was wrong. He got the oversized chair, and two ordinary ones, from the bed of the truck, and they settled in along the first base side of the closest ball field, as though they were watching the six-year-olds play their version of baseball. She and Isobel sat side-by-side, and Cuffs just beyond Isobel, at enough of an angle so that Kirsten could see his face. They were far enough behind the parents and other spectators – only a handful, since it was a Friday morning – so they could talk privately . . . and so Cuffs' language and demeanor wouldn't cause the game to be called on account of terrorism.

Cuffs wore khakis, a sleeveless gray sweatshirt, and a too-small Yankees baseball cap. Isobel, who had her hair in a ponytail, wore flip-flops, loose-fitting jean cut-offs, and a baggy, extra-large Che Guevara tee that hung down almost as far as the shorts did.

'You guys been to a resale shop?' Kirsten asked.

'Yes, actually,' Isobel said. 'Two of them. That's been our entertainment.'

'How are you feeling?' Kirsten asked.

'Oh, I'm fine.'

'Hell,' Cuffs said, 'you told me this morning you were about to puke your guts out like you did yesterday.'

'What I *said* was that I felt a little nauseated again.' Isobel spoke right up to him, and didn't seem quite so terrified as before. 'But I didn't throw up today,' she said, turning to Kirsten, 'and I feel fine now.'

'Cuffs told me you've been putting in long days.'

'Yes, I've been—'

'Watch it, for Chrissake!' Cuffs sounded as though he might punch someone. 'What did I tell you?'

'Oh. Sorry.'

'My fault,' Kirsten said. 'I shouldn't have brought it up.' Cuffs obviously didn't want Isobel giving away where they were hiding. 'So . . . the two of you are getting along OK?'

'I guess so,' Isobel said. 'OK enough.'

Cuffs just waved his hand, as though to say Kirsten should

skip the crap and get on with what was on her mind. She noticed, though, that his eyes never stopped scanning the surrounding area. The guy was a machine.

'Obviously you don't know this yet,' Kirsten said, 'but last night Tyrone Beale was murdered.'

'Oh my god, *no*.' Isobel's hand went to her mouth. 'Oh, Jesus.' Eyes wide, she stared at Kirsten. 'I haven't seen or heard any news this morning. You . . . you're sure?'

'I saw his body. He has a brother, Andrew. He saw him first, and called me. I called the police.'

'Why the hell didn't *Andrew* call the police?' Cuffs, an ex-cop, wasn't even looking at her when he spoke.

'He's . . . got a history. He didn't want to face the cops alone. He had nothing to do with it, believe me.'

'Was it . . . like . . . a robbery?' Isobel asked.

'I don't think so. It happened at his apartment. In his office there. I think they caught him outside somewhere and made him take them there. I don't have to go into detail. He was beaten up, then shot. I think the killers were looking for something . . . or for someone.'

Isobel stared at her. 'When you say "for someone," do you mean . . . for me?'

'Who do you think?' Cuffs said it casually. 'Who am I being paid the big bucks to take care of?'

'So it isn't the police, then, that are looking for me. It's someone else.'

'This all started,' Kirsten said, 'with you getting the feeling someone was following you, watching you. And I think you were right. And even though it was your father's men who picked you up that night, it wasn't your father's men following you then, and it's not the police now. The police don't consider you missing.'

'I guess I knew that, but I was hoping . . . I mean . . . those men at Mr Beale's door, your husband said they were police.'

'No, he said they *looked* like police to him. Same as the two men in the car outside your father's house looked like police to you. But you don't *know* they were. You—'

A shriek of laughter came from the ball game spectators.

'Finally a kid hits the ball more than ten feet,' Cuffs said, 'and then he runs like hell toward third base.'

'But there's something else, Isobel,' Kirsten went on. 'There's the FBI.'

That got even Cuffs to turn his head in her direction, but he didn't say anything.

Isobel did, though. 'What are you talking about? The FBI?'

'Yes. Two FBI agents are looking for you.'

'You don't mean . . . is that who was at Mr Beale's door?'

'No. Dugan saw those two, and they weren't the FBI, or at least not the FBI agents who spoke to him, and later to me. The agents didn't say you were a suspect in any crime. What they told me is that they think you might have information related to a criminal enterprise.'

'What?' She seemed truly mystified. 'Why would they think that?'

'I don't know,' Kirsten said, 'but tell me about Hit the Rock.'

'Hit the Rock? This is crazy.' Isobel spread out her hands. 'Hit the Rock's not a criminal enterprise.'

'I didn't say it was. And the FBI didn't either. It's just something that came up when we talked. So tell me about it.'

'It's a non-profit group, sponsored by a church. They work in Guatemala, bringing fresh water to rural villages where women have to walk miles and miles to get water. I signed up to go down and work with them this year, but the program got canceled. I don't even know if it's still in existence.'

'Because the man who ran it got murdered.'

'Yes,' Isobel said, 'but what's—' She stopped. 'That can't be why the FBI wants to talk to me. That happened in Washington, DC. He'd rented a car there, and the police said someone was trying to steal it.'

'Right.' Kirsten paused. 'I guess you must have known the man, right?'

'Yes, of course. His name's Miguel Parillo. I knew him from Tufts, where I went to school.'

'Was he a minister in the church?'

'Oh no. He just worked for Hit the Rock because he'd been to Guatemala and he saw the need. He has . . . had . . . a PhD in anthropology, and he was a visiting professor. I took his classes, both last year and this. It was an informal class, like a seminar. He and I got to be close, like . . . friends. He really impressed me and . . . well . . . I guess I talked about him so much that some of my friends teased me that it was getting to be more than just a teacher–student thing.'

'But it wasn't?'

'Of course not.' Isobel's face reddened. 'Miguel was way older, like thirty-five or something. He was getting ready to write a book, like a memoir of his work in Guatemala, and a friend and I were helping organize his notes and materials. I told Jamison all about it. Anyway, Miguel recruited me, and a few other students, to give a year after graduation to Hit the Rock.'

'He must have been quite a guy.'

'He was a wonderful man. A good man. Jamison met him, too. A few months ago, during spring break, here in Chicago when I was home. Miguel was giving a lunch hour talk to this business group downtown. Born-again Christians, but with real money. I went, and Jamison, too. He got a chance to speak to Miguel, and he liked him. And the next thing I knew . . . Miguel was dead. I was devastated. I still am.' Tears shone in her eyes.

'Have they arrested anyone yet for his murder?'

'No. Not that I know of. At first I was checking every day on the Internet. I even called the DC police one time. But they had no suspects, and after that I just . . . well . . . I stopped checking. I guess I tried to put the whole thing out of my mind. I suppose that's the coward's way out, but . . .' She lowered her head, as though staring down at her lap.

'I don't think you're a coward,' Kirsten said. 'An awful lot's been happening. You plan to spend a year volunteering, and the man in charge gets murdered. You come home, where it should be safe, and someone's watching you, stalking you. Someone breaks into your apartment. You're told your baby sister will be deported if you don't break-up with your boyfriend.' She paused. 'Your father thinks that threat came from Jamison's mother, you know.'

'I know,' Isobel said, still staring downward. 'But I can't believe it's her. The thing is, I can't believe *anybody* would make such a threat.'

'Well, anyway, all that, and now . . . Tyrone Beale. Hard for anyone to handle.'

'No one asked me,' Cuffs said, 'but when one person knows two guys who get gunned down, just a few months apart, I gotta ask myself . . . coincidence or connection? And coincidence never gets my vote, 'cause that's a dead end.'

Isobel lifted her head. 'You think there's . . . ? But that's impossible.' She turned to Kirsten, and there were tears welling up in her eyes.

'What I think,' Kirsten said, having already crossed coincidence off her ballot, 'is that we're going to figure this out. We're going to help you. Dugan and I. And Cuffs.'

Isobel stared at her and nodded, but said nothing. Finally she lowered her head again and wiped her cheeks dry with the hem of her tee shirt, and when she looked up this time she said, 'Mr Beale couldn't have told them where I was, right? Because he didn't know.'

'That's right.'

'And still they killed him.'

'They thought he must know where you are. So they . . . they questioned him. And when it was over they killed him. Even if he'd known . . . and had told them . . . they probably would have killed him.'

'And,' Cuffs said, pointing at Kirsten, 'they think *you* must know, too.'

'Yes,' Kirsten said. 'And Dugan, as well. And Andrew, Beale's brother.'

'Yeah, but you're the one who's in front of my face. I oughta snatch you right up now and put you in the truck with Isobel and drive away.' He shook his head. 'But if I do that, goddammit, who the hell's gonna find out who these bastards are?'

THIRTY-FOUR

'We don't even know for sure it was Isobel they were looking for,' Dugan said. He was playing devil's advocate as he, Kirsten and Andrew gathered chairs around the desk. It was Juan Cho's desk, in Juan Cho's office, and they were waiting for the timer to go off and announce that the pizzas were done.

After he and Andrew had picked up Andrew's clothes, Dugan got a call from Kirsten. 'We've got the *perfect* place to hole up,' she said. 'Wancho's Towing. It's in a mostly deserted area, but still close to everything. It's been closed for a few days, and I checked it out and it's secure. Also, it's a place no one would ever think we'd go.' She gave him a list of supplies to pick up for the three of them, including more clothes, a bunch of throw-away cellphones, some flashlights, a kitchen timer, and sleeping bags and air mattresses.

Dugan and Andrew had spent the day shopping, going from store to store in the Tribeca Dugan had borrowed from Fred Schustein, constantly on the watch for anyone following them. On the downside, Andrew was driving him nuts. It was under-standable, sure, but the guy hardly said one word all day, mostly staying in the car when Dugan went into the stores, showing no interest in anything they bought . . . or in anything else. He did join Dugan in a clothing store and picked out a pair of pants and a shirt for himself, and wore them when they left. All in all, though, it had been a long, long day, made longer because Kirsten insisted they not show up at Wancho's until after it was dark, and by then Dugan was tired, and irritated, and bored out of his mind.

She had met them on foot by a rear entrance she'd described, one that was reached by going around the block to the north and then driving back south on a gravel lane that ran between the railroad embankment and the fence along Wancho's west border. The entrance itself – with a sliding gate, just like the front entrance off the street – was off that lane, and very near the north end of the property. She opened and closed the gate and got in the back seat. He drove to the rear of the building and parked next to her borrowed Malibu, and they'd gone inside.

Now here they were, sitting in Cho's office, down the hall from a small kitchen Cho provided for his employees. Kirsten had picked up Pepsi and frozen pizzas. She said she thought it best, under the circumstances, to avoid alcohol. Dugan wasn't so sure, but he kept that to himself.

'I mean,' he said, popping open a Pepsi and continuing his argument, 'what could Isobel possibly have, or know, that would make someone kill a man to find her?'

'I don't know, not yet, but what else could they have been after, if not Isobel?' Kirsten turned to Andrew. 'Did your brother have any other clients lately? I mean, besides Jamison Traynor?'

'I dunno,' Andrew said, looking at the wall beyond her.

'Andrew,' she said. 'I know this is bad for you. But you can't just space out. Look at me.'

He looked at her. 'Sorry,' he said. 'I . . . I'll try. I don't think he had any other clients for . . . I don't know . . . a couple of weeks, anyway. I know I asked him did he have anything for me to do, and he said he was kind of in a dry spell.'

'Maybe so,' Dugan said, amazed that Andrew had just spoken about twenty times the number of words he'd managed the entire rest of the day. 'But even if Beale didn't have any other clients, that doesn't prove the killers were looking for Isobel.'

'True enough,' Kirsten said, 'but she's my client, so I have to assume she's the one they're looking for, and make sure she stays safe. If I'm wrong, no harm done.'

'I'll buy that.' Dugan paused to swig some Pepsi, then turned to Andrew. 'I don't know if you heard Kirsten or me telling the police we were at your brother's place last Tuesday and two guys showed up and knocked on his door. He didn't let them in, and they left.'

'Yeah, I heard that.'

'The thing is,' Kirsten said, 'we're pretty sure they're the ones who killed your brother. And we have pictures of them.'

'What pictures?'

'We'll look at them after we eat.' Dugan shook his head. 'That damn detective . . . Romero? I told him about them and I couldn't believe he wasn't more interested. I wonder if they found your brother's copies in his apartment.'

'Which reminds me, Andrew,' Kirsten said, 'is there anywhere Tyrone might have kept things like that? I mean, besides at his apartment?'

Andrew frowned. 'I can't think of anywhere.'

'So if the cops *didn't* find the photos,' Dugan said, 'the killers did, and took them. And they'd have *left* them there if they were pictures of somebody else.'

'And your brother's security camera,' Kirsten said. 'And his laptop. I didn't see those, either.' She got out her cell. 'I'm calling that younger dick, Smits. You got their cards, Dugan?' He fished a card from his wallet and gave it to her, and she tapped out the number. She waited, then identified herself and asked for Smits. 'Oh,' she said, 'well sure, that'll be fine.' As she waited she said, 'He's gone for the day. They're getting Romero.'

'Hell,' Dugan said, 'he'll tell you to take a hike, and—'

She held up her finger to cut him off. 'Yes, right. Right. Sorry to bother you, Detective, but I'm just wondering if you found the photos of those two men who came to Beale's office Tuesday morning.' She waited, frowning. 'I understand that. But we told you we had— No, hold on. *You* wait. This has nothing to *do* with how you do your job. I'm just saying that if you didn't find those photos, we can supply copies.' She waited, rolling her eyes, then said, 'Look, I don't give a damn *what* you don't appreciate. If you don't want these photos, say so, and I'll deliver copies tomorrow to Deputy Chief Corrado. He can decide whether security cam photos of two men acting suspiciously around a murder victim's home, just days before he was killed, might *possibly* be of interest to the investigators assigned to the case.' She paused. 'OK, fine, yeah. You *do* that . . . if he'll take your call. He *will* take mine. I guarantee it.' She folded the phone. 'Guy oughta take his pension and go fishing.'

'Does he want the photos?' Dugan asked.

'Yeah. They didn't find any. Plus he says *he'll* call Corrado. See if I'm bluffing.'

'*Were* you bluffing?'

'Are you kidding? Sandy Corrado and I go way back.'

'OK, so besides delivering the pictures, what do we do tomorrow?'

'First of all, did Fred say how long you can keep his car?'

'He said as long as I want.'

'Because we don't know how long you'll be away from your office. You shouldn't call in. Tomorrow's Saturday. Don't even call Larry Candle to see what's going on. All anyone knows is we've dropped out of sight. No one knows where we are. Or whether we're OK.'

'Great, I'll pretend I've been suspended.' He didn't mention that he'd already called in about five times that day. He wondered how hard it would *be* not to call in.

'You and Andrew should stay together at all times. In the morning you can deliver copies of the photos to Romero, and then . . . well . . . just wait for a call from me.'

She went on to stress how careful they all had to be that no one saw them leave or enter Wancho's. Only Cho himself, who'd gone to China, and the big guy with the heavy fist – 'Luis,' according to Kirsten – knew they'd be there. Cho had left them keys to the building, along with two openers for the electronically operated gates.

Meanwhile, they had the place to themselves. Not exactly the Four Seasons, and to Dugan's mind not exactly 'the *perfect* place to hole up.' But at least they had a kitchen with a stove. And right now there were Home Run Inn pizzas in the oven, and the timer had just gone off.

THIRTY-FIVE

The wall of glass fronting the sidewalk meant they weren't able to use the cashier's area and the customers' waiting room – if you could call people ransoming their cars 'customers.' That left Cho's office and the kitchen, a smaller space, for sleeping areas. Dugan and Andrew would sleep in the office, both of them on the floor, since the lumpy, saggy sofa was useless, and Kirsten had the kitchen floor to herself. The thermostat for the air conditioning was in there, and she set it in the mid-sixties and crawled into her sleeping bag.

Sleep didn't come quickly on that hard floor, air mattress or not. She hadn't thought of pillows, and the little inflated mound built into the end of the mattress was useless. She lay there, fully clothed, with her head on a rolled-up bath towel, staring into the dark and listening to traffic pass by on the street out front. There wasn't much traffic, and most of it passed at a pretty good clip.

It was the occasional vehicle that drove by slowly that had her nerves on edge. Each time that happened, she was sure *this* time the car would stop, and its occupants would jump out and bang on the door . . . or smash their way through the plate glass. She consoled herself by remembering that the door between the cashier's office and the rest of the building was locked and solid . . . and that she had her little Colt 380 semi-automatic on the floor beside her. Also, even if she never got to sleep, the A/C was working, and so far she hadn't seen – *or felt, thank God* – any rodents or creepy-crawly things.

The next morning, Saturday, Kirsten woke first, giving her first claim on the tiny bathroom, with its ancient rusting shower stall. There was plenty of hot water, though, and when she was finished she made coffee and woke up her co-refugees. They all compared their various aches and pains from a night spent in sleeping bags on air mattresses on a vinyl-tiled concrete floor.

They gathered around Cho's desk again, and drank coffee and shared a few doughnut holes she'd picked up the day before . . . and made their plans. How long they'd have to stay under the radar they didn't know, but they agreed that whenever they left Wancho's they'd leave together. They'd take all their belongings with them, Dugan and Andrew – and what Dugan called their 'bedrolls' – in the Subaru, and Kirsten with her things in the Malibu. They'd keep in close touch, using the throwaway cellphones, and they'd stay away from Wancho's all day. In the evening, they'd rendezvous at some prearranged spot and then, after dark, head back together into what Dugan kept calling their 'hidey-hole.'

Kirsten had insisted on all that because, if their hiding place were to be discovered somehow, she wanted all of them to be out of there – or even all *in* there, God forbid – and able to work together. 'United we stand,' she said, 'et cetera.'

Kirsten operated best on her own, of course, and would have preferred not to have Dugan to worry about. And Andrew was even more of a concern. He was bright enough – his idea to have her with him when the police got to his brother's apartment proved that – but his brother's death, and the grisly condition of the scene, had him still moving around in something of a daze.

She didn't want him left alone, without Dugan, and she couldn't expect the two of them to stay shut up all day and watch TV. So her first suggestion was to put them both in the Subaru Tribeca, with lots of cash, and point them toward Oregon. In fact, Andrew agreed to that. He would have agreed, it appeared, to anything at all she suggested. But Dugan was having none of it, and there was no sense arguing.

So the two men would go somewhere for a real breakfast, and then have copies made of the photographs and deliver them to Smits and Romero up at Area Three police headquarters. After that they'd drive around somewhere and wait for a call from her, and then make plans for the rest of the day.

By nine o'clock they had everything packed into the cars, including their trash – to be tossed into a dumpster elsewhere – leaving Wancho's Towing looking to possible inquisitive eyes as if no one were camping out there.

They used the rear exit, of course, with Kirsten going first. She
checked to make sure Dugan closed the automatic gate –
she trusted him, but couldn't help herself – and then drove along
the railroad embankment to the street. This whole area was pretty
deserted even during the week, and that day being Saturday she
didn't start seeing moving traffic and people until she'd gone a
couple of blocks. When she got near Kedzie she pulled to the
curb and waved at Dugan and Andrew going by in the Subaru.
Then she threw a U-turn and went the other way.

They'd be going north, she knew, but she drove south, headed
eventually for I-290, the Eisenhower Expressway. But first she
needed a decent-looking place for breakfast. She found one, and
ordered two soft-boiled eggs, with toast and coffee. She knew
where she wanted to go that morning, and who she wanted to
talk to. Like Cuffs, she was always suspicious of coincidence.
When two men with ties to Isobel were murdered, just months
apart, even if one went down in DC and the other in Chicago,
she had to proceed as though there were a connection. And that
possibility was strengthened by the mention of Hit the Rock by
the FBI agents who were looking for Isobel.

She'd researched Hit the Rock, and the church that sponsored
it, and found nothing that failed a rudimentary smell test. But
the man who'd been at the very heart of it was dead. Why?
When you had nothing to go on, money was always a good bet,
so while she ate she mentally rehearsed the approach she'd take.

Half an hour later she was back in the Malibu and ready to make
a call. Not really sure whether her iPhone use could be tracked,
she took out one of her new throwaways and tapped out the
number, She got an answer on the first ring.

'Good morning and God bless you,' the woman said, and
sounded as though she really meant it. 'Almond Hill Community
Church. Can I help you?'

'Reverend Skogland, please.'

'Oh, I'm sorry, hon. Pastor Steve's awfully busy just now. Can
I take a message?'

'Actually, it's very important. I need to see him . . . today. But
for only a few minutes.'

'Gosh,' the woman said, 'I'm afraid Pastor Steve couldn't
possibly see you on such short notice, dear. Especially not on

Saturday. I can make an appointment for you, though, for some time on Monday if it's urgent. Could you tell me what it's about? That is, would it be for pastoral counseling? Or a prayer session? Or about membership?'

'Well,' Kirsten said, 'here's the thing. Um . . . what's your name?'

'*My* name? Margaret. Margaret Hansel.'

'Really? I always *loved* the name Margaret. It's so pretty, and so—' She stopped. Best not to lay it on *too* thick. 'Well anyway, Margaret, it really *has* to be today. I need to find out more about your Hit the Rock project.'

'Is that right? So you've heard of Hit the Rock?'

'Oh yes. A friend of mine went to this fund-raiser, back in the spring you know? And she said one of the men being honored ran a program called Hit the Rock, and my friend was just *so* impressed with the program. And since then I keep saying to myself, "Kay, you have to get *out* there and *talk* to that pastor about it." And then just today, knowing I'd be out your direction, I said to myself, "Kay, you get yourself *over* there. That might be just the charity for you and William to give to." She was sure that would get her a quick appointment.

'Oh, honey,' Margaret said, 'you don't know how glad I am to hear that. Hit the Rock is so dear to our hearts here at Almond Hill. I was on the committee when we started it up. But I'm sorry. Pastor Steve's Saturdays are just too full. There's no chance of talking to him today.'

Kirsten was genuinely surprised. 'Darn,' she said. 'I was hoping . . .' She paused. 'Say, you were on the committee. You think I could talk to *you* about it?'

THIRTY-SIX

Parker Gillson's Malibu had a GPS, so Kirsten didn't get totally lost along the curving blacktops of unincorporated Kane County, some forty miles west of the city. When she found Almond Hill she discovered that it was, indeed, a church set on a hill – or at least a gentle mound, possibly a landfill site – and surrounded by several acres of just about the greenest grass she'd ever seen. What almonds had to do with it, though, wasn't so clear.

She turned on to the long drive that curved up the hill, passing a large sign that announced:

WELCOME HOME TO
ALMOND HILL
REV. STEPHEN SKOGLAND, PASTOR

The building itself surprised her. She wasn't sure why, but she'd been expecting ultra-modern curves and soaring arches that swept up towards heaven.

In fact, the style was quite traditional. Colonial, she thought; all red brick and white trim, with a row of white columns across the front. Except for the sign, and the simple white cross at the peak of the roof, it might have been a courthouse or a town hall. But it was a church, and it reflected a comfortably successful and prosperous congregation.

At the top of the hill the drive swept around to the rear of the building and a huge parking lot. There were maybe thirty cars parked in a lot that had space for at least three hundred more. There were three yellow school buses, too, with a crowd of teenagers milling around them, obviously waiting to board. She was impressed. This many adolescents awake and about before noon on a Saturday? And at church?

She parked and headed for the door Margaret Hansel had told her to use, and went inside and up a few stairs and along a wide hall, following the arrow on a sign that said *Church Office*. She was struck by the clean scent of floor wax, and by how bright and shining everything was. And that included the people she encountered on the way: first a couple of men in shorts and tee shirts, carrying soccer balls; then several nicely dressed women, late thirties–early forties. Everyone seemed genuinely friendly as they smiled and greeted this visitor in her well-worn blue jeans and lightweight jacket over a red tee.

'Can I help you?' a woman asked, just as Kirsten tried the office door and found it locked. 'Are you looking for someone in particular?'

'Margaret Hansel. She's expecting me.'

'Oh, I just *saw* Margaret,' the woman said. She was forty-five or so, in yellow Capri pants and white sneakers, walking alone and carrying a tall stack of what looked like kids' books. 'In the great hall, I think it was. I'll show you. My name's Mimi, by the way.'

'No thanks. You look pretty busy. Just point me in the right direction. I'll find it.'

'Oh, goodness no, I'll show you.' The woman crouched and set the books on the floor against the wall. 'You could get lost for days in these hallways.' She laughed. 'Well, it's not *that* bad, but I'll show you, anyway.'

Kirsten followed her, and it *was* a little tricky. Around a few corners and down some steps, Mimi chattering about their new children's library, Kirsten scarcely paying attention to anything but how damn *nice* this woman was.

They passed a framed poster on the wall that showed two hands reaching out to each other, and said: LOVE ONE ANOTHER, *John 13*. Kirsten felt as though she'd stepped into an alternate world where people actually *did* that. Then they passed a poster that showed a man smiling down on a worshipful woman and two perfect kids, and the saying was: WIVES, BE SUBMISSIVE TO YOUR HUSBANDS, *1 Peter 3*.

OK, so even paradise isn't perfect.

Mimi led her to the 'great hall,' which proved to be a reception room near the front entrance. A rectangular area about twenty-five by fifty feet, with a high ceiling, a carpeted floor and lots of sofas and chairs. 'There she is,' Mimi said, pointing toward the only person in the room, a woman sliding a carpet sweeper back and forth. 'Margaret never stops working,' she whispered. 'But don't worry. She loves to talk, too.' Mimi smiled, then hurried away.

Margaret was a small woman, probably in her mid-sixties, with short gray hair and wearing a navy-blue knee-length skirt and a white blouse. She looked up as Kirsten approached and quickly set the carpet sweeper aside. 'You must be Kay,' she said. 'I'm so sorry I wasn't in the office, but I ran down here to do a little last minute check. There's a wedding this afternoon, and—'

'That's fine,' Kirsten said. 'I won't keep you long. Can we just sit here and talk a few minutes?'

'Sure,' Margaret said. 'Or we could go back to the office. We have some brochures about the Hit the Rock Foundation there.'

'Actually, I've been on the Hit the Rock website and I've talked to some people, so I have a good understanding of the program. Let's just sit here and talk.'

'OK, sure.' They sat facing each other on two small upholstered chairs. 'So . . . is there anything in particular I can tell you?'

'First, Margaret, thanks for seeing me. Oh, and please excuse my attire. The jeans, I mean, but I'm on my way to a child's birthday party, and it might get a little messy.'

'Don't give it a thought,' Margaret said. 'It *is* Saturday and—'

'Thanks.' Kirsten paused. 'OK, let me get right to the point. I'm very impressed with everything I've learned about Hit the Rock so far.' That was the truth, actually, and she thought she might as well start there.

'Oh, that's so nice to hear,' Margaret said, smoothing her skirt across her thighs.

'And you know,' Kirsten said, moving on now to the lies, 'so far it's been just a wonderful year for my husband's business. And now, I'm *this* close,' she said, holding her thumb and forefinger a quarter inch apart, 'to deciding about—' She stopped, remembering the poster in the hallway, and said, 'Of course, the final decision is William's, you know. But he has to decide how to divide a substantial sum of money he's earmarked for our charitable giving for the year.'

'That's *so* nice. Our blessings all come from God, so how can we keep from sharing?' Margaret gave no sign of the sort of grab-the-check-and-run impulse that representatives of even the most legitimate charitable enterprises – and Kirsten was pretty sure Hit the Rock was one of them – must feel when they hear words like *substantial sum*. 'We know ours is just one of thousands of causes competing for people's support. And you need to feel confident about how your gift will be used.'

'I'm so glad you understand,' Kirsten said. 'And that's why I really need to talk to someone familiar with . . . well . . . with the financial aspect of the project. We need to assure ourselves of the program's financial stability.'

'Well,' Margaret said, 'in the office there are copies of the financial report.'

'I always find it hard to get the facts out of a financial report. I prefer to talk to someone in person, someone who can answer any questions I might have. I thought Pastor Steve might be the one.'

'Well, as I said, Pastor Steve can't meet with you until Monday.' Margaret sighed. 'I should say, though, that he's not really the one to talk to about finances. The stewardship committee makes all the financial decisions for the church, and also for the Hit the Rock Foundation. Pastor Steve tries to stay as far from that sort of thing as possible. I mean, he and Marilyn . . . Marilyn's his wife . . . went down to Guatemala themselves last year, as volunteers, but I doubt he's ever even *looked* at a Hit the Rock financial report.'

'Oh. Well, then . . .' *Don't give up, dammit!* 'So who *could* I talk to? I've put this off way too long. Is there . . . well . . . maybe an accountant I can meet with?'

'There *is* an accounting firm that handles the finances for Hit the Rock. It's a small firm, run by Marilyn's . . . Pastor Steve's wife's . . . brother. His name is Roger Krupa, and his office is in Forest Park.' She paused, then added, 'Roger . . . well . . . he doesn't go to church, but he's very generous. Marilyn says he provides financial services to quite a few non-profit organizations, for a very nominal fee. Actually, he wouldn't charge *anything* for his Hit the Rock work but the stewardship committee insists on paying.'

Kirsten looked at her watch. 'You think Roger ever works on Saturday afternoons?'

'My goodness, you *are* in a hurry. But actually, Marilyn says that's one of her brother's problems. He works all the *time*. Every Saturday. Even lots of Sundays.' She lowered her eyes and shook her head, maybe saying a prayer for Roger. Then she looked up. 'I could call his office and see if he's in and— But gosh . . . what about that birthday party you mentioned?'

'Oh, yes . . . I mean . . . no. You're right. Don't call. Today's out of the question. Darn.'

'Oh, I *know*, dear. You're thinking your husband will be upset. It's so hard for men not to be impatient. It's always go, go, go. My husband was like that himself, before he accepted Jesus. And that's Roger, too. With both their kids grown and living away from home now, Roger still insists on maintaining that beautiful big home in River Forest. He *is* very successful. But working on Sundays? That's the *Lord's* day. It just breaks Marilyn's heart.'

THIRTY-SEVEN

Dugan and Andrew left Wancho's in the Subaru, with Dugan at the wheel and Andrew obviously still lost somewhere inside himself. It was natural that Andrew would be shocked and stunned by his brother's brutal murder, but the man seemed so down, so far-off, that Dugan wondered about his ability to function. He thought he should do something about that, or at least test it. After all, who knew *what* they might be facing in the next couple of days? The cops again, for example, almost certainly. But who else?

'You have a valid driver's license, right?' Dugan asked.

'What?'

'A license? A driver's license?'

'Oh,' Andrew said, 'yeah, I got one. It's from Kansas.'

'Right. So . . . why don't you drive?'

'You mean . . . *me*?'

'Yeah, well,' Dugan said, pulling to the curb and stopping, 'there's no one else in the car.' He said it as kindly as he could. 'You know, I can't even imagine how bad you must feel. But the thing is, those guys want Isobel Cho. They want her bad, and they'll be coming after us, too, thinking we can lead them to her. You need to stay alert, awake, paying attention. We both do. So I'm thinking, if you drive you *have* to pay attention.' He got out of the car and went to the passenger side.

Andrew got out and went around and slid in behind the wheel. He took a moment to adjust the mirrors and the seat, which in itself was encouraging to Dugan, then started the car and pulled out into the street.

Dugan waited a few minutes and then asked, 'You OK?'

'Yeah, I'm OK.'

It was a warm day, probably headed into the mid-eighties. And it was Saturday, so traffic was heavy. Area Three Headquarters was at Western and Belmont, on the northwest side, and when they got near there, Dugan directed Andrew first to a restaurant he knew about which was just two blocks away. Andrew handled the car perfectly well, but unless Dugan asked him a direct question he never said a word. Not while driving; and not when they got into the restaurant.

The place smelled great, like bacon grease and coffee. It was large and bustling with the clatter of dishes and a roomful of people chattering away, but they were seated quickly, and served coffee. After Dugan ordered his breakfast – eggs over easy, sausage, hash browns, wheat toast – the waitress, a thin, energetic-looking African-American who could have been seventy years old, turned to Andrew. 'How 'bout you, sugar?'

'Nothin',' he said.

'Not even a biscuit and jam? Or orange juice or somethin'?'

'No,' he said, 'just the coffee.'

'I don't know,' she said. 'Husky man like you should—'

'He's suffered a loss,' Dugan said. 'Why don't you just bring him the same as I'm having?'

'Good idea,' the woman. She smiled down at Andrew, and when he didn't look up, she patted him on the shoulder. 'I'm *so* sorry, baby,' she said, and turned away.

While they waited Dugan read the *Sun-Times*, but newspapers didn't take long to get through these days, so then he killed time by deciding which of their fellow breakfasters, the ones not in uniform, were cops. Investigator Romero's doubts Thursday night about cops looking alike notwithstanding, Dugan thought picking them out wasn't that difficult. And there were quite a few just then. So, even if the food here might clog your arteries, it seemed an unlikely place to get gunned down.

The waitress returned with their breakfasts and they started in. 'When I was an assistant state's attorney,' Dugan said, trying to make conversation, 'I used to eat here a lot. There are branch courtrooms in the same building as the police station and I was assigned there for awhile.'

'Uh-huh,' Andrew said, obviously not interested in Dugan's career history.

They took their time eating, in silence, and Dugan was at least glad to see Andrew cleaning his plate, even downing both pieces of toast. Dugan took care of the check and they left. Next stop was a nearby print shop where the clerk scanned and printed high-quality copies of the photos of the men who'd knocked on Andrew's brother's door Tuesday morning. Andrew had only glanced at the photos the night before, but now he studied them with care – which Dugan took as another positive sign – and said he didn't recognize either of the men.

By the time they got to Area Three headquarters it was close to eleven. They could see cars driving slowly through the parking lot, looking for spaces that obviously weren't opening up. That surprised Dugan. He'd thought that on Saturdays, with the courtrooms closed, there'd be lots of parking. Finally, he left Andrew in the car to drive around the block a couple of times, while he went inside to deliver the photos.

He walked along Belmont Avenue, and when he reached the corner of the building he turned, and was surprised by the number of people he saw around the entrance. Maybe it was the warm weather, or maybe continuing fallout from some street gang craziness the night before, but there were an awful lot of people coming and going for a late Saturday morning. Weary-looking cops, uniformed and not; defiant young punks pretending they weren't afraid of the police or of anything else; other civilians, mostly middle-aged, probably arrestees' and victims' families both. Everyone chattering, hyped-up; occasionally yelling at each other, with the louder, angrier cries back and forth mostly in Spanish.

Dugan joined the melee, and when he got inside he found the action centered where he'd expected it would be, at the Nineteenth District station on the first floor. Where he was headed, though, Area Three headquarters, was on the second floor, separate from the district station. He knew his way around, and skipped the elevator and took the stairs. He waited maybe ten minutes up there at the Violent Crimes Division desk before someone finally told him that Smits and Romero were both off that day. That was fine with him, and he left the photos with another detective, who promised to pass them along. Dugan wrote out a receipt and the detective, whose name was Moon, complained that he didn't have to sign a receipt. Dugan said Romero insisted he bring the photos, and if they got lost somehow he didn't want Romero on his ass.

Moon eventually signed the receipt and returned it, and Dugan was headed back down, alone in the stairwell, when the buzz of a phone startled him. It took a few seconds for him to realize it was one of the throwaways he was carrying. 'Yes?' he said.

'It's me,' Andrew said. 'Those men. I seen 'em.'

'What men? You mean . . . the guys in the photos? Jesus. Where?'

'Right here. In the parking lot. I went in looking for a place an' I seen 'em. Green Tahoe . . . two guys . . . just sittin' there.' Andrew was breathing hard. 'It was them, goddammit.'

'Are you still in the lot?'

'No. I kept going. They didn't even see me.'

'OK, I think I know a back way I can go out. I'll meet you on Belmont Avenue. OK?'

'Yeah, OK. Jesus.'

Dugan walked through the district police station on the first floor like he belonged there, and no one paid any attention to him. He found the rear exit close to where, in his day, prosecutors could park when they had to come in at night and review cases and approve felony charges. A few minutes later he was walking on the sidewalk along Belmont, and pretty soon Andrew pulled to the curb in the Subaru.

Dugan slid into the passenger seat. 'OK,' he said, 'Let's just—'

'Cops,' Andrew said. He threw the car into *Park*. 'It was fucking cops killed Tyrone.'

'Hey, hold on,' Dugan said. He laid a hand on Andrew's arm. 'We don't *know* they're the ones. And we don't *know* they're cops. Are they still in the lot?'

'I had to keep moving 'cause there was cars behind me, but I don't think they came out. If they ain't police, why they here?'

'They *might* be cops, yeah.' Dugan looked around. 'But why would cops just be sitting in the lot? Maybe they're not cops, just two guys thinking they'd come here and watch. Thinking you and me and Kirsten might have to come in today and answer more questions from Smits and Romero. But those two are both off today.'

'Yeah, they out playin' golf or shoppin' with the kids. 'Cause they don't fucking *care* who killed Tyrone.'

'Yeah, well . . . anyway, we can't sit here on the street and hope the Tahoe passes by. We're too much out in the open, and it's a traffic lane.' As if on cue, a blue-and-white pulled even with them and the uniformed cop at the wheel motioned them on. Dugan waved back to him and got out and hurried around to the driver's side. 'I'll drive,' he said.

'Yeah,' Andrew said, 'but—'

The cop gave a blip of his siren and a more impatient wave, and Dugan pulled the door open. 'C'mon, hurry!'

Andrew got out and ran around to the passenger side, and Dugan slid in behind the wheel and they drove off. 'We need to follow those guys, and I've got experience with that stuff.' Actually, he'd tailed another car only once before in his life, and while the people he'd been following that time weren't exactly friendly, they also weren't the sort to shoot him down if they spotted him.

He drove around the block and came to one of the entrances to the police parking lot, and pulled in. And, amazingly, found an open slot right away and parked.

'See there?' Andrew said, pointing. 'Two rows over, up in the front? Green Tahoe. That's what you said, right?'

'Yeah, I see it, and a couple guys in it, but I can't see who they are.'

'It's the ones in the pictures, man. I seen 'em. Well, *one* of 'em, the one looks like a frog.'

'Bingo,' Dugan said, remembering Toad, and the thin guy Kirsten said looked like a weasel, on the third floor above Lo-Kee Cleaners and the White Hen. 'We'll just wait here.' He paused. 'Tell you what, though. You should get in the back seat.'

'Bullshit. Why?'

'Because when they leave we're going after them, and if they notice two guys . . . a white guy and a black guy . . . pulling out behind them they might take a closer look. So you'll have to stay ducked down, out of sight, and that'll be easier if you're back there.'

'Yeah, well, I guess.' Andrew switched to the back seat.

They waited, with the windows lowered and no breeze, and the sun beating down and the heat in the car rising.

Dugan wondered whether they'd seen him go into the building, and recognized him, and were waiting now for him to come out. Or maybe they missed him and were waiting for one or all three of them – him and Andrew and Kirsten – to show up and go in to talk to the cops. They could fairly easily have found out what he and Kirsten looked like. But Andrew? Maybe not so easily. Still, he wasn't going to trust the driving to Andrew.

Finally, at just about noon on the button, the passenger door of the Tahoe opened and a man got out. 'Down!' Dugan said, and he himself slid lower in his seat, peering through the steering wheel. It was the thin guy, Weasel, and he didn't look their way. He slammed the car door shut and half-walked, half-trotted to the police station and went inside.

'Y'know what?' Dugan said. 'I don't think they're cops. I think they're just two guys who decided to wait here all morning, thinking we'd show up. Maybe they were here yesterday, too. Now one's going inside, probably to see if Romero and Smits are even working today.'

Ten minutes later the man came back out.

'Stay down . . . down . . . down,' Dugan urged Andrew, as he watched through the wheel and saw the man walk back to the Tahoe, then saw the Tahoe back slowly out of its slot.

Dugan started the Subaru's engine and backed out also. There were at least two other cars cruising the lot now for parking spots and as the Tahoe, two rows away, headed toward the exit, Dugan moved with them, keeping his distance. When the Tahoe, with Wisconsin plates now, turned west on to Belmont, he followed.

THIRTY-EIGHT

Kirsten left Almond Hill Community Church, wondering if she was losing it. How could she have forgotten about that damn birthday party for a group of kids, only a few minutes after she'd made it up? She consoled herself with the idea that at least she'd managed to keep Margaret Hansel from calling up the accountant, Roger Krupa, and telling him that some woman had shown up out of nowhere and wanted to talk to him about Hit the Rock's financial stability.

Poking her nose into Hit the Rock might amount to nothing, but she'd long ago learned to take at least a brief look down any path she stumbled on to. She *knew* the FBI was looking for Isobel. She didn't know why. She *assumed* Tyrone Beale's killers were also looking for Isobel, and she couldn't believe their interest was coincidental, and unrelated to the FBI's interest.

She *knew* Isobel had been close to Hit the Rock's Miguel Parillo, shot dead in Washington, DC, and if she didn't assume, she at least *wondered* whether the interest in Isobel, from wildly different directions, had something to do with Miguel Parillo, and Hit the Rock. If that were true, his murder might not have been the botched car-jacking the DC police took it to be.

At any rate, Margaret had given her the address of Krupa's office, and Kirsten's drive back to the city would take her right past Forest Park. So . . . what the hell? She just wasn't sure whether she hoped he'd be in, or hoped he'd be out. Did she want a conversation . . . or an uninterrupted look around?

Dugan continued to insist that Andrew keep his head down so the men in the green Tahoe couldn't see him, and Andrew, thank God, was following orders so far.

'What the hell's goin' on?' From his bent down position in the back seat, Andrew's voice was muffled. 'What's all this turnin' around and shit?'

'The Tahoe turned south off Belmont,' Dugan said, 'but those are residential streets and if we'd followed them in there they'd have spotted us for sure. I had to hang back and make a U-turn. My guess is they were just circling around, to go south on Western Avenue. So that's where we are now. On Western, I mean. I think they're up ahead somewhere.'

Andrew's head popped up to Dugan's right. 'You *think*. But you don't know, right?' Chasing after his brother's probable killers was putting some life into the guy.

'Yeah, well, they're off Belmont and I haven't seen any Tahoe going *north*. So, unless they stayed in that little section that's hemmed in by the expressway, they gotta be headed south on Western.'

Andrew obviously had no answer to that. He sank into the back seat, but sitting up now, and Dugan didn't bother telling him to get down. He decided that if the two guys in the Tahoe were very alert, they might catch on to a Subaru Tribeca that seemed to go wherever they went. But if so, it would be the car they picked up on, and not the people inside the car.

Traffic on Western Avenue was still heavy, and Dugan threaded his way among the cars until, three blocks later . . . there it was. 'Got it,' he said, letting up on the accelerator.

'So if they up there, why you slowing down?' Andrew was leaning forward again, peering through the windshield.

'We're not trying to *catch* them. We're trying to see where they go, learn what we can about them. And if you're not gonna stay down, at least lean back.'

'I been away from Chicago five years and I'm not exactly famous,' Andrew said, sitting back. 'How they gonna recognize me?'

'I don't know how they'd recognize you, or me, or Kirsten, or anybody. But they wouldn't have to recognize your face to know you're a black guy in a car being driven by a white guy, and hey, the car seems to be following them.' He paused. 'Hold on. OK . . . let's see what they do up here. Uh-huh . . . west on Diversey. I bet they hop on the Kennedy.'

And hop on they did. The Tahoe first passed under the Kennedy Expressway and then took a hard left on to the two-block-long southbound ramp. Dugan got caught by a red light, but wasn't too worried. He'd catch up with them again.

It was close to one o'clock when Kirsten turned on to Madison Street in Forest Park, a suburb whose signage boasted 'Big City Access, Small Town Charm.' And sure enough, looking east along Madison she could see Loop skyscrapers rising up through the haze just ten miles off. The sky was beginning to fill with wisps of thin clouds, but it was still warm, and no sign of rain.

Madison here was bustling. Not only lots of street traffic, but lots of people on the sidewalks, too. Moderate to upscale retail businesses lined both sides of the street for several blocks in both directions, with a good sprinkling of restaurants and bars to fortify and lubricate the Saturday shoppers.

She parked in a municipal lot in the seventy-four-hundred block and walked across the street to a two-story brick building which, like most of the buildings along this strip, had been carefully renovated. She looked for the street entrance to the second floor offices, and found it next to the door to an independent bookstore on the first floor. She went inside and up one flight, and then down the hall to the door that said *Krupa & Associates*. This door was locked, so she pressed the button on the jamb and heard a mellow set of door chimes sound inside. In quick response, a buzz and a click announced the opening of the lock.

She pulled open the door and went inside, and found herself in a thickly carpeted reception area. It was small, but elegantly furnished, with English hunting scenes on dark wood paneled walls, and four matching chairs upholstered in plush, deep red.

'I'm coming,' a man called from somewhere deeper in the suite. 'You're early, dammit. You said you—' He stopped as he appeared in the doorway opposite her, obviously startled. 'Oh,' he said, and a few drops of coffee splashed out of the mug in his hand, and landed on the carpet. 'Sorry. I was expecting . . . someone else.'

'Roger Krupa?' Kirsten asked, and when he nodded she said, 'I'm Kay Hendricks. Sorry to drop in unannounced like this, but I wonder if you could give me a few minutes.'

Krupa glanced at his watch and said, 'Well, I suppose I *do* have a *little* time. Oh, pull on that door, would you. The latch doesn't always catch, and with no receptionist I feel better when it's locked.'

She pulled and the latch caught, and she followed him down the hall and into his office. He went through all the right motions: offering her a comfortable chair; giving her a choice of coffee, tea, or a soft drink; assuring her that her unexpected appearance wasn't a problem. 'We're *all* too busy these days, aren't we? But I like to think I've always got time for folks who need my exper- tise.' Motions appropriate for a professional whose success depended on convincing potential clients that their matters would be in good hands with his firm.

But Kirsten quickly found that she wasn't comfortable with Roger Krupa. Was it the script that seemed just a little too pat, a little too well-rehearsed? Was it all those nervous gestures – the constant finger-tapping on his desk, the furtive, too-frequent glancing at his watch – that didn't match the gracious words? Or was it that she was just too damn ready to find a crook, to get to the bottom of this business and set Isobel Cho free to live her life?

Whatever. Just get on with it.

Krupa was somewhere in his fifties; tall and thin, with a slight stoop he really ought to pay attention to or it would only get worse. His crisply pressed khakis and pinpoint Oxford blue shirt, with the sleeves turned up to mid-forearm, were casual, but expensive. His hair was cut short, reddish-brown, and retreated from his broad, smooth forehead in tight curls. All in all, he was nice-enough looking, although his features – eyes, nose, mouth – were squeezed in a little too close together on his face.

'I do have other commitments,' he said, 'but we can at least start exploring what it is you'd like us to do for you.' He took a sip from his coffee. 'We're a small firm, you know, and that gives us the opportunity to offer uniquely personalized service. Estate and tax planning are—'

'Not to cut you off,' she said, cutting him off, 'but I understand that you have among your accounting clients a number of non-profit charitable groups.'

'Yes, that's true. And I'm quite proud of that.' Although he seemed less proud than curious, possibly even concerned. 'So . . . are you seeking services on behalf of a non-profit?'

'Actually, I'm not seeking any services at all.'

'Oh?' He tilted his head slightly. 'Well then—'

'Please don't misunderstand.' She gave him her most sincere smile. 'I'm not here to waste your time. My husband and I are in the process of planning some charitable giving.' She gave him the spiel about their good fortune. 'We've looked round, and something that's gotten my husband's interest is a non-profit called Hit the Rock. It's sponsored by Almond Hill Community Church out in Kane County.'

'I see,' he said. 'So you're thinking of making a donation.' Her phony story didn't seem to be going down as smoothly with Krupa as it had with the church lady. His demeanor was bordering now on . . . what? Suspicion? 'Still,' he said, 'what brings you here?'

'The thing is,' she said, 'we're talking a substantial sum of money here, low six figures, and we're concerned about the financial stability of some of these groups. I mean, we'd hate to pour a lot of cash into a dying program. Does that make sense?'

'Absolutely,' he said. 'But I'm still—'

'So I went out and consulted with the folks at Almond Hill. They said you handle the financial aspect of the project. And they suggested I come and see you directly. So here I am.'

'Well, I don't think I can help you. I just do the accounting, try to keep the IRS happy, that kind of thing. They should really have given you the financial reports, so you—' His phone rang. 'Excuse me,' he said, and picked up the receiver. 'Roger Krupa here.' He paused, then said, 'Uh . . . sure.' He looked at his watch. 'Right. Ten minutes. But I should tell you I'm with someone just now, but . . .' Listening, looking at her and nodding. 'Of *course* I didn't forget.' He paused, then seemed to reach a decision. 'And you know what? The woman who's here right now? She stopped by unexpectedly, to ask about Hit the Rock.' He listened. 'Uh-huh, right. A possible donor. Wondering about its finances. Whether it's sound.' Listening some more. Frowning. 'Uh . . . yes, I'll try to do that. I'm sure she can wait ten minutes. Of course . . . I understand. Ring the bell when you get here.' He hung up and stared at the phone.

'I guess that was your other commitment, right?' Kirsten asked.

'Yes,' he said. 'In fact, one of my associates. The one who . . . you know . . . actually does the work on the Hit the Rock account. So you're in luck. We're *both* in luck. You just sit tight, and he can fill you in on everything.'

But Roger Krupa didn't look like he was in luck. He looked scared to death.

THIRTY-NINE

The light went green and Dugan sped forward, turned, and pulled up on to the long ramp, and then on to the Kennedy, where the Tahoe had gone. The expressway was busy, but not bumper-to-bumper.

When he spotted the Tahoe again it was entering Hubbard's Cave, where the Kennedy passed under Hubbard Street, north of downtown. The tunnel was just a couple of blocks long, and they were quickly out in the sunlight again, Dugan holding back, sticking to the right lanes.

Just south of the Loop, at the Circle Interchange, the Tahoe exited the Kennedy and headed west on the Eisenhower. Traffic was lighter here, and Dugan had to stay further back. Maybe ten minutes went by and they were getting to the western suburbs, and he was certain they hadn't been spotted. He was getting the hang of this.

'So,' Andrew said, 'what's the plan? I mean, we follow them to wherever they're going . . . and then what?'

'We play it by ear.'

'You got a gun?'

'Jesus, Andrew, I told you . . . we're not gonna confront these guys. Just watch where they're going. See who they are, what they're up to.'

'Yeah, alright, but they killed my brother. I gotta get a gun.'

'Forget that. We need some evidence. We need— Damn! They're getting off.' He had to veer across two lanes of traffic to make it into the far left lane, in a hurry, because the Tahoe had its turn signal on, as though to exit at Harlem Avenue, a rare exit off the Eisenhower from the left lane.

The Tahoe did, in fact, take the exit, and turned north. Dugan followed. Harlem, a main business artery, was bumper-to-bumper just then, slow going for everyone, which wasn't so bad. Dugan and Andrew were a block back.

'What town is this, anyway?' Andrew asked. 'Oak Park, or what?'

'We're on Harlem Avenue, and Oak Park's on our right. But look.' Dugan pointed ahead through the windshield. 'They're turning left on Madison. That'll put them in Forest Park.'

Thinking the men must be close to wherever they were going, Dugan dug out one of his phones, ready to call Kirsten.

'So,' Roger Krupa said, 'we'll just sit here and wait, and my . . . my associate will be here.' He looked around the room, everywhere but at Kirsten. 'Um . . . are you sure you wouldn't like something to drink?'

'What I'd like,' she said, 'is the truth about who's coming.' She was taking a big leap here, but if she wasn't right, the only downside was having an accountant in Forest Park who thought she was nuts. 'And I'd like to know why you're so damn scared.'

'Scared?' He finally did look at her. 'I . . . I don't understand. Scared of what?'

'Look, time is short. Someone's coming, and you don't like whoever it is. You're *afraid* of whoever it is. And you made a point of telling them there's a woman here asking about Hit the Rock, and its finances. I'm going to assume there are two of them coming, two men. They may be "associates" of yours, but they don't have a key to the office. They don't work for you. You work for them.'

He stared at her, his eyes narrow, his mouth open. 'You're out of your mind,' he said. But when he looked at his watch again and seemed desperate, she knew she was right.

She stood up, went to the door of his office, and turned back to him. 'No, *you're* the crazy one, if you think your dealings with these men are ever going to have a happy ending. They've already killed two men they saw as a danger to them. And sooner or later, if you continue to help them . . . and you *have* been helping them . . . they'll see you as a danger, too. And they *will* kill you. Make no mistake about it.'

'My God, how did . . . I mean . . . what makes you say such—'

She held her palm up toward him. 'Spare me the bullshit. I'm on my way. You choose. You either continue down this insane road with them until they put a bullet in your brain, or you tell them that I insisted I had to leave. That I actually seemed to be the potential donor I said I was, and that you couldn't stop me, not without creating big trouble for yourself . . . *and* them . . . if I was telling the truth.' She paused, saw him glance again at his watch. 'I can help you out of this mess, you know.' She turned away, then back to him once more. 'And believe me, whichever path you choose, you're going to hear from me again.'

He was calling to her as she went through the door to the hall, but she didn't stop to listen. She saw a sign for a rear exit from the second floor and she went out that door and down a set of exterior wooden stairs into a small parking area, accessible from an alley running parallel with Madison. By then enough time had passed that if she walked down the alley to the street, and from there to where she'd parked the Malibu, she might walk right into the arms of the guy Dugan called 'Toad,' and that other guy, 'Weasel.' *If* she was right about them being the ones on their way.

She hesitated, then headed for the rear door to the book store. Just as she got there her throwaway cell rang and she dug it out of her purse. 'Hello?'

'It's me,' Dugan said. 'Long story short, we're right on the tail of the two guys in the Tahoe. Toad and friend.'

'Good. They're in Forest Park, right?' She tried the door. It was locked and she rang the bell. 'On Madison Street?'

'Damn, how did you know that?'

'A lucky guess. Are they still in the car?'

'Yeah, but they seem to be looking for somewhere to park. No, wait . . . they just turned north on a side street.'

'Stick around. They'll park in the alley behind the stores and go up to meet a guy.' She heard someone unlocking the bookstore door. 'When they leave, stay with them.' The door opened. 'And don't get caught at it.' She ended the call.

'Hi there.' A guy with a friendly smile stood in the bookstore doorway. 'You here for the meeting?'

'Uh . . . yeah,' she said, stepping inside and closing the door behind her, and locking it. 'Hope I'm not late.'

'Just a little,' he said. 'This way.'

The guy turned to lead her through a cluttered storeroom that smelled like paper dust and boiled coffee, but she stayed right by the back door and looked out the little window. She saw the Tahoe pull into the parking area and squeeze into the only open slot. Two men got out. The one from the passenger seat was Weasel, and he went straight to the stairs to the second floor and up. The driver – she couldn't see his face, but he was a short guy – went down the alley. That would be Toad, and he was carrying a blue gym bag. He'd be going up to Krupa's the front way.

'Psssst.' It was the bookstore guy trying to get her attention, and she turned around. 'This way,' he said, half-whispering. 'You don't wanna miss the argument between Doctor Watson and Teddy Roosevelt. It's great fun.'

FORTY

'She already knew where we were . . . or at least where *they* were.' Dugan slipped the phone in his pocket. 'I wonder how she knew that.'

'I dunno,' Andrew said. 'Now what do we do?'

'She thinks they'll park in the alley and go inside. When they leave we'll follow them again.' By then they'd reached the street where the Tahoe had turned north. Dugan was about to turn there, too, but saw Toad walking back toward Madison, carrying a blue gym bag. So Dugan went straight, hoping the guy hadn't noticed them.

He circled the block, came back and, not seeing Toad or Weasel anywhere, drove into the one-way alley. Halfway down, he spotted the Tahoe sitting in a little concrete parking area behind one of the buildings. He continued on to the next cross street, where he found an open spot half a block away, and parked where he and Andrew could keep an eye on the alley.

'When they come out,' he said, 'they'll most likely turn south, to go back to Madison.'

'You're parked by a hydrant,' Andrew said.

'Yeah, I know.' He took out the cell and called Kirsten.

'Can't talk now,' she whispered. 'Call me back as soon as you see the two bozos again.' He heard laughter and applause behind her . . . and then she was gone.

He and Andrew waited, and twenty minutes later he saw the Tahoe nose out of the alley. He called Kirsten again. 'They're leaving,' he said.

'Both in the car?' Still whispering, with voices in the background.

'Yeah.'

'Nobody else with them?'

'Not that I can see.'

'Stay with them.'

'OK, and what are—' But again she was gone.

The bookstore specialized in history and mystery, and the 'meeting' Kirsten had barged in on – actually, the dozen or so people seated on folding chairs seemed thrilled to have a new face among them – was a series of enactments of fictional conversations between historical figures. Probably entertaining, and educational as well. Probably. But Kirsten's mind was one flight up, on Roger Krupa, and how *his* meeting, with his two 'associates,' was going.

Dugan called twice, and the second call came just as the presentations ended and people were getting coffee and chatting. As soon as he said the two men had left, without Krupa, she ended the call, and started toward the exit. Then she thought she really should buy something. She owed *that* much to the guy

– Augie, everyone called him – who'd let her in the back door. He seemed to be the owner, and he had saved her a lot of trouble – and maybe saved her life. Plus, he had such a happy round face, and such a great shy smile. She grabbed a paperback by someone named Alexander McCall Smith – the slim little book would fit easily in her purse – and paid cash for it. Augie tried to give her a schedule of coming events at the store but she hurried out to the sidewalk and back up the stairs to Krupa & Associates.

Not surprisingly, the spring latch hadn't caught properly, and the hall door was unlocked. Kirsten pulled it open and went inside. It was very still, very quiet in the suite. 'Mr Krupa?' she called.

No response.

A chill ran through her, and she stepped farther into the elegant waiting room. 'Hey! I'm back.'

'I'm . . . I'm in here,' he called. His voice seemed weak, and strained, but at least he was alive. She was able to exhale again.

She found him sitting in his office, his head hanging low over his hands, which rested, one on top of the other, on the desk before him. 'Remember me?' she said. 'I *told* you I'd be back.'

His breathing was deep, and clearly audible, but he didn't look up. There was a sour odor in the room that hadn't been there before.

'Are you . . . OK?' she asked. He didn't answer and she stepped close to his desk and leaned forward . . . and saw a blue gym bag on the floor near his chair. 'Look at me,' she said. 'Are you OK?'

He finally looked up at her, his face very pale. 'I . . . I guess so.' He lifted his right hand from the desk, took hold of his wrist and raised his left hand up in front of him. The little finger stuck out at a terrible, impossible angle from the rest of his hand.

'Jesus.' Kirsten swallowed down the breakfast that rose in her throat, and that's when she first noticed the drying vomit on Krupa's chin, and on his shirt. The sour smell. 'Tell me what happened,' she said, and sat across from him in one of his client's chairs.

'I don't know. I . . . I tripped.' He laid his hand back down, wincing when it touched the desk. 'Caught my finger on the edge of my desk.'

'Uh-huh,' she said. 'You keep rehearsing that line till you get it right. Maybe someone will believe it.'

'It hurts . . . really bad. I feel like . . . I feel faint.'

'Lay your head down on the desk.' He did as he was told, and she leaned forward. 'You need to get to an emergency room. They'll give you something for the pain, and they'll set that finger.' *But meanwhile,* she thought, *I can use that pain to get at some facts.* 'You can't drive, so I'm going to take you.'

He moved, as though to get up.

'But not yet.'

He raised his head. 'What?' Anger flared in his eyes, which was probably good for him.

'First, tell me what you told those two goons when they got here.'

'I can't . . . I mean I don't . . . Oh God, I just don't know.'

'Tell me, dammit. Then we'll go to the ER.'

'I . . . OK . . . they were mad when you weren't here. I told them you . . . that you really seemed to be what you said. Interested in giving money. I told them that, even so, I tried to get you to wait for them, but you said you had to go, that your husband was waiting for you. I said I couldn't talk you into staying, and I couldn't physically restrain you. That if I did, and if you were what you said, we'd all be in trouble.'

'What did *they* say? What happened?'

'The tall one said he thought I was lying, that I must have *let* you go. The short one said maybe not. He didn't know. But he said one thing he knew for sure . . . that I hadn't done what they told me to do. And he . . . he took my finger . . . and he . . . he did this.' Nodding at his hand. 'He said this was a hint of what happens when people don't do what they're told.' He paused, and she could see his eyes overflowing now with tears of pain. 'Can we go, please?'

'In a minute,' she said. 'You need to tell me everything. Exactly how they're using you. Because if you don't I'll eventually find out anyway. And without me on your side it's only going to get much, much worse. I'm the only chance you have.'

'No,' he said, obviously close to breaking into sobs. 'I have no chance at all.'

'You can believe that if you like. And if you do . . . then it's true. But if you choose to believe I can help you, then you have a chance to get out of this business alive. Not a sure thing, and no way you'll ever escape without *some* consequences. But I'll help you as much as I can.'

'So . . . if I promise to cooperate, you'll take me to the hospital?'

She thought for a moment. 'No, that's not the deal. The deal is: I'm taking you to the hospital. While you're there, you think things over. And when the doctors are through with you, you tell me whether you're with me or not.' She stood.

He stood, too.

'Oh,' she said, pointing to his waist, 'I need your cellphone.'

'You can't—' He winced, as though hit by a fresh wave of pain. 'Uh . . . OK.' He unclipped the phone from his belt and handed it to her.

She put it in her purse, thinking he'd probably have given her his wallet, or the key to his safe deposit box, if she'd insisted. 'You'll get it back when we're finished at the hospital. But for now, let's go.'

He came around the desk, clutching his left hand to his body, either not noticing or not caring that he'd vomited his lunch down the front of his expensive shirt. They went through the waiting room, and she let the door fall closed behind them.

But when they were just a few yards down the hall he stopped. 'Wait, I should lock that door.'

Damn, she thought. But what she said was, 'I think I heard it lock.'

'It's *supposed* to, but it doesn't always catch. Anyway, I should use the key, turn the deadbolt.'

The key, though, was in his left pants pocket and he struggled to get at it with his right hand. 'Relax,' she said, 'I got it.' Slipping her hand into his pocket, she pulled out a leather key-case, and hurried back to the door. She fumbled with the four keys in the case, found the one that worked, and locked the door. 'See?' she said. 'You need me.'

His face was very pale and there were tears in his eyes, and he didn't seem to see any humor in her remark. She slipped the key case back in his pants pocket . . . the left pocket again.

They went down the hall, and on their way down the stairs she said, 'Don't forget what I told you. Say no to me, and it may take me a *little* longer, but I *will* find out what's going on. And you? You'll be on your own. With your two friends. And with lots of other body parts for them to work on.'

FORTY-ONE

Dugan didn't mention it to Andrew, but heading down the Eisenhower he couldn't help wondering: How long could one car tail another, in broad daylight, without even the most inattentive of tailees failing to catch on? On the other hand, it did seem as though well over half the cars on the road were SUVs, and there wasn't much about the look of the Subaru he and Andrew were in that set it apart from any other silver-gray SUV in the world.

So they stayed with the chase, all the way into the city. Once they were off the Ike, he was forced to give the Tahoe a two-block lead, until finally it pulled to the curb in the middle of a complex of high-rise condo buildings, just west of the Loop. Weasel got out and disappeared among the buildings, but which one he went into Dugan couldn't tell.

The Tahoe drove off, headed south, and ten minutes later slipped into a covered parking space behind a string of row houses near the Chicago campus of the University of Illinois. Toad got out and went into one of the units, and again, from his vantage point Dugan couldn't tell which unit it was. He could see, though, that the guy wasn't carrying a gym bag. And Weasel hadn't been, either.

Dugan turned to Andrew. 'I'm hungry,' he said. 'You like Italian beef?'

'I don't care.' Either Andrew was sliding back into his funk, or he'd never really come out of it.

'Yeah, well, Al's is real close.'

They drove just a few blocks to Taylor Street and a low brick building with a red sign that said AL's #1 ITALIAN BEEF in white block letters. It was a popular place, boasting friendly urban ambiance and quick service. 'Damn good sandwiches, too,' Dugan said.

'I dunno. I guess I don't feel like eating.'

'You'll change your mind. You'll love it.'

They went inside and Dugan ordered large Cokes and beef-and-pepper sandwiches for both of them. 'To go,' he said, because it suddenly occurred to him that maybe Toad ate at Al's, too. Around here, who didn't?

They took their drinks and sandwiches – and about five paper napkins apiece, to protect the Subaru's interior from Al's spicy tomato sauce – and went back to the car. 'You might as well get in the front,' Dugan said. 'I don't see us doing any more tailing today.' He got behind the wheel and started the engine. 'We'll drive somewhere else, and stop to eat. These things are too big and too messy to eat in motion.'

They didn't have to go far. There was a public library around the corner from Al's. 'We should be good here for as long as it takes to eat,' Dugan said, pulling into an employee parking space. 'I doubt Toad visits the library very often.'

Andrew sat in silence, and Dugan gave up trying to figure out what to say to a man who, less than forty-eight hours earlier, had discovered the battered, lifeless body of his only brother. He ate his sandwich, and Andrew ate about half of his, and Dugan wadded up the debris leftover and stuffed it into the take-out bag and put it on the floor of the car. He looked at his watch. 'Damn,' he said, 'is it really only three o'clock?'

Andrew didn't answer. He seemed to be studying his thumb.

'So,' Dugan said, thinking he should at least try to be helpful, 'you feeling OK?'

'What about the funeral?' Andrew said. 'There's gotta be a funeral.'

It took Dugan by surprise. 'Yeah, well, sure. And Kirsten and I . . . we'll be helping you with that.

'You will? Why?'

'Because . . . well, because we owe you.'

'Owe me?'

'What, you don't remember? We'd probably be dead if you hadn't done what you did.'

'You mean . . . back five years ago or whatever? I was just trying to save myself.'

'Maybe so. I was in no shape to know *what* the hell happened. But anyway, so what? We owe you. Tomorrow's Sunday, so on

Monday we'll call those two detectives . . . if they haven't already
called *us*, to tell us to come back in again. Anyway, we'll find
out when they'll be ready to release the . . . release your brother's
body. We'll get a funeral director lined up. Maybe even a church.
Your brother belong to a church?'

'I don't think so.'

'Well, anyway, we'll get a place for a funeral.'

'Who's gonna come to it?'

'Jesus, Andrew, how do I—' He stopped. 'I'll come, and
Kirsten, and you. And maybe your landlady . . . that friend of
your mother's? What about Jamison Traynor? Maybe even Isobel
Cho. And maybe some sheriff's deputies, or other people he used
to work with at the sheriff's office. We'll put a notice in the
paper. Who knows?'

'That's good,' Andrew said. 'There's gotta be a funeral.'

FORTY-TWO

I t was a fifteen minute ride to the hospital, in Maywood, just
west of Forest Park, and Kirsten walked Krupa into the ER.
The sign said it was one of only ten 'Level 1 Trauma Centers'
in metro-Chicago. That, plus being just blocks from an interstate
highway, meant there must have been plenty of broken, bloody
bodies carried through those doors. So the look on the intake
person's face when she saw that little finger, sticking out crazily,
terribly swollen, and looking like maybe only skin kept it attached
to Krupa's hand, seemed significant. He was also moaning softly
now, non-stop, and he really did look as though he might faint
any minute . . . or maybe throw up again. They took him back
into the treatment area right away.

Kirsten sat in the waiting area with just two other people: a
mother and a little boy, maybe eight years old, sitting side-by-side.
The woman held the boy cradled against her. He was sound
asleep and she was nodding off, and Kirsten couldn't tell which
was the patient . . . or if they were just waiting for someone
being worked on inside.

Twenty minutes later a stout, concerned-looking black woman

in a gray lab coat came out and introduced herself as Michelle Coleman, a trauma physician. 'Are you the friend who brought Mr Krupa in?'

'Yes,' Kirsten said. 'And I'm worried sick about him. I'm a client as well as a friend. I went to his office to see him, and when I got there I saw he'd broken his finger. He was in terrible pain, but I think he was embarrassed to call an ambulance. Poor man. I knew he should see a doctor right away. He'd fallen, he said, and caught his—'

'Yes, he told *me* that, too. A freak sort of accident, certainly, and preliminary X-rays show an odd combination of fractures. I've given him something for the pain, and as soon as the orthopedic surgeon is available he'll be going into surgery. He may need some blood vessel repair as well. It may take some time, I'm afraid.'

'I see. Well, can I talk to him for a few minutes before all that?'

'No, that's not a good idea. We've taken him upstairs already. He's sedated, anyway.'

'So . . . will he be here . . . overnight?'

'I'm not certain. Probably not. That'll be up to the surgeons, primarily the vascular surgeon, if he's needed. But either way, today or tomorrow, he'll need transportation home. He said his wife is out of town and that he has no relatives nearby. They'll have the hand demobilized, so it'll be awkward for him . . . dressing and undressing, things like that. But except for no driving for a few days, he should be able to manage on his own.'

'He has a sister, I think,' Kirsten said. 'I'll check on that. And I'll see that he gets home. Either I can take him, or I'll make arrangements.'

'Do we have a number for you? Or does he?'

'No, I won't be going home tonight, and my cell's not working. But I'll stay in touch with the hospital. Can you put a note in the chart? That Kay Hendricks will be calling?' She spelled out Hendricks. 'I don't want them telling me they can't say how he's doing, or whether he's ready to go home.'

'I'll see to that.' The doctor paused. 'I guess that's it. It was very kind of you to take the time to get him here.'

'Yeah, well, thanks,' Kirsten said. 'But you know what they say: "Do unto others . . ." and all that.'

They wished each other well, and ten minutes later Kirsten was in her borrowed Malibu, wondering whether Doctor Michelle Coleman was still pondering Roger Krupa's phony story about catching his finger on the edge of his deck, or asking herself what sort of trauma could cause such an 'odd combination of fractures.'

Meanwhile, Kirsten was headed back to Forest Park, with the key she'd taken earlier from Krupa's key-case.

Again she parked in the municipal lot, walked across Madison Street, and used the door next to the bookstore entrance. Up on the second floor she walked slowly along the corridor, but heard nothing behind any of the closed doors. It seemed that Krupa was the only tenant up here who worked on warm Saturday afternoons.

She unlocked his door and went in, locked the door again behind her, and went through the suite to his private office. The smell was still there, and so was the vomit, pretty dry now, mostly on the hard plastic mat on the floor under the desk chair. But more interesting to her was the zippered gym bag, the blue one the driver, Toad, had been carrying when he left the Tahoe behind the bookstore.

Ever since her days as a homicide investigator, she routinely carried latex gloves in her handbag, and she slipped a pair on and crouched down and opened the gym bag. And found cash. Wrapped and stacked. Various denominations. She didn't bother to count it. Thousands, anyway.

She left the bag there and took a look around the suite of offices. There was no office or station for a receptionist or a secretary, but there were two accountant's offices in addition to Krupa's, and a storage room in the rear crowded with office supplies, old computer equipment, and other assorted junk. One corner of that room, near a door into a tiny bathroom, was set up as a sort of kitchen, with a dorm-room refrigerator sitting next to a kitchen cabinet. On top of the cabinet were a toaster oven, a coffee maker, and a roll of paper towels standing upright; inside, she found paper plates and cups, and plastic utensils and the like, along with some plastic bags and several paper shopping bags with grocery store logos. She took two of the paper bags and reinforced one of them by putting the other inside it, and took that, and a couple of unopened packs of copy paper, back to Krupa's office, and left them there.

She went through the suite again, more thoroughly this time, but it took just fifteen minutes to conclude that she wasn't about to find any information related to Hit the Rock, or anything else that might be useful. There were no papers or records lying around in any of the offices. There was a safe in a closet off Krupa's office, but it was locked, as was every file cabinet in the entire suite. And all the computers were password protected.

It was only about two thirty, and she was sure Krupa wouldn't be ready to leave the hospital for quite some time. But there was nothing more to be accomplished in his office. So she went out the door and locked it carefully behind her. And if her search had been more successful maybe she wouldn't have left the two reams of copy paper in the blue gym bag behind Krupa's desk, and wouldn't have taken the money out with her in the reinforced shopping bag. Maybe.

FORTY-THREE

Dugan was about to back the Subaru out of the library parking space when his throwaway cell rang. He cut the engine and answered.

'It's me,' Kirsten said. 'What's up?'

He gave her a quick review of their day, starting with Andrew spotting the two men in the Tahoe, down to Toad dropping Weasel off, and then driving to the row houses and going inside. 'We were already pushing our luck with the shadow stuff,' he said. 'So we went and had lunch.'

'Good idea. And Andrew?'

'Hanging in there,' Dugan said. 'Not great. But anyway, where *are* you?'

'I'm at a hospital out in Maywood, waiting for an accountant who's having his little finger put back together. He suffered a few complicated fractures during a pep talk your friend Toad gave him.'

'Um . . . I guess I get the gist of it.'

'I can't go into the details now, but it has to do with Hit the Rock . . . and maybe a bunch of other small, probably legitimate, non-profits . . . and what I'm guessing is a money laundering scheme.'

'OK. And that has what, if anything, to do with Isobel?'

'If I'm right, it means I have to wake her up.'

'In the middle of the afternoon?'

'I think she's asleep,' Kirsten said, 'but in the sense of that old "She who knows, but knows not that she knows" saying.'

'Right, I got it. I think.'

'So I need to meet with her again.'

'If someone needs to meet with her again,' Dugan said, 'let's make it *we*, not just you.'

'That's fine,' she said, which surprised him. 'I'll talk to Cuffs. Set something up.'

'For later today?'

'Probably tomorrow. I need to be right here when the accountant gets out. When his pinkie hurt like hell and looked like it was about to drop off, he was starting to cooperate with me. But he's scared to death of Toad and friend, so once he gets his finger straightened out and gets some pain relief, he might backslide . . . and need another little nudge from me.' She paused. 'Meanwhile, you guys'll just have to drive around and wait for my call. Stay safe.'

'Wait, don't go yet. I got something to say.'

'Oh? What's that?'

'Just that Andrew and I are scared shitless of those two guys, same as that accountant is. And I'm hoping you are, too. You get what I'm saying?'

There was a long silence, then, 'I understand. And I love you.'

'You, too,' he said, and put away the phone.

'Not me,' Andrew said.

'Not you what?'

'I'm not scared of those fuckers.'

'I hope that's just talk,' Dugan said. 'Not talking scared is great. Not *acting* scared is even better. But not *being* scared? That worries me. 'Cause we *are* going after those guys, and I'd feel a lot safer if we were all scared.'

FORTY-FOUR

Kirsten was back at the hospital, having left the Malibu in the parking garage, with a double-strength shopping bag full of cash in the trunk. When she said she was Krupa's ride home the woman at the front desk made a call, and then told her he was in outpatient surgery, and that it looked as though he'd be discharged that evening, but she couldn't say definitely when that would be.

'He suffered a very serious multiple fracture of one of his fingers,' Kirsten said, 'and I'm worried about him. May I see him as soon as the surgeon's finished with him?'

The woman directed her to outpatient surgery and told her to check in with the nurse, and that there was a waiting room up there.

It was nearly five o'clock when a middle-aged man in a light blue lab coat came into the waiting area, looked around, then walked over to her. He introduced himself as the orthopedic surgeon.

'How's he doing?' she asked.

'He's resting comfortably. He'll be fine. It was a strange break, but I'm sure that hand looked worse to you than it was. We didn't need a hand specialist or a vascular surgeon.'

He went on to describe the procedure, and what follow-up Krupa needed, but all she was really interested in was how soon the patient would be ready to go, and what his mental status would be.

'He'll be out in about a half hour,' the surgeon said. 'He's mentally alert. We used a local anesthetic, which will last for quite a while. We're sending him home with pain medication for when that wears off.'

Forty minutes later the doors swung open and Roger Krupa came into the room, being pushed along in a wheelchair by a young Hispanic man. She rushed over. 'How *are* you, Roger?'

'I have nothing to say to you.' He was scowling.

'I *know* you don't like hospitals, Roger,' she said. 'But I *had* to bring you in. You'll be *so* glad I did when you're feeling better.' When he didn't answer she turned to the man pushing the chair. 'Isn't he able to walk?'

'Oh, he can walk OK. It's procedure. After surgery, you leave by wheelchair.'

None of them said a word as they rode the elevator down to the first floor, or as they proceeded along the corridor toward the lobby. Krupa was fully dressed, and his left arm was in a sling. His entire hand, except for the index finger and thumb, was encased in what was either a bulky bandage or a cast. She couldn't tell which.

When they reached the lobby Kirsten turned to the Hispanic man. 'If you wait here with him,' she said, 'I'll run and get the car, and meet you at the entrance.'

'No,' Krupa said, twisting his head toward the man behind him. 'I'm not going with her. I want a cab.'

'Well,' the man said, 'I guess it's up to you. You'll have to call one. You have a cellphone?'

'Yes, but she has it.' Pointing at Kirsten.

'Me?' Opening her eyes wide.

'Yes. You took it. Give me back my phone.'

'Oh my *Lord*, Roger,' Kirsten said. Then, looking at the Hispanic man, 'Is he, like, taking . . . pain medication?'

'I don't know,' the man said. 'I'm just patient transport. You have to ask the nurse, or the doctor.'

'I tell you what,' she said. 'I know you're busy, so let's just take Roger over and let him sit on that sofa and rest awhile, get his bearings.' She pointed to a waiting area near the hospital entrance. 'I'll wait with him there, and when he's ready I'll get the car.'

'No,' Krupa said. 'She took my phone. I want a cab.'

The patient transport guy looked worried. 'I don't know. Maybe I should get security.'

'Oh, that's not necessary,' she said. She leaned down toward Krupa. 'Roger honey, you remember that gym bag your friend brought you?'

'What?' He stared at her.

'Oh, *you* remember. The gym bag. The one your friend brought to your office? I *knew* you'd be worried about it. And your friend? He'd be *really* worried. So . . . I took care of it.'

'Jesus,' he said.

'Yes.' She gave him a big smile. 'I *knew* you'd be pleased. Now, why don't you let me take you home?'

Once they were in the car he asked, 'What did you do with it?'

'The gym bag? As far as I know it's still in your office. I mean, it was there when we left. I bet there was a lot of money in it, right?'

'You . . . you're crazy.'

'Yes, sometimes I surprise even myself.'

'You have no idea who you're dealing with,' he said. 'And I don't mean me. I mean *them*. You just don't know.'

'You're right about that. Which is why you're going to tell me. Not just who they are, but everything you know. And eventually you're going to tell the police, or the FBI, or some other law enforcement agency. And when you do, I'm going to work as hard as I can to get you a good deal. You might even avoid the federal country club.'

'I can't tell anyone. Those men . . . they'll kill me if I do.'

'And do you think they *won't* kill you, anyway, once they decide you're more dangerous than useful? Which, sooner or later, *will* happen, even if I disappeared from your life forever. Which, by the way, *won't* happen.'

He slumped in his seat. 'God, how did I ever get into this?'

'Oh, I think you *know* how you got in. It's how to get out that's important. So, do you want to go to your office or your home? The home's in River Forest, right? And isn't that beautiful big house feeling a little empty these days, what with the wife out of town and the two kids living on their own and all?'

'I don't know where I want to go.' His head was hanging low. 'I don't know what I want to do.'

'Well, cheer up. I can help you with that second part. What you want to do is to put this all behind you. You want to tell me what you've been doing, how you've been . . . what? . . . cooking the books? Is that the appropriate accounting term? And explain how many, if any, of those non-profit clients of yours know what you're doing. What you want is to give yourself a chance to collect your social security.'

'Oh my God,' he said. 'Take me to my office.'

FORTY-FIVE

'So this Krupa . . . maybe not that bad a guy, you think?' Dugan dipped his last three French fries together in ketchup and shoved them in his mouth.

'Not exactly a model citizen,' Kirsten said, 'but more a gambler than a crook. Loves to play poker.'

'You mean *lives* to play poker. It's that damn addiction thing. You get in over your head, and . . . well . . .'

'And the piper has to be paid.'

Dugan hesitated. 'Right,' he said, deciding this wasn't the time for a crack about mixed metaphors. He sucked some Dr Pepper up through a straw and glanced at Andrew, sitting silently beside him. He wondered again, as he'd wondered all afternoon, what was going on in the guy's mind. Other than that he wished he had a gun.

He and Andrew had both seen Tyrone Beale's body at more or less the same time Thursday night, and since then he himself had been struggling to erase that gruesome, sickening scene from his consciousness. If it wasn't easy for him, and he'd hardly known Tyrone Beale, what must Andrew, the man's brother, be going through?

He sure wasn't saying much of anything. And he wasn't eating, either. He'd done great at breakfast, then ate about half his lunch, and now hadn't even touched the fish sandwich sitting in front of him, getting cold.

Kirsten had met them here, in a Burger King parking lot, and they'd gone inside and ordered their meals 'to go.' Then she'd joined them in the Subaru, Kirsten in the back seat, he and Andrew in front. The plan was to eat and wait right there until it was fully dark, and then head back to Wancho's for the night. Meanwhile, Kirsten was telling about her encounter with Roger Krupa. Dugan wondered whether Andrew was even listening. He was just so damn—

'Hey,' Kirsten said, 'is anybody paying attention?'

'Yeah,' Dugan said. 'I mean, no. Sorry, I got distracted.'

Andrew didn't answer. Just sat staring ahead through the windshield into the gathering darkness.

'I was saying,' she said, 'how Krupa told me this money laundering thing's been going on for two-and-a-half years. The basic scheme is pretty simple. He's always had a bunch of non-profits on his client list. He does all their financial stuff: keeps the books, handles federal and state reporting requirements, sometimes gives a little financial advice. They're all fairly small, low profile, legitimate outfits that don't get a lot of attention from the government, or from anyone else.'

'How many does he have? Three? Five? Ten?'

'Nineteen. He goes easy on their fees, and he's gotten sort of a name for it. Although he says he's refused to take on any new non-profits since this started.'

Dugan sipped the last of his Dr Pepper. 'It's getting dark. We should be able to leave pretty soon.'

'Yeah, but let me finish this first,' Kirsten said. 'The way it works is that either Toad or the other guy, Weasel . . . sometimes both, but never anyone else . . . brings him a bundle of cash. He puts it in the accounts of one or more of his clients and records it as from anonymous donors, or from named people who don't exist. Later, he pays the entire amount out from the client to one of several companies as fees for "fund raising services" or "consulting services". The services, of course, are never performed, and the companies, as far as he knows, are shells. By the time some individual gets it, maybe in the form of salary from one of the companies, it's clean money, and taxes are probably paid on it. Once he pays out the so-called "fees," Krupa's not part of it.'

'Sounds simple enough,' Dugan said.

'Yeah, well, it took him a little longer to explain. He claims not one of his clients knows a thing about it. They never get more, or less, than what comes in as legitimate donations. He keeps two sets of books for each client . . . not physical books, because it's all done on computers . . . and the clients and their directors see a financial report that's just slightly different from what he files with the government. It gets a little complicated around the edges and I'm not sure I understand everything. But I got it all recorded. Digitally.' She held up what looked like a fat pen. 'And as soon as I get a chance . . .' She put the pen back in her bag and took out a memory stick. 'It'll be on one of these.'

'Krupa gets a cut?'

'A small one, but he never sees it. It goes toward paying off his debt.'

'And the money comes from where? Drugs? Gambling? Prostitution?'

'Maybe all of the above.' Kirsten said. 'And maybe these guys sell guns to street gangs and get paid with drug money. *Somebody's* doing that in this city. And across the state, too.'

'And from here to Mexico and beyond. How much are we talking about?'

'Krupa says they brought him about four hundred thousand last year.'

'Jesus, that's what? Eight thousand a week?' Dugan paused to do some calculating. 'But . . . let's see . . . nineteen clients? If you round that out to twenty, that's an average of only about twenty thousand a year to be run through each client's accounts.'

'More through the bigger ones. Less through the smaller ones. Not enough to draw attention.'

'But what about the people who run these non-profits? Don't they ever look at the documents he actually files with the government?'

'He says if they ever *did* see exactly what the government sees, most of them wouldn't notice the difference. In fact, though, in case they ever ask, he has a false set of government filings for them, which matches the financial reports he prepares for them.'

'And the only people he deals with are these two guys?'

'Right, and he has no idea who they are. He says the revolving poker game where he lost the money has been shut down for two years now. When he'd lose he'd borrow money from the house to cover it. Eventually it got to where he owed way too much, and was running up some ungodly weekly interest. That's when the two goons showed up.'

'They mob-connected?'

'They could be,' Kirsten said. 'He doesn't know, doesn't *want* to know.'

'So he *does* have an occasional sensible thought. What do *you* think?'

'I think probably not. Or if they are, they're doing this on the side. You'd think the big boys would operate on a bigger scale, use larger accounting firms, more sophisticated systems, foreign banks. All that.'

'But four hundred thou a year, even pre-tax, isn't bad for two guys . . . or even three or four guys . . . and they might even have more than one Roger Krupa in their stable.'

'And maybe a murder is worth it to them,' Kirsten said, 'to keep the river flowing.'

'And to keep themselves out of jail.'

'Hold on.' Andrew finally spoke up, swiveling in his seat to face them. 'I got a question.'

'Good,' Dugan said. 'I was starting to think you weren't listening. Go ahead.'

'These are the guys, right? They killed Tyrone? But why?'

'Can I prove it to a judge or jury?' Kirsten asked. 'No. But here's what I think. A man named Miguel Parillo was recently shot dead in Washington, DC. He ran a non-profit organization that was one of Krupa's clients. I think Parillo found out somehow that they were using his organization in this money-laundering scheme, and was about to blow the whistle. And they killed him. Parillo was close to Isobel Cho, and they think she knows something, or has something in her possession, that's dangerous to them, and they're looking for her. And like I said before, I think they killed your brother when he wasn't able to tell them where she was.'

'He wouldn't have told them even if he knew,' Andrew said.

'No,' she said, 'probably not.'

'For *sure* not.'

'You knew him better than anybody,' she said, 'so I'm sure you're right.' She tried to think of something besides Tyrone Beale's battered, bloody remains. She turned to Dugan. 'There's something I didn't mention before. When I talked to Cuffs and Isobel yesterday, Cuffs told me she'd been putting in long days, and she'd been sick.'

'Long days?' Dugan asked. 'What the hell's that about?'

'I have no idea. But he said she hadn't been feeling well. Or, to put it in his words, she puked up all over his fucking car. That was the day before yesterday. Then yesterday, she said she'd been a little nauseated again, but didn't throw up, and when we talked she said she was feeling fine. Cuffs thinks it might have been food poisoning.'

'Yeah,' Dugan said, 'God knows where and what they're eating.

Plus, a large dose of just plain Cuffs would give anyone a nervous stomach.'

'Anyway, I hope she's alright.'

'We better go.' Dugan said. He turned to Andrew. 'You gonna want that sandwich later?'

Andrew, staring out through the windshield again, gave a little wave of his hand. 'Uh-uh.'

Dugan took the cold fish sandwich and the wrappings from his own meal, and from Kirsten's. 'I'll get rid of this stuff and we'll head back to our hidey-hole.'

'I don't know,' Andrew said. 'I don't feel so good.' He opened his door. 'I gotta go to the bathroom.'

'Jesus, can't you—' Dugan caught himself. 'OK, take your time,' he said. 'We'll leave as soon as you get back.'

Once Andrew was out of the car, Dugan asked, 'Anything we should talk about while he's gone?'

'Just that we have to remember how bad this is for him.'

'Right, and it's impossible to know just what's going through his mind.' He gathered the trash and all their cups. 'I'll take care of all this.' He took everything out and dropped it in a barrel. When he was back behind the wheel he said, 'Y'know? This afternoon, out of nowhere, Andrew started talking about a funeral, wondering where it would be, who would come, that kind of stuff.'

'We should help with that.'

'I know. I told him you'd handle everything.' Dugan looked at his watch. 'Damn. Where *is* he? I hope he's not really *sick*.' He opened the car door. 'I'll check on him.'

A few minutes later he was back.

'So?' she asked.

'I don't know whether he's sick or not. But he's definitely gone.'

FORTY-SIX

Andrew had been carrying one of the cellphones they'd just bought, so they tried the number . . . and got voicemail. 'It's my fault,' Dugan said. 'He was being way too quiet. But what's he think he's gonna do?'

'I have no idea,' Kirsten said. 'But I do know that we can sit here and ask each other why he took off, or we can drive up and down the streets in the dark looking for him. One thing's as useless as the other.'

'And the El is . . . what? A block-and-a-half away? He could be on a train already.'

'He's got numbers for both of us, so he can call if he wants to.' Kirsten opened the car door to get out. 'Let's go to Wancho's.'

They left the Burger King in tandem, Dugan in the Subaru and she trailing him in the borrowed Malibu. She was concerned about Andrew. Even if he wasn't thinking straight, she hoped he had enough sense to stay out of sight. But she had lots of other things to think about, too. Mostly about Isobel. She'd seemed strangely subdued when they'd talked, and there were tiny lines of red showing in her eyes. Was she really sick, or just exhausted and stressed out? And why wouldn't she be? It was bad enough that Eleanor Traynor – or *someone* – was threatening her little sister. But having killers looking for her, and not even knowing why, was much worse. Plus, was there something she wasn't talking about? And was that deliberate?

Kirsten liked Isobel. There was something about the girl – and she couldn't help thinking of Isobel as a girl, a youngster – something that had instantly drawn Kirsten to want to help her. Or maybe it wasn't Isobel at all. Maybe it was the result of Kirsten's having just spent that week in Seattle, caught up in the midst of marital spitefulness that threatened the future of a little child. Whatever the mix of unconscious motives might be, when Kirsten had walked into Tyrone Beale's office Tuesday morning and found Isobel there, she'd felt as though someone – God? the universe? fate? – was setting her in front of a person who needed her help. A person to take care of. It was weird, maybe, but Kirsten felt as though she'd suddenly discovered a younger sister she'd never had.

Something startled her out of those thoughts, and it took her a second to realize it was her phone, vibrating in the purse on the seat beside her. Not one of the throwaway phones she and Dugan and Andrew were carrying these days, but her usual cellphone.

That phone had rung several times throughout the day. She

hadn't answered any of the calls and each time, when she checked, there'd been no voicemail message and the caller had been 'unknown.' Was it silly not to answer? After all, even if Beale's killers were looking for her – and she had to assume they were – it seemed unlikely that they had the equipment and capability to work the coordinates and locate a subject who answered a single cellphone call.

Still, though . . .

She didn't answer.

She waited a few moments and then, after stopping right behind Dugan at a red light, she took the phone from her purse. Again, there was no voicemail message. But this time there was a number for the last caller, a number she didn't recognize . . . and no name.

Oh, why not?

She put the bud in her ear and pressed the call back button.

'Thank you for returning my call.' The man's voice was familiar, but she couldn't place it.

'Uh-huh,' she said. 'What do you want?'

'Not I,' he said. 'The senator.' *Of course, Erik Decker.* 'She would like to speak with you.'

'So? Put her on. I can spare a minute.'

'She's not available now. I called earlier today, several times.'

'I've been busy. What does she want to talk about?'

'Tomorrow's Sunday,' he said. 'The senator will be at church in the morning. Will you be available at, say, noon?'

'I have an appointment at . . .' She paused. 'You know what? Noon will be fine. You'll call me?'

'No, the senator would like an in-person meeting.'

'You're kidding. Unless you want to put her on a plane.'

'She's home for the weekend, in Illinois. She'll be attending fundraisers tomorrow afternoon and evening, on the North Shore. Do you know where the Baha'i Temple is?'

'Of course,' she said. 'But it's supposed to be a beautiful day tomorrow. And it's Sunday. There'll be a lot of people coming and going.'

'The main parking lot is closed. There are several construction crew trailers in the lot. One of them is red. The senator will meet you in that one at noon.'

'Not to repeat myself, but what does she want to talk about?'

The light turned green and Dugan drove forward, and she followed him.

'I understand,' he said, 'that you're a witness in a homicide investigation.'

'What makes you think so?'

'I try to learn what I can about incidents and persons the senator might need to know something about. The murder of a man recently hired by her son is that sort of *incident*.'

'And am I that sort of *person*?'

'Possibly.'

'Is that why you had someone go through my hotel room?'

'Please, that would have been illegal. And my methods are . . . entirely legal and non-intrusive.' He was quoting her own words to Eleanor Traynor almost verbatim. 'At any rate, the senator may be able to be of assistance to you.'

'In regards to what?'

'That would be better addressed in the in-person meeting,' he said. 'But I can say this: you may have been thinking of the senator . . . or even of *me* . . . as hostile. But that need not be.'

'That's comforting,' Kirsten said, but not at all convinced. 'I'll be there. But I'll meet the senator *outside* the trailer. We'll go in together.'

FORTY-SEVEN

'So,' Dugan said, after Kirsten told him about the phone call from Erik Decker, 'I guess it's safe to say your visit to Washington succeeded in getting the senator's attention.'

'I thought it would.'

They were in the little kitchen at Wancho's Towing and he saw now why, as they'd passed a supermarket on the way here, she'd called and told him to wait while she 'picked up a few things.' He had thought she must be thinking of something for breakfast, but apparently the next day's meeting with the senator had prompted her to pick up a bottle of Chardonnay . . . and a corkscrew.

'Here,' she said, handing her purchases to him, 'take care of this.'

'Glad to.' He went to work on the cork. 'The Baha'i Temple, you know, is one of my favorite places.'

'I know that,' she said. 'But what I don't know is what's on Traynor's mind. I don't have a clue.'

'It might be some sort of trick.' He poured some wine into a plastic tumbler and handed it to her.

'Possibly.' She took a sip of the wine. 'And possibly I'll learn something I can use to help Isobel.'

'So,' he said, 'you're definitely going?'

'Of course. Wouldn't you?'

'I would, yes. And I *will*. I'll be there before you get there.'

They talked it over, and in the end she didn't object to having him there to cover her back. 'As long,' she said, 'as you stay out of sight and you don't interfere.'

'Unless there's trouble,' he said.

'Uh-huh. But there won't be.'

The Baha'i Temple was easy to get to. North on Lake Shore Drive until it fed into Sheridan Road, and then a straight shot up Sheridan – although 'straight shot' didn't really describe the curves and corners Sheridan took as it worked its way along the lake front out of the city, through Evanston, and into Wilmette.

Dugan got there at eleven thirty. He'd seen the place dozens of times, taken the guided tour twice, and he never got over being impressed. A sparkling white edifice, sitting on a knoll and with a dome rising nearly a hundred and fifty feet above the ground, it resembled something out of ancient Persia, magically transported to the shore of Lake Michigan. Appearing at first sight to be round, in reality the building had nine sides, nine entrances, and nine panels forming its domed roof. Nine being a sacred number to the Baha'is, the temple was built on nine pillars, each sunk ninety feet into the ground, and was set in the center of nine acres of lush gardens, pools, and fountains.

The day was bright, but with a surprisingly cool breeze off the lake, and there were probably a couple of hundred people – some in their best Sunday attire, others in shorts and flip-flops – wandering the grounds, and in and out of the temple itself. Dugan, who'd stopped on the way and bought a cheap camera at

Walgreens, did his own wandering, taking snapshots of one entrance after another – even though each one looked pretty much like the other eight. He had a plan, though, and paused when he came to the west side of the building. From there he could look down, across the trees and reflecting pools, to the parking lot. As predicted, there was a chain across the entrance, and the lot was filled with construction equipment and materials, including a red trailer used as an office.

At about five to twelve he watched a dark blue Ford sedan – probably a rental – pull up close to the chain across the entrance. A man exited from the front passenger side and held the back door open and a woman got out. Both were dressed casually: he in a navy sport coat and tan pants, she in a light blue raincoat buttoned up over a skirt or a dress. The driver stayed in the car and the car stayed where it was, by a sign that Dugan knew said *No Parking, No Standing,* while the man and the woman walked into the parking lot and headed straight for the red trailer.

'They're here,' Dugan said into his cellphone. 'The man's going up the steps to the door of the trailer. He's unlocking it . . . but not going inside. Now they're both just standing there, looking around. Unless someone's been sitting in that locked office for about half an hour or more, the two are alone.'

'I'm on my way,' Kirsten said. 'This won't take long. I'll see you when we're done.'

Less than a minute later he saw her walk past the Ford and go into the parking lot.

He'd earlier spotted a white-shirted security guard on duty, barely twenty years old, who seemed to have nothing to do but walk around and answer visitors' questions, and tell drivers where they might park when they discovered the lot was closed. Dugan hurried down the steps from the temple entrance and went over to the guy.

'Excuse me,' he said, and pointed out the blue Ford. 'That's my brother-in-law. He dropped the rest of us off and now he's waiting because he's too lazy to go park somewhere and then walk back a block or two.' He held out a twenty. 'I'll give you this to go over and tell him he has to move the car.'

'I don't know, sir,' the guy said. 'I don't think—'

'Aw, c'mon. Take the twenty and go for it. And if he actually

moves, come back and I'll give you this.' He held up a fifty.
'He's a great guy, and he and I have a lot of fun with each other.'

'Yeah, well, I guess there *are* signs there. I'll give it a try.'

Dugan waited, and five minutes later the Ford had pulled away,
and the security guy had what was probably the equivalent of
an extra day's pay in his pocket. Dugan walked to the trailer. He
went up the metal steps to the door, knocked, and immediately
opened it, calling, 'Anybody in here?'

The three of them were sitting on folding chairs and their
heads were all turned his way. Kirsten was obviously as surprised
as the other two, but he hadn't been about to let her walk in here
when neither of them knew what the hell she was walking into.
'Hey,' he said, 'you people aren't supposed to be in here. This
here's private property.'

The man who must have been Erik Decker stood up. 'We have
permission.'

'Yeah?' Dugan said, standing in the doorway. 'From who?'

'The man who owns the company that owns this trailer. Mr
Joel Conrad. He gave me the key.'

Dugan didn't recognize the name, of course, but he had to
assume it was real. 'Oh.' He held up his hands. 'Well then, sorry.
I'm one of the foremen, you know? Just checkin'.'

He left, closing the door behind him.

FORTY-EIGHT

Kirsten had stood patiently while Erik Decker, using an electronic device about the size and shape of a cellphone, proved
to his own satisfaction – and correctly – that she was neither
armed nor wired. Then they'd all sat down, and Decker and Eleanor
Traynor had gone into a recital about how everything said here was
off the record. They made vague references to 'possible prosecu-
tion' if certain matters mentioned here were repeated.

And that's when 'the foreman' burst in.

Once the intruder was gone, Decker and Traynor withdrew to
one end of the trailer and spent some time whispering together.
In the end, whatever their suspicions, they decided to go ahead.

'To begin with,' Traynor said, 'as you may or may not know, I am a member of the Senate Intelligence Committee.' She paused a few seconds, apparently to let Kirsten begin to appreciate her importance and to conclude that she had access to certain classified information. 'That membership brings with it a significant responsibility,' she said, 'and I take that responsibility quite seriously.'

'Makes sense to me,' Kirsten said. She wanted to hear what these two had in mind, but she also wanted them to know she had an agenda, too. 'Of course you're also angling for a vice-presidential nod, right?'

Traynor seemed ready for that one. 'I'm sure there are any number of potential running-mates being considered by any number of potential presidential candidates.'

'And you're one of them, and that's why you want to keep a distance between your family and Juan Cho's family. Because he might drag you down.'

'Ah,' Traynor said, giving the sort of superior, condescending smile she might have used with an eleven-year-old, 'if only things were that simple.'

'Excuse me.' Decker leaned forward in his chair. 'Your fixation on the senator as the source of so-called "threats" concerning Mr Cho's younger daughter is, quite understandably, misplaced. I am certain that Mr Cho, also understandably, withheld certain facts from you.'

'OK,' Kirsten said, thinking it was time to shut up and see where this was going.

'Let me explain it this way. In these volatile times, our nation's defenses rely to a large extent on information-gathering.' He paused. 'Do you follow me?'

'If I fall behind,' Kirsten said, 'I'll raise my hand.'

'Good,' he said. 'Persons with long-standing relationships in certain foreign countries, and whose positions require frequent travel to and from those countries, can sometimes be of great assistance in that regard.' He paused, the teacher giving the student time to digest what had been said. 'Now if such a person were to suddenly find himself the object of a great deal of national, and even international, attention . . . well . . . this would tend to restrict the freedom of activity he previously had. He would be less—'

'Hold on a minute,' Kirsten said. 'Are you telling me that Juan Cho is a spy?'

'Understand me, please. I'm speaking in generalities.'

'Yeah, well, I'm not *hearing* in generalities. What I'm hearing is that Juan Cho's entry into the public eye would make him no longer useful in the "information gathering" game. I'm hearing that when you warned him to keep his daughter away from Jamison Traynor, and thus to keep himself out of the public eye, it wasn't to protect the senator's career, but to protect Mr Cho's usefulness. You're suggesting that when you threatened to snatch away his child it was for the sake of national security.' She turned to Traynor. 'Am I hearing right, Senator?'

'What you *hear* is your business,' Traynor said. 'But I assure you, it's not helpful to throw around terms such as "threatening" people, or "snatching away" children. Especially when you suggest possible involvement on my part.'

'Let me continue,' Decker said. 'It's important to keep in mind that sometimes people freely enter into what you call the "game" because they desire, and receive, a benefit from . . . if you will . . . team management. Later, if the player becomes no longer of value to the team, management may feel it appropriate to withdraw the benefit.'

Kirsten thought about that for a moment. 'So . . . you're telling me that's how Cho got his daughter out of China and into the US? By agreeing to be a spy?'

'Again,' Decker said, 'I'm speaking in generalities.'

'But,' Traynor put in, 'if we *were* speaking of some particular individual, that person's situation, and the outcome of any arrangement he had with his superiors, would be matters beyond the control of any individual senator.'

'Actually,' Kirsten said, 'what happens seems to me to be entirely *within* your control. You could choose to avoid the extra scrutiny of yourself – and those close to you and your family – that comes with being a candidate for a very high office. In other words, if it's going to cause a nine-year-old to be ripped from her family, or mess up your own son's life, don't make the run.'

'Breaking up with that girl,' Traynor said, a new hard edge in her voice, 'would hardly "mess up" my—'

'Forgive me, Senator,' Decker said. He turned to Kirsten. 'I suggest we move away now from generalities, and get specific. I have a proposal to make.'

'Alright, then,' Kirsten said. 'And I suggest you make it in plain English.'

'You have undertaken to help Isobel Cho.' He paused, as though waiting for a reply, so she nodded and he went on. 'You are helping her with at least one serious problem which is entirely separate from her relationship with the senator's son.'

'Am I?'

'Yes. We know that the man hired by the senator's son to be Ms Cho's bodyguard, Tyrone Beale, has been murdered. We also know that certain signs indicate to you that his killer, or killers, appear to be seeking Ms Cho.'

'OK, let's assume that's something I'm working on,' Kirsten said, guessing Decker had gotten this from the Chicago cops. 'So what's your proposal?'

'We propose that you and Isobel drop any interest in the senator or her affairs. In return, we will work to see that those persons who appear to be targeting Ms Cho will be . . . well . . . let's say that they will no longer be in a position to harm her.'

'Oh? And do you know who these "those persons" are?'

'No. Not yet. But I'm certain that the resources at our disposal will be able to identify them more quickly than you can, and more quickly also than the Chicago Police Department. And our resources will see to it that the individuals, once identified, are apprehended, and no longer a problem to Ms Cho.'

'That would be great,' Kirsten said, 'but it wouldn't solve everything. One of Isobel's main concerns is the threat that her sister will be taken away from her family and sent back to China. Trying to make sure that doesn't happen is part of my job, and that part *does* involve the senator.'

Decker stared at her, then shrugged. 'Unfortunately,' he said, 'one cannot always have everything one wants. Ms Cho wants her sister to remain in this country, and you say she's been offered a way to accomplish what she wants, by making a choice she prefers not to make. Then you offer the senator a way to accomplish what Ms Cho wants, by making a choice the senator prefers not to make. If it were left to me, I would resolve this easily, by making the lives of both you and your client extremely difficult if you continue to pursue Ms Cho's wishes in ways which may be detrimental to the senator. However, the senator has asked me to try to resolve this in another, less confrontational, way.'

'OK, so run the deal by me again.'

'What we offer is assistance . . . effective assistance . . . in identifying those who killed Mr Beale and who you believe threaten Ms Cho's life, and in seeing that they are apprehended or otherwise rendered harmless. In return, you and Ms Cho will abandon all interest in the senator and her affairs. No other issues are included.' He paused. 'The deal is on the table. Take it or leave it.'

'I understand, and of course it's not up to me. I have to talk to Isobel.'

'Fine.' Decker stood up. 'You have my number.'

FORTY-NINE

'You almost blew it, you know,' Kirsten said, staring at Dugan, trying her best to look angry, when in fact she wasn't.

'Worth the risk, I thought. Who knew what they had planned for you inside that trailer?'

The two of them were settled in a corner table after an initial run through the lunch buffet line at a restaurant in Evanston. It was called Mount Everest and it featured Nepali food, which seemed a lot like Indian food, something she knew Dugan wasn't crazy about. Still, the place had several advantages: it was far off their beaten path; it was only minutes from the Baha'i Temple; and there didn't seem to be any other diners near their table who spoke English. Dugan seemed willing to give it his best shot, with tiny portions of six different entrées on his plate.

'What they had planned was conversation,' she said. 'They'd just finished trying to scare me with talk about national security and official secrets, when you came in. After you left they huddled. Whether they recognized you or not . . . maybe from your website photo . . . I couldn't tell, but they weren't buying the construction foreman bit. I'm sure they figured you were on my side, which didn't help my self-reliant Wonder Woman image. Anyway, whatever they thought, at least they didn't walk away.'

'And . . . ?' he asked, frowning down at what Kirsten thought was a piece of marinated goat meat.

'And it's a complicated business, and there's lots they're not telling.' She paused. 'But here's how I read it. First, Eleanor Traynor *is* in line for a vice-presidential nod, but won't get it if the Cho family is mixed up with her family . . . and there's a whole lot more to that than just people thinking Cho's a lowlife thug. Second, Decker says he and Eleanor can summon up resources that will help find the guys who tortured and killed Beale and are now targeting Isobel . . . and us . . . and have them apprehended or, as he put it, "rendered harmless."'

'The first part sounds intriguing, but I guess the second part's more crucial just now. So . . . I don't suppose they'll "summon up" those resources just because it's the right thing to do.'

'Not exactly. Here's the deal.'

After lunch Kirsten drove to Parker Gillson's neighborhood and left his Chevy Malibu on the street about a block from his house. She locked it . . . but kept the key, just in case . . . and joined Dugan in the Subaru. Andrew hadn't called, and with him gone there seemed little need to break up and travel in two cars.

By four o'clock they were on their way to Horner Park to meet with Cuffs and Isobel, to talk over Erik Decker's deal. But before they got there Cuffs called. 'Forget the park,' he said. 'It's wall-to-wall people. And no parking for blocks.'

'Any other ideas?' Kirsten asked.

'Nice weather like this, every damn public place in the city's gonna be full. Your place is out. My place is *definitely* out. Place I've had Isobel stashed is out. Hell, I need to find a new place for her, anyway. It's overcrowded there, and we're wearing out our welcome. Plus Isobel's not feeling so good. She was tossing her breakfast again today.'

'Really. I was wondering . . . has she ever suggested asking her boyfriend, Jamison Traynor, to help find her a place?'

'Nope. I brought it up, but it got voted down. Just as well, too, since we don't need one more person in the loop.'

'That's true,' Kirsten said. 'OK, hold on a minute.' She muted the phone's mike and turned to Dugan, who'd just stopped at a light. 'We need a place to talk to Isobel, and she needs a new place to stay. What about Wancho's? At least for one night?'

'Why not? It's Sunday. That whole neighborhood will be deserted.'

She went back to Cuffs. 'You still there?'

'Hell no, I got offended and hung up.'

'We can meet and spend at least one night at Wancho's Towing. Know where that is?'

'Yeah, I know Wancho's. But that's no good. That place'll be jumpin' today and tonight.'

'No, they're closed. Juan Cho left for China Wednesday. There's a rear entrance off a roadway along a railroad embankment that's—'

'I *told* ya, I know the place. That's where you been staying?'

'Yes. Pick up Isobel's stuff, and yours, if you're staying too. Call me when you're close to Wancho's and we'll meet you at the gate and— Oh, we only have three sleeping bags and air mattresses.'

'I got air mattresses.'

'We just need one more. Andrew's gone. So one of us can use—'

'Gone when? Where?'

'Last night. Just took off. God knows where. Poor guy's been pretty much in another world. This thing with his brother hit him pretty hard.'

'Damn! You shouldn't have let him get away, for Chrissake.'

'Yeah, well, he wasn't a prisoner, y'know.'

'Yeah, yeah. Where's he live?'

'Somewhere around Forty-third and Vincennes. Dugan knows his exact address, but—'

'Get it. Gimme a couple hours. I'll call you when me and Isobel are near the gate.'

Kirsten was nervous about arriving at Wancho's in broad daylight. They took their time, picking up groceries and supplies along the way, and when they got close they drove around the area a little first and made sure – for about the thousandth time in the last couple of days – that no one was following them. Dugan was right, though; the entire neighborhood was deserted. The factories and warehouses, the few that were still in operation, were shut down for the weekend; and there were no retail stores, big or small, and no bars or restaurants. The nearest residential street was two blocks to the north.

They drove in through the rear gate and parked behind the building and went inside. Dugan headed straight for Juan Cho's office to watch the end of a Cubs game, and Kirsten unloaded the grocery bags and puttered around the tiny kitchen . . . doing nothing at all but feeling anxious. She realized that Cuffs' obvious concern about Andrew having taken off had awakened a heightened concern in her, as well.

Not that she hadn't been worried about Andrew, but he'd barely been gone when Erik Decker called, and from then on she'd been focused mostly on Isobel, and wondering what Decker and Eleanor Traynor had in mind. She'd called Andrew a few times, but he obviously had his phone off. She decided he'd probably mope around awhile, and eventually he'd either call them and come back, or – what else could he do? – he'd go home. And 'home' was a bed to sleep on in somebody's basement. From what he'd told her, she was sure he had no legal residence there, got no mail, paid no bills. Anyone looking for him would never find him there. Still, it was almost twenty-four hours now since he'd disappeared, and she'd expected him to have called by now.

All of that was bouncing around in her mind when, at about six o'clock, her phone rang. It was Cuffs, saying he and Isobel were close. She took the Subaru and drove the hundred yards or so through the nearly empty lot to the back gate. Cuffs was already waiting there in his pickup, and drove in when she opened the gate. He stopped the truck just inside and Isobel got out, carrying a duffel bag, along with a blanket and a pillow. As soon as she closed the truck door, Cuffs backed up, obviously to turn around and leave.

'Hey!' Kirsten called. 'Where you going?'

Cuffs' window was down. 'You got that address?'

'Yeah, but—'

'Gimme the address. I don't like Andrew runnin' around out there on his own.'

With Cuffs gone, Isobel threw her stuff in the back seat, and Kirsten closed the gate and they drove back to the office. 'I had a meeting today with Jamison's mother and that Erik Decker guy,' she said. 'You ever meet Decker?'

'No, but Jamison's mentioned him a few times. Jamison doesn't like him.'

'I don't think he gets paid to have people like him. Anyway, he did most of the talking at our meeting, and he had a proposal to make. Dugan's inside. We'll get something to drink, and we can all talk about it.' She paused. 'Um . . . you feeling OK?'

'I'm fine. Just, you know, tired. I haven't been sleeping too well.'

'Last time we talked, Cuffs said you were putting in long days.'

'Yes, I— Well, he said I could tell you now, since we're not going back there any more. Remember that women's shelter I told you about?'

'With the nun running it? Is that where you've been staying? And Cuffs, too?'

'Yes. I've been sleeping in a little room, like a closet, by the kitchen. He sits outside the door all night. He sleeps some, too, I guess.'

'I bet the nun loves Cuffs.'

'Well, she's *impressed* by him anyway, and he actually tries to be *nice* around her. Except sometimes he forgets and says things that— Anyway, she runs the shelter on almost no money and doesn't have much staff. So he told her he and I would help with some cleaning and painting and fixing stuff up.'

Kirsten parked the car. 'OK, we'll go inside and talk about Decker's proposal. And then, since there's nothing much to do around here, maybe you can get rest up and deal better with this . . . this stomach flu . . . or whatever.' She opened her door.

'Wait, please,' Isobel said. 'Before we go in, I need to tell you something.' Kirsten turned to face her and Isobel burst into tears. 'It's something no one knows but me. No one.' She was wringing her hands as though they were cold, and through her sobs she said, 'I . . . I'm not really sick.'

Kirsten stared at Isobel, then smiled and laid a hand on her arm. 'You know what?' she said. 'I'm not as surprised as you might imagine. In fact, I think some part of me must have known this, or felt it somehow, all along. You're not sick. You're pregnant.'

FIFTY

Half and hour later they were in Juan Cho's office, and Isobel obviously didn't like what Kirsten was saying. She set her glass down hard, splashing water up and out over Juan Cho's desk. 'You're saying my father's a *spy*? That's not possible!'

'I'm telling you what Decker told me,' Kirsten said, 'with Jamison's mother, who's on the Senate Intelligence Committee, sitting right there. Is it *true*? I can't be absolutely certain, but I think it is. It's certainly very possible. You told me yourself that for years he's made frequent business trips back and forth between the US and China.'

The three of them – Isobel, Kirsten, and Dugan – were sitting in Cho's office, drinking water and Diet Pepsi and Moose Drool, respectively. The two women hadn't said another word about Isobel being pregnant, other than Isobel begging Kirsten not to tell anyone, and Kirsten agreeing. They'd gotten out of the car and gone in through the door into the kitchen, with Kirsten saying that they had an awful lot of other things to talk about just then.

So they'd all gotten their drinks and gathered in Cho's office, and Kirsten had begun to tell Isobel, as gently as possible, what she'd learned from Erik Decker, as well as from Juan Cho himself, about Cho . . . and about Luisa. She knew much of it would be difficult, almost impossible, for Isobel to accept, so she'd started with what she hoped would be the least disturbing: that Isobel's father was working in an 'information gathering' capacity for the United States government.

There was so much more to tell: that it was at the urging of Luisa's mother that Cho had managed to get Luisa out of China and into the US; that he had done so illegally, but with the clandestine help of a government agency, probably the CIA; and, what would certainly be the most disturbing of all, that Cho was not Luisa's biological father, which meant that Luisa was not Isobel's sister . . . not even a half-sister.

Kirsten was concerned that having all this dumped on her at

once might overload Isobel's emotional circuitry. But it had to be done, and she did it, and at each step she met the expected resistance, along with anger and denial. Dugan had heard all of it already, but she'd wanted him to be present as she told it, maybe as a kind of anchor . . . for her as well as for Isobel. So he stayed and listened, and hardly moved except to sip his beer. He didn't say a word, and Kirsten loved him for his silent presence.

In the end Isobel did not break down, or stalk away in fury, or withdraw into herself. 'First of all,' she finally said, 'Luisa is my sister, blood or not. And secondly, none of this means that my father is a bad person.'

'What it means,' Kirsten said, 'is that he's the man you described to me from the start: a man who, when he knows what has to be done, does it.'

'You know,' Dugan added, breaking his silence, 'not many guys would be smart enough, and tough enough, to do what he did.' He drained his second Moose Drool, and stood up. 'I'd like another beer,' he said, 'but I guess I better go make some coffee instead.'

When he was gone, Kirsten said, 'Last Wednesday I was furious with your father, Isobel, when he told me he was taking off for China, with all that's going on. But now I know that it could have been that he had no choice.' She had other suspicions now, too, about Cho's trip, darker suspicions, but those she kept to herself. 'Anyway, you and I still have a lot more to talk about.'

She began to describe for Isobel the proposal set out by Erik Decker, and eventually Dugan came back with three cups of coffee. There were no windows in the office, and he surprised them with the news that it was almost sundown.

Neither of the women touched her coffee as Kirsten continued. When she finished laying out the proposal, it was Dugan who spoke first. 'I've been thinking about this deal. Decker claims his "resources" can identify Beale's killers and stop them from coming after Isobel . . . and us. Is there any chance that that's because the killers are working for him?'

'My God!' Isobel was wide-eyed. 'If they're working for Mr Decker, they'd be working for Jamison's mother. Are you serious?'

'I'm not saying it's true,' he said. 'I'm saying it's something to think about.'

'I *have* thought about it,' Kirsten said, 'and the answer I get is "no."' She turned to Isobel. 'I'd been convinced at first that it was Decker, acting on Jamison's mother's orders, who told your father that if you and Jamison didn't break up, Luisa would be sent away. But I'm no longer certain at all about that. What I *am* certain of, though, is that Beale's killers . . . we've been calling them Toad and Weasel, by the way . . . are coming from an altogether different direction. I mean, I don't *like* Eleanor Traynor much, or Erik Decker either. She's a lightweight with exaggerated ambitions, and he's a thug with a high-class vocabulary. But I don't think the two of them are running a couple of hired gunmen. They're smarter than that.'

'So,' Dugan said, 'if the killers aren't working for him, do you think he can really handle them?'

'I think he can get it done.' Kirsten nodded. 'When he talks about his "resources," he must mean federal law enforcement. Probably the FBI. We know they're already looking into some matter they think Isobel might know something about.'

'I already *told* you,' Isobel said, 'I don't know anything about—'

'I know, I know.' Kirsten raised her hand to cut Isobel off. 'And we'll get back to that whole "What-*might*-you-know?" topic later. Right now, though, let's stick to Decker's proposal. The cops don't seem to be moving ahead very quickly on the Beale case, and they certainly aren't interested in any input from us. Decker claims he can get the Feds involved quickly, and get these killers put away. The fact is, I believe him. In return, of course, I have to stay away from Eleanor Traynor, and not do any snooping into her affairs.'

'I didn't know,' Isobel said, 'that you *were* snooping into her affairs.'

'I haven't been. But I've threatened it. And for whatever reason, she and Decker seem more than a little worried about it. That's the point of their proposal.'

'Well,' Isobel said, 'I can't keep hiding forever, so maybe I should agree. Plus, I just can't believe that if I don't break up with Jamison his mother would actually send Luisa to China. I mean, she doesn't think much of me, but she's his *mother*. I can't believe she would do such a thing.'

'And, when you think about it,' Kirsten said, 'I've only been *assuming* that Eleanor is the one who threatened that. With what we know now, I think it's more likely that the threat came from the people who helped your father get Luisa into the country. They'd certainly want him to stay out of the public eye, and keep himself useful to them.'

'That's all interesting speculation,' Dugan said, 'but let's get back to Decker's proposal. I know no one's asked me, but here's how I look at it. Whatever Isobel decides, we're still gonna have the Luisa problem. But if she *does* OK the deal, Decker gets the Feds to go after the killers, and we stay away from Senator Traynor. If she *doesn't* OK the deal, we're stuck with the local cops . . . or us . . . identifying and neutralizing a couple of pretty bad guys. I'm not a big FBI fan, but I prefer the first alternative.'

'That's right,' Kirsten said. 'And as to Luisa, if the government *does* start deportation proceedings, we won't beat them back by me digging up some sort of dirt on Eleanor Traynor.'

'Then why waste any more time?' Isobel said. 'Why not just call Mr Decker and tell him I agree to his proposal?'

'Let's think about that overnight.' Kirsten looked at her watch. 'It's eight thirty and Dugan said it was getting dark out. I don't want to use any lights in the building that can be seen from the street.' She looked at Dugan. 'We didn't bring Isobel's things in from the car, so . . .'

'At your service, ma'am. And I'll get some more coffee.' He stood. 'Any takers?' They both shook their heads and he left.

'There's still one more thing to talk about, Isobel,' Kirsten said, 'and that's *why* those killers are after you. I think it has to do with Miguel Parillo.'

'Miguel?' Isobel's eyes widened. 'Why do you say that?'

'Because I think the killers . . . Toad and Weasel . . . believe that you have certain information Miguel had, or at least that you have access to that information. It's about Hit the Rock, I'm sure of it.'

'But I *told* you, I don't have—'

'Even if you don't know what it is, it's something Toad and Weasel don't want getting out. The FBI agents I talked to don't seem to know what it is, either. In fact, they don't seem to know anything at all about Toad and Weasel, or their connection with Beale's killing.'

'Whatever any of them think,' Isobel said, 'or what you think either, the fact is that Miguel never gave me any secret information about Hit the Rock. I mean, I told you that this other girl and I were helping organize his notes and materials. It was for this memoir he wanted to write about the work he'd been doing. But it's not like he gave me any secret documents.'

'There could have been something you didn't recognize as important. When did you last see him?'

'It was on the Sunday he went to DC, a few days before he was killed.'

'Tell me about that,' Kirsten said.

'Well, he was taking the train to DC from the South Boston station. He called and said he had some more notes about Hit the Rock he wanted to give me before he left. I knew he didn't have a car, so I borrowed one and drove to where he was staying, and then drove him to the station. On the way, he gave me a memory stick with more of his notes on it. He was having meetings that week, about Hit the Rock. I think they were about its financing, and raising funds. I remember it didn't seem like he really wanted to go. Before that he always seemed to enjoy all the travel and stuff he did, but that day . . . that day he seemed uneasy about it.'

'Uneasy?' Kirsten leaned forward. 'Uneasy how?'

'I don't know. Like saying he wished he didn't have to go, and he hoped everything would go all right. That's the first time I ever heard him talk that way about anything. He was always so positive, and upbeat. Then a few days later he was robbed and killed, and . . . well . . . I know it sounds strange, but afterwards I wondered if he had some kind of premonition of death or something.'

'Yes,' Kirsten said. 'Or something.' She stood. 'I'd like to have Dugan in on this. Let's take a break, and go see where he is, and—' Her cellphone rang and made her jump. She reached into her bag on the table, took out the phone and flipped it open, and saw it was Cuffs. 'Hello?'

'You still at Wancho's? Everything alright?'

'Sure. We're just—'

'I'll get there as fast as I can. But get the fuck outta there. I found Andrew. They sawed off one of his fingers before they shot him.'

FIFTY-ONE

er heart pounding, Kirsten put her cell back in the bag and slipped the strap over her shoulder. 'Wait right here, Isobel,' she said, and ran out into the hall. 'Dugan?' she yelled. He didn't answer, but the kitchen light was on and she was sure she heard him coming in the door from outside. 'Dugan! C'mon! We have to hurry.'

But when she got to the kitchen there were *two* men there, and Dugan wasn't one of them. The thin man, Weasel, held a gun pointed at her, a nine millimeter semi-automatic. The wide, squat one beside him was Toad, and he held one hand out, palm toward her. He pressed his other forefinger to his lips, warning her to stay silent.

Weasel angled the gun barrel up and down twice, just slightly, but she got the point. She raised her hands up near her shoulders.

'Smart girl,' Toad said, his voice barely above a whisper, but still harsh and guttural. He raised his index finger. 'Stay smart. Don't say a word.' Several seconds of silence passed, until Toad lowered his hand and said, 'Call him again.' He gestured toward the door to the hall behind her.

'What?' She kept her voice as low as his.

'I said—'

'I heard you, but— Oh,' she said, raising her voice a little, 'you think *Dugan* is back there?'

'Don't play with me, bitch,' he said. '*Call* him.'

'Dugan!' she yelled. *'Dugan!'* She shrugged. 'This is stupid. He's not back there.' Not shouting now, but loud enough. Hoping Isobel could hear. 'There's *no* one back there. The hall leads to Juan Cho's office, where I came from. And past that is the front, with the cashier's office, and the waiting room.' Wouldn't Isobel know she could get through to the waiting room? And wasn't there just a knob to open the deadbolt to get out the front door?

Toad's hand went under his sport coat and came out with a

gun. 'Move,' he said, and when she stepped aside he went past her into the hall.

Weasel hadn't said a word. He still stood near the door to the outside, his nine pointed at her. The window in the door reflected the interior light, so it must have been fully dark outside by then. She wondered if Dugan was out there and—

Her cellphone rang. It was in the bag hanging from her shoulder. 'I should get that,' she said.

'No.' Weasel's voice was as Dugan had described it. Thin and strained, as though he had throat problems. Maybe that's why he hadn't spoken so far.

'But it could be Dugan,' she said.

'Give me the phone.'

'Well, OK, but . . .' She fumbled in her bag and came out with her Colt 380, and shot Weasel square in the chest . . . or she would have, except that he moved and she hit him closer to his right shoulder. His own shot dug into the wall a yard to her right.

He didn't go down, but sank back against the refrigerator, staring at her, his left hand pressed to where blood was beginning to flow out from his wound. The gun dropped from his right hand and hit the floor. Then his knees buckled and he slid down, his back against the refrigerator, until he was sitting on the floor, his hands tucked into his chest, his torso and head bent forward almost to his legs. There was a lot of blood, and she wondered if she'd hit an artery.

Keeping an eye on the door to the hallway, she snatched up his gun, meaning to throw it out the door, but by then the door was open and Dugan was coming in, and she gave it to him.

'I saw through the window,' he said. 'I went to get Isobel's bag, and thought I heard a car slow down out front and ran to look. And when I got back around again I—'

Screams broke out from down the hall, beyond Cho's office. They were Isobel's screams, and they were coming closer. And then they stopped.

Kirsten was facing the hall door, the Colt raised, when Isobel appeared, Toad beside her. He was shorter than she was, but clearly much stronger. She wasn't screaming now, but moaning. She had one hand pressed to her face, covering her mouth and nose, and there was blood oozing out around her fingers. Toad's right arm was wrapped around her middle, and his left hand held the barrel of his gun shoved into the side of her neck, angled upward.

'Toss the hardware on the floor,' Toad said. 'Or she's dead.'

Kirsten was ready to comply, but Dugan, with Weasel's nine also trained on Toad, spoke up. 'No,' he said. 'You won't shoot her, because you know that as soon as you do, *you're* dead. You can't fire and then have time to re-aim and shoot even one of us, much less two.' He paused, then added, 'So . . . my advice . . . let's talk this over.'

'I got nothing to talk over.' Toad shoved the gun harder into Isobel's neck. 'Jimmy!' he said, not taking his eyes off Kirsten and Dugan. 'Get up.'

'I . . . I can't do it,' the man on the floor said. 'I'm shot.'

'You think I don't *know* that, for Chrissake? Get up and out the door. We're outta here.'

'I don't think so,' Dugan said

'Yeah? Well I *do*,' Toad said. 'Jimmy! Up off your ass, pussy. You're not dying.'

To Kirsten's amazement, Weasel . . . Jimmy . . . sat upright, then got to his feet. Doubled over, half-crouching, one hand still pressed to his bloody shoulder, he stumbled to the door . . . and out.

'He'll bleed to death,' Kirsten said. 'He needs medical attention.'

'Yeah, right,' Toad said, 'so he can die in lockdown.'

By then Isobel was showing no resistance at all, but Kirsten could still tell how powerful – and how crazed – Toad was as he lifted the girl's weight off her feet and carried her sideways with him to the open door . . . without once taking the gun barrel from her neck.

'You have to know you'll never make it,' she said.

'We cut our way in,' he said, 'and we'll get out . . . the girl with us. And if I see you coming after us? Or I hear cops coming? She's dead.' He paused in the doorway and stared back at them, a sly, reptilian look shining in his eyes. 'But the bitch is no use to us now,' he said, 'so . . . if we get to the car, and get a few blocks from here? With no one following? I let her go. She lives or she dies. It's up to you.'

And then he dragged her away.

FIFTY-TWO

'He's lying,' Dugan said. 'He won't let her go. He'll kill her.' He started for the open kitchen door.

Kirsten grabbed his arm. 'No! He'll see you and shoot.'

'He's twenty yards away by now. He won't waste time looking back. We need to—'

'Wait. Let's find out.' There was a grease-stained gray windbreaker hanging on a hook by the door and she grabbed it and waved it across the doorway, and two shots rang out, the slugs slamming into the wall opposite the door. Another shot came through the window.

'I was right about the twenty yards, anyway,' Dugan said, as they both crouched near the floor. 'Probably forty by now. And he's got Isobel, for Chrissake. We need to call 911.'

'No! Didn't you see his eyes? He's way over the edge. If cops come screaming up he'll know he's done for, and he'll kill her out of sheer rage. Right now, though, he knows he still *needs* her.'

'So what the hell's *your* plan?'

'I don't know. I guess . . . I just want to keep them in sight.' She pointed to the wall above Dugan, and a gray electrical box. 'The switches for the floodlights are in there. Turn them on, but stay away from the window.'

He stood and opened the metal door and threw every switch in the box. Kirsten killed the kitchen light and went to the open door, knowing Toad couldn't see her now. She saw *him*, though, forty or fifty yards off, moving faster than she'd thought he could, dragging Isobel along with him. She wasn't screaming. Maybe she couldn't, not with her nose broken.

Toad said they'd cut the fence to get in, and they'd have done that a long way from the building to avoid being heard. Kirsten scanned what she could see of the fence, and through the scattered trees up at the north end she spotted the opening he had to be headed for. At a hundred yards away or more it looked like a small black square, low to the ground in the north fence, near the corner where the north and west fence lines met, just beyond the rear entrance off the gravel road.

Toad was nearly halfway there, dragging Isobel along.

Dugan came up beside Kirsten with car keys in his hand, but the Subaru's hood was up. 'Damn,' he said. 'I bet they pulled some wires or something.'

'Turn off all the lights except around that gate,' she said, pointing. 'That's where they cut the fence. Then get that car going. We need it.'

Dugan went back into the kitchen and, as she trotted after Toad, the lights started going off, section by section. When the area closest to the gate went dark, those lights came on again right away, and then all the remaining lights went out.

Toad and Isobel hadn't yet reached the lit-up area yet, but with the illumination beyond them she could see their outlines. He might have been tiring, because he'd slowed to a walk and seemed to be pulling Isobel along sideways. Maybe looking back to see if anyone was coming; maybe with the gun barrel at Isobel's neck again.

Her own weapon still in her hand, Kirsten slowed down, too. She was unsure what she could do even if she caught up with them before they reached the hole in the fence. She was convinced Toad would kill Isobel if he knew he was going down. Still, she felt she at least had to stay close, had to keep them in sight. And Toad's car would be out on that gravel roadway.

Why doesn't Dugan have the Subaru going yet? And Jesus, where's that damn Weasel . . . or Jimmy or—

She heard something. Was that a car? Stopping on the street in front of Wancho's? Then, definitely, muffled voices from back at the building. She spun around and looked. In the dark she could barely see the outline of the Subaru with its hood up. But she couldn't see anyone working under the hood.

'Dugan?' she called.

No answer.

'Dugan! Are you—'

A shot rang out behind her and she dropped to the ground . . . too late, of course, if the bullet had been on target. But it wasn't. And Toad wasn't wasting another shot. Hearing the car start up again and drive away, headed west on the street behind her, she stood up and saw Toad, under the lights now, dragging Isobel. The girl was resisting, arms flailing, but he was pulling her toward the hole in the fence, with just twenty yards or so to go.

That's when Kirsten heard the car turn north on to the gravel road between the west fence to her left and the railroad embankment beyond that. She couldn't see much through the slats woven into the fence, and thought it might be Cuffs in his pickup. But as the vehicle got close to the gate, the gate started sliding open. Cuffs didn't have an opener. She and Dugan did, but who else? Cho's manager, Luis, probably had one, but why would he be here?

Toad, who should have been hurrying even faster toward the hole in the fence, was apparently as shocked as Kirsten was. He seemed unable to move, frozen in place, staring at the opening gate. His gun – in his left hand – hung down by his leg and Kirsten stopped, took a shooter's stance, raised her weapon. But at that distance, aiming between a couple of trees, and with Isobel struggling and pulling on Toad, she couldn't chance a shot.

What drove in through the gate wasn't a pickup truck. It was a white Ford Explorer, the kind of vehicle Juan Cho arrived in when he met Kirsten at McDonald's a hundred years earlier. It was empty except for the driver. A man, she thought, so maybe it *was* Luis.

Whoever it was, he must have seen Toad and Isobel, because he slammed on the brakes and slid to a stop just inside the gate. Kirsten saw his door open, but it was on the side of the car away from her. She saw him reach for something on the floor of the car as he got out, and then heard him scream something – *roar* something – in Spanish. The only word she caught was, '*Isobel!*'

And Isobel screamed back. '*Papá! Ayúdame, papá! Ayúdame!*' At the sight of her father she suddenly tore free of Toad's arm around her, and her momentum carried her sideways and on to her hands and knees on the ground.

'Bitch!' Toad howled. 'Bitch!' He swung his gun hand around toward the crawling, scrambling girl. But her father roared again – no words Kirsten understood, if they were words at all. Toad swung back to see Cho just five yards from him now, waving a two-foot-long, shiny steel rod – a crescent wrench – in front of him. Kirsten raised her gun again at Toad, but the Ford was in the way now and the angle was wrong . . . and her own hands were shaking.

Cho, like a roaring, raging bear, charged, but Toad held his ground, and from maybe ten feet away he shot Cho in the chest. Cho slowed, but didn't stop, and Toad fired again, twice more. Then Cho was on him, swinging the wrench down, hard. Toad ducked aside and the wrench missed his head, but slammed on to his left shoulder and he howled in pain, and the gun fell from his hand.

By then Kirsten had moved closer, and sideways, to where neither the Ford nor any trees blocked her view, but still she couldn't shoot without possibly hitting Cho. And suddenly there was Isobel, her face a mask of blood, running toward her. She raised her hand, but the girl kept coming, arms outstretched. Kirsten turned aside and grabbed Isobel's hand. They both turned back to see Toad on his knees, his left arm hanging limp, reaching around for his gun with his right hand. Cho, unsteady and wobbling from side to side, stood over him and slammed the wrench down on his upper back. Once, twice. Kirsten, almost sick herself, wrapped her left arm around Isobel and turned the girl's head away from the carnage.

Cho brought the wrench down a third time and it landed on Toad's back with a thud. Toad, though, managed to get a grip on the gun and then, as he struggled to stand upright, one more blow landed. No thud this time, but a terrible crack of forged steel against skull bone, and Toad fell face down on the ground.

Cho stood over him, staring down as though daring the lifeless man to move again. But he himself was more and more unsteady. His torso rocked from side to side, then forward and backward. Isobel tried to turn and look, but Kirsten, her gun under her belt now, held her tight in both arms. She kept Isobel turned away while Cho gave out a loud moan, dropped the wrench, and fell forward on top of the man he'd just beaten to death.

Only then did Kirsten hear Dugan calling out to her, only then heard sirens screaming in the distance through the night.

FIFTY-THREE

Two weeks later, on a Monday afternoon, Dugan was on his way to pick up Kirsten at Isobel's house – the house she was raised in, and where she lived now, with Luisa and the nanny. It was in the Sauganash neighborhood, on the city's north-west side. He was driving Kirsten's Camry, the car he'd been rescuing from Wancho's Towing the night this whole Isobel Cho thing began.

Isobel was a beautiful girl, no doubt about it. Smart, too. And Kirsten insisted she was 'tougher than you think.' But she was also very young, and in Dugan's opinion she was going to be in a fragile state for a very long time.

The physical stuff was the easy part. Scratches, bruises, sore muscles and joints, even the broken nose the plastic surgeon said had been a snap to fix – the 'snap' part being the surgeon's little joke – were the stuff of ordinary human existence. And finding yourself pregnant when you weren't counting on it? Not generally a terminal condition.

But the psychological wounds? Dugan had thought Isobel was already a basket case when she showed up at Tyrone Beale's place, asking Beale to get help from some guy – a man she didn't know from Jeffrey Dahmer – just because the guy 'didn't waste time thinking about it' before he'd manhandled Beale. OK . . . get help with what? Well, it seems someone broke into her apartment, someone's stalking her. Of course maybe it's just her father, trying to get his obstinate daughter's attention. But no, it's actually a couple of psychopaths who'll torture and kill to get at her, and she doesn't know why. Oh, and meanwhile, someone's threatening to ship her little sister off to China.

Although Isobel had resisted being put into protective custody with the ever-charming Cuffs Radovich, in the end that was about the only thing that didn't work out badly for her. It was only after she'd left Cuffs' protection that her world finished caving in. Watching her own father murdered? Watching him beat his murderer to death? Dugan knew she'd carry those terrifying images with her forever. Along with all those unanswerable questions about whether she'd been somehow responsible for everything.

All in all, saying Isobel was 'in a very fragile state' was an understatement. Even so, he'd given up reminding Kirsten about it, because all she did was smile sadly and say, 'I know, I know,' and then run off to 'do whatever I can' to help Isobel . . . and Luisa.

Meanwhile, back at Dugan's office Larry Candle had taken the reins and was keeping the practice going, and seemed to be doing his genuine best not to drive Mollie crazy. And when Parker Gillson found a grocery bag full of cash in the trunk of his Malibu it was Larry who, after removing a nice fee for Cuffs, delivered the remaining seven thousand dollars, as a gift from an anonymous client of his, to a nun who ran a women's shelter on the north side.

Dugan was in the office maybe half-time, spending the other half tying up loose ends . . . and encouraging Kirsten. He knew she was haunted by the horror of having shot and killed a man, as monstrous as the man was. And Dugan was having his own recurring dreams about that. In fact, Weasel – Dugan preferred that name to 'Jimmy' – had almost survived. And Dugan could possibly have saved his life.

It hadn't taken long to realize he'd never get the damn Subaru started, and he'd been about to go after Kirsten when he heard strange, suspicious noises. He went to look, and there was Weasel, who'd somehow blundered his way around to the side of the building away from the action. He was sitting on the ground, both hands clutched to his shoulder, trying to stop the bleeding.

Just then a car drove up and stopped in front of the building. Dugan couldn't see through the fence, but heard someone get out and pull on Wancho's front door. He raced around, went in through the kitchen door and down the hall, and ran into Juan Cho, frantic, wild-eyed, yelling that he couldn't reach Kirsten, and where was Isobel. Dugan got as far as saying they were both out near the rear gate by now, when Cho ran back out and jumped into the Ford Explorer and took off.

At that point Dugan thought to hell with Kirsten's fears about Toad killing Isobel, and called 911. Then he ran to help Kirsten. Not until too much later, after the cops were there awhile, did he think again of Weasel. He ran back to try to help . . . but the man had bled out. No great loss, true, but keeping him alive would have kept Weasel's specter from dogging Kirsten.

Both Toad and Weasel were ID'd as transplants from Florida. Both had been cops in Miami, both discharged and nearly indicted for torturing confessions out of suspected drug dealers. An Outfit guy who hired them for occasional odd jobs in and around Chicago was also identified, but trying to tie that guy to any money laundering scheme the two thugs had going was certain to be, in Dugan's opinion, a waste of law enforcement resources.

The police investigations into the murders of the two Beale brothers would eventually be closed, marked 'Primary Suspects Deceased,' as, probably, would the Parillo case in DC. Cuffs had found Andrew's mutilated body at his brother's apartment, and the cops opined that he'd gone back there to look for the gun he knew his brother kept hidden under the floor of a kitchen cabinet, because they found those boards lifted up. But the cops had already found the gun and taken it. The killers must have been watching the place, and caught Andrew there.

The FBI agents were, of course, not about to explain much to mere mortals like Dugan and Kirsten, but apparently Miguel Parillo had called an FBI hotline, requesting a meeting to discuss information he had about possible criminal activity, and mentioned Isobel as someone who was holding his materials and who knew how to reach him. Miguel had emailed Isobel from DC on his Blackberry – which the cops eventually found in Toad's town house – to remind her about the memory stick he'd given her. He said it held 'crucial' information, and told her to be sure to store it with his other 'important' notes and photos. She'd put it with other materials he'd left with her, in a safe deposit box at a bank near Tufts, waiting for use in the book he was planning. Knowing nothing about his family, not even what country they lived in, she'd simply left everything in the box.

Dugan, armed with Isobel's authority, flew to Boston, drove to the bank, in Somerville, and emptied out the box. The only document on the stick spelled out what Miguel had discovered about an accountant manipulating Hit the Rock's accounts. Nothing in the document led any farther than Roger Krupa, but everyone knew he'd have given up Toad and Weasel in a heartbeat.

At Kirsten's suggestion, Krupa hired Dugan's own lawyer, Renata Carroway, who was hoping to broker him a deal that called for complete cooperation, extensive addictions counseling, and no jail time.

Dugan got to Isobel's house just before two. It was a large frame home in a sort of faux-Victorian style, on a quiet shady street. Kirsten came out as soon as he pulled to the curb. She was carrying the shoulder bag she used for short trips, and another little red suitcase he didn't recognize, obviously something Isobel gave her.

Kirsten waved goodbye to Isobel and to the three or four other

young women who came out on the porch, and then she ran out
to the car so quickly he barely had time to get out and around to
take her in his arms. She'd been spending a lot of time here the
past two weeks, but this time she'd stayed overnight, two nights,
keeping Isobel company and helping take care of Luisa while
the nanny took some time off. He was so glad to see her, to feel
her body pressed against his, that he got teary-eyed . . . and
didn't want to let go.

When they heard all the giggling from up on the porch, though,
they finally broke their embrace. He put both bags in the back
seat and opened the front passenger door for her.

'I'll drive,' she said.

'Really?' She'd been leaving the driving to him during those
two weeks, and when they were both in the car and she was
pulling away from the curb, he asked, 'Does this mean we're
getting back to normal?'

'I don't know. I don't know what normal is.'

She didn't sound terribly sad about that, but still he had no
answer for it. 'How's Isobel doing?' he asked.

'She's OK,' Kirsten said. 'She'll be fine. Except for Luisa she
hardly has any family. None nearby. But she has real good friends.
Girlfriends.'

'And she has Jamison Traynor.'

'Maybe. That's another whole story. She hasn't said anything,
but . . . well . . . this pregnancy? I think there's a reason she
didn't just run to Jamison for help from the start.'

He was stunned. 'You can't be serious. You mean . . . Miguel
Parillo?'

'It's a feeling I get. But later for that. Right now there's something way more important. I can't believe how lucky it was that
I was with her this morning.'

'Oh?'

'Two people came to see her, unannounced. A man and a
woman. From Washington, the State Department. Actually, they
were quite nice.' She stopped at a red light. 'They said it was
fine for me to sit in on the conversation, and that maybe it was
even better if she had a friend with her.'

'That sounds scary,' he said. Then, when the light turned green
and she drove forward, he added, 'Kirsten? You should have
turned there.'

'No. See?' She pointed. 'Sauganash Park.' She pulled to the curb beside a lovely little park, full of grass and trees, and play-ground equipment . . . and a group of little kids gathered around a couple of teenagers near the fieldhouse, and some adults, probably parents, standing around. 'We can sit here where it's peaceful, while I finish telling what happened. Then we have to pick— We have an errand to do, and then we'll go home.'

'Uh . . . yeah. Sounds like a plan.'

'OK. So these two people . . . agents or whatever . . . they said it was a sensitive issue, but not really confidential. They were in Chicago on a matter having to do with Isobel's father, they said, and there was something they wanted her to hear first from them, and not from someone else.'

'Jesus! You mean they verified he was a spy?'

'That's what I was thinking, too. But no, not that. The woman did most of the talking. She said the US was contacted by the Chinese government several days ago, and informed that Juan Cho was about to be indicted . . . or whatever they call it in China . . . and they'd be starting extradition proceedings to get him back and stand trial.'

'Trial? For what?'

'Homicide. It happened a couple of weeks ago, when Cho was on that trip to China that made me so mad.'

'Damn! They think he killed someone?'

'The victim was a man who lived with his wife and son in the same village where Cho was part-owner of a business. The man was strangled with a piece of rope. The body wasn't found until several days later, after Cho had left the country. The victim didn't come home one night, but his wife said he was a drunk and a drug addict, and he'd often disappear for days at a time, and the whole village verified that.'

'Cho left Chicago on a Wednesday,' Dugan said, 'and was home sometime the following Sunday. I mean . . . he hardly had time to get there and back. And certainly not a lot of time to kill someone.'

'That's what I said, but the Chinese police have traced his movements and they say he had time and opportunity. Apparently he paid a small fortune to set up last minute flights to and from China, and two chartered flights inside China.'

'So . . . they have proof he's the killer?'

'Whatever the evidence is, the Chinese say it's conclusive. Not that it makes much difference now. The State Department, of course, notified them that Cho is dead, so the matter ends there. But it's of public record in China, and public to some extent here in the States, although no one but a few government officials may ever hear about it. Still, the government thought Isobel should be notified.'

'She must have freaked out.'

'When the agents left she sort of shut down, a lot like Andrew did, and I was glad it was already set up that some girlfriends were taking her to Wisconsin with them for a few days. But pretty soon she broke into tears again, and I held her and told her what I tell her every day, that I'm going to help her, and that she's going to be fine. And that she's going to have a beautiful baby, and I'll help her with that, too. I reminded her that Luisa is the sweetest child in the world, and that I absolutely adore her . . . which you know is the truth.'

'Well, I wasn't sure,' Dugan said, 'since you only say it twenty times a day.'

'You're sweet, too,' she said, 'so don't start worrying that you'll be replaced.'

'I'm not worried. I'm thrilled. I have no idea what's going to happen next, but the prettiest woman in the world looks . . . well . . . tired, and a little stressed. But somehow better than ever.'

'Shut up, will you? You'll have me crying, and I need to finish my story first. When I got to the part about adoring Luisa, Isobel wiped her eyes and finally looked up at me. "That man my father killed," she said, as though there wasn't any doubt that he'd done it, "he was Luisa's real father, wasn't he." It wasn't a question, and I said, "Yes, I'm sure he was." And Isobel said, "Luisa's mother begged my father to take Luisa. So now there's no one to claim that he took her against her parents' will." She started to cry again, and then her friends came, and we didn't get to talk about it any more.'

Again Dugan didn't know what to say, so he said, 'I love you. Let's go home.'

'Right. But first, come on.' She opened the car door, and pointed toward where the little kids were splitting up, running to their mothers, and a few fathers. 'Day camp's over,' she said.

'We have to pick up Luisa. She'll be staying with us while Isobel's in Wisconsin.'

'A kid? At our condo?'

'Sure. She'll sleep in the nurser— She'll sleep in the room Andrew used. She'll love it. And y'know what? She'll especially love her Uncle Dugan.'